STEALING HOPE

A KIMBELL TEXAS SWEET ROMANCE
BOOK FIVE

ANGEL S. VANE

BONZAI
MOON

BonzaiMoon Books LLC
Houston, Texas
www.bonzaimoonbooks.com

CHAPTER 1

L UKE

~

"It's time for you to step away from putting out grass fires and saving cats from trees. Come back into the ring where you belong." Herbert's voice crackles through my phone

I close my eyes, willing away a resurgence of the life I left behind. The thrill of campaign strategy, the satisfaction of seeing polling numbers shift, and, more importantly, to see communities impacted and lives changed. How did I end up here, covered in baby vomit and confronting ghosts from my past on a dreary Kimbell morning?

Let's rewind about ten minutes …

The smell of maple syrup and bacon drifts from Gwen's Country Cafe, mingling with the earthy scent of newly mowed grass from Bell Park as I head to the tax office, hoping to beat the line as the first one there. Children's laughter rings out from the parking lot of the daycare as parents line up to do morning drop-offs. I'm halfway to my destination when I hear a desperate plea.

"Hold Baby, please!" Tara Stafford says.

My arms extend instinctively, gripping the ten-month-old daughter of Tara Stafford under her arm pits. Her little face scrunches up like a disgruntled garden gnome.

Tara bolts away, running faster than a world-class sprinter to grab her two older daughters by the neck before they start playing Frogger across Main Street in Downtown Kimbell.

And I use the term 'Downtown' loosely. The moniker is less about skyscrapers and more about a sense of community. The quaint town center serves as Kimbell's beating heart, where government buildings jostle for space along cherished local haunts. Main Street slices through the center, flanked by a patchwork of eateries, boutiques, and gathering spots that define small-town charm.

Tara chides her daughters, dragging them back toward her sister's daycare, leaving me alone with Baby.

I pull the child's thin body into my chest. Her onesie hangs loose on her like a coat hanger. Her round blue eyes stare daggers at me. She doesn't look too happy to be in my arms.

"Or maybe you're not happy that your mommy named you Baby. I'm sure that's going to lead to a lot of arguments when you get older," I say, rocking her slightly from side to side.

Baby lets out a low wail as her face reddens.

I glance at my watch. I still have plenty of time before the Tax Office opens. Spending a few minutes with this little one to help Tara isn't a burden.

In fact, some would say situations like this are my M.O.

And by some, I mean my closest friends—Ronan O'Reilly, Darren Manning, Wiley Alexander, and my best friend, Nate Bell. We make up the A-Shift of the Kimbell Fire Department. One of their favorite things to do is roast me about being in a convenient place at a convenient time to lend a helping hand. They think I'm addicted to being a do-gooder and hero.

Smoothing a hand over Baby's head, I peer at her frowning face. She feels warm and squirms in my grasp. "Don't worry, Baby. I'm not trying to be a hero by helping your mom out. I'm just as uncomfortable holding you as you are being held by me."

Baby stiffens in my arms, her little fingers gripping my shirt as she grunts. Seconds later, the stench almost knocks me out. Yep, she's taking care of her business while cradled in my arms.

Glancing over my shoulder, I'm relieved to see Tara walking briskly toward us. I decide to meet her halfway, turning quickly to head toward her.

Wrong move.

Baby hiccups, then hurls projectile green vomit onto my white dress shirt. I jerk her away, holding her an arm's length away from the mess she just made. She responds with a giggle.

I let out a sigh as Tara grabs her from my arms. "Luke, I'm so sorry. Let me pay for your dry cleaning."

"Don't worry about it," I say, then point to Baby's diaper. "I think you have more important things to take care of."

Tara raises Baby in the air and sniffs, then groans. "I'll make this up to you, Luke. I promise." She dashes back to her car as my phone buzzes in my pocket.

The call I shouldn't have answered.

"What are you talking about, Herbert?" I ask, although I know what prompted this call after years of silence.

"Don't try to pretend you weren't glued to your TV as the poll results came in on the primaries."

So what if I was? That doesn't mean I want to discuss the results with him. He's waiting for a response, but I play this game much better. Silence is a strength.

"Okay, I'll cut to the chase," Herbert says, his words tumbling at a fast pace. "Madeleine needs you. You were the best campaign manager she had. You're a natural political strategist. Every decision you made in her mayoral campaign got her elected. We need that same Luke magic to get her the governorship. What do you say?"

I grip the back of my neck, trying to release the throbbing pain from my tight muscles. Making it to a run-off in the primaries is a long way off from being on the ballot in November and even further from being elected governor of Texas. She's facing an uphill battle.

"I'm not working on another campaign for Madeleine Rice. Ever."

"Come on, isn't it time to get over what happened back—"

"You have my answer. Don't call me again." I shove the phone back into my pocket and push through the doors of the tax office.

CHAPTER 2

L UKE

~

Bobby Lee Junior, Lasso County's tax assessor-collector, lifts a hand toward his mouth as his brows furrow into a deep frown. I swear he's turning as green as—

"Is that vomit on your shirt?" He looks at me as if I'm a walking manifestation of the bubonic plague coming to destroy him. "Now, if you're sick, you should go back home." The man looks ready to flee.

I swivel toward him, which is another mistake.

His body lurches in a dry heave.

"I swear I'm fine." I almost cross my arms over my chest to hide the stain, then think better of it.

"Vangie!" He yells, disdain painted across his face. He reaches for the bottle of hand sanitizer resting on the worn oak counter and pumps it for a good twenty seconds until his hands are dripping wet. "Can you grab a large polo from the stock closet and bring it up front?"

"Extra large," I whisper.

"What?"

"Not sure I can squeeze into a large."

Bobby Junior stiffens, his face turning dark red. "Make that an extra large, Vangie!"

Seconds later, a petite woman rounds the corner, her soft brown hair framing a face with girl-next-door charm. An infectious giggle escapes her lips as she points at me, eyes dancing with glee. "You're Mr. March! I love what the calendar says about you." She clears her throat, and adopts a sultry, Irish accent as she says, "Eyes as green as the March clover and ready to save your day."

I can't help but laugh since her Irish accent is horrible.

Vangie thrusts the shirt toward me. "How are you still hot covered in puke? What happened?"

"Baby Stafford …" I say, thankful for the change of clothes. I unbutton my shirt quickly, dropping it to the floor, and pull the Polo on.

Bobby Junior averts his gaze as Vangie lets out a low whistle.

"Thanks for the shirt—"

"Oh, it's not free," Bobby Junior says.

"No, it will cost you an autograph!" Vangie says, then sprints to her desk. Drawers jerk open frantically until she finds what she's looking for. In a blink, she's shoving her way between me and Bobby Junior with the Firefighter Hunks calendar.

Bobby Junior crosses his arms over his chest. "What were you thinking posing commando in a calendar? Never thought you'd do something like that." He shakes his head with disdain.

"Only my chest was bare, and it was for a good cause." I remind myself of the meals that will go to kids living below the poverty line this summer. They'd normally miss out on healthy meals when the schools aren't open. It makes the unexpected attention from the ladies bearable.

"An excellent cause. We haven't met yet. I'm Vangie Tarkington,"

She gives me a sweet smile. "I grew up in Kimbell, moved away for too many years for reasons we don't need to discuss, then came to my senses and moved back home about a month ago."

"Luke Diamond. Nice to meet you," I say, flashing her a smile. She makes an exaggerated fanning gesture. Grabbing a marker from a brass pen holder, I pause as she flips the calendar pages to March. "How do you spell your name?"

"Oh, it's not for me," Vangie says. "This copy is for my cousin, Kennedy. She's moving today, and this is her housewarming gift."

"You know Kennedy?" Bobby Junior asks.

"Nope." I write her cousin's name. "I've only lived here for a little over five years. That's not enough time to have met everyone."

"You may not know my cousin, but you know her." Vangie beams. "If you drive into Downtown Kimbell from the east, you can't miss her. She's the girl on the billboard."

The marker clatters to the floor as realization strikes me.

"That's your cousin, Kennedy?"

The billboard woman I stare at while waiting for the light to change to green is real and local. I'd convinced myself she was some stock photo model, carefully chosen by a bunch of old men running an accounting firm to put a much friendlier face on their business.

But I was wrong.

The woman is … Vangie's cousin, Kennedy.

My mind races, recalling the details I admire on my daily commute —her mesmerizing mahogany eyes, the full lips curved in a smile both professional and playful, and those dark loose curls framing her flawless face. She's a timeless beauty, graceful and sophisticated, yet with a twinkle in her eyes that makes her approachable. Suddenly, my drive home holds a new kind of anticipation.

"She's a real pretty girl," Bobby Junior says.

"Not that it profits her much," Vangie adds, her eyes hiding a cryptic message.

"What does that mean?" I feel compelled to ask.

A flash of embarrassment and unease crosses Vangie's face. "Let's just say she's gorgeous enough to hook them but can't for the life of her reel them in."

"That's a great way of putting it," Bobby Junior says.

I must admit I'm a bit surprised a woman like Kennedy could have any problems in the relationship department, but I know looks aren't everything. I grab my ruined shirt and toss it in the trash bin behind the counter.

"What brings you here so early?" Vangie asks.

"Just dropping off payment of my property taxes." Reaching into my back pocket, I pull out the five-figure check and hand it to her.

Bobby Junior says, "I appreciate you staying on top of this."

"It's two months late," I point out.

"Better late than never. We've had a spike in delinquent property owners now that property values around town are going through the roof. We really need the money," Bobby Junior says. "With the influx of tourists and new residents with vacation properties by the lake, we're struggling to fund all the infrastructure and transportation upgrades needed."

"The increases this year gave me sticker shock," I admit.

"Not sure how you managed it on your fire fighter salary. You guys serve the community tirelessly but don't get paid a lot for your efforts," Bobby Junior says.

The answer is simple. "I promised Gramps."

My grandfather's weathered face flashes in my mind, his eyes crinkling as he surveyed the land he lived on for over sixty years. With a frown creasing his eyebrows, he said, "This land's got Diamond blood and sweat in every acre. Don't you forget that." His calloused hand squeezed my shoulder. "All this will be yours someday. Don't let nobody take it away from you when I'm gone." The memory tightens my chest. He was gone too soon for my liking.

"Here's your receipt, Luke." Vangie hands me a printout. "And thanks again."

"Anytime," I say as my cellphone emits a shrill beep. I say a quick goodbye, then head outside. Part of me wants to ignore the text, but I can't because I know exactly who it's from.

Tapping the screen, I read the message.

UNKNOWN NUMBER
We need to talk soon -M

CHAPTER 3

K ENNEDY

~

"YOU'VE GOT TO BE KIDDING ME!" I STAND AT THE EDGE OF my property, staring in disbelief at the innocent-looking barbed wire fence separating my land from the land owned by the descendants of the late Frank Diamond. The fence that, apparently, is electrified.

Granny's laughter echoes in my memory. Her words fuel me. "Nothing worth having comes easy, Ken. You just have to keep fighting to get what you want."

That's precisely what she did her whole life. My grandmother, Alice Butler, did it when she clawed her way from poverty growing up in East Austin to become one of the top horticulturists in the state, designer of the award-winning Bell Botanical Gardens, contracting her gardening services to the rich and famous.

She also did it every time Frank Diamond, the town's resident recluse and curmudgeonly land baron, tried to run her off from being his neighbor. For decades, he was a thorn in Granny's side, planting invasive poison ivy along the property line, accidentally spraying herbicide on Granny's prized roses, and luring an army of squirrels to be a nuisance in her trees.

I was amazed she never let the old fool bother her. Granny said that our family was meant to own land in Lasso County. Her father had lost land here in a dispute in the early 1900s when she was just a teenager, and it devastated our family. They moved to Austin to start over, but she never forgot her childhood home or how much she loved living in Kimbell. The first chance she got, Granny moved back and bought property here to honor her father and his original dream to raise his family in this quaint small town.

And now she's passed the land on to me.

"I wish." Orlando Watson, the amateur home renovator with out-of-this-world skills, gives me an apologetic look. "Having a jacuzzi nearby raises the risk of electrocution. It's a no-go unless your neighbor agrees to disable the electricity from the fence."

An electrified fence was overkill, even for crotchety old Frank Diamond. Was the old man afraid Granny would beat him up with a handful of Texas wildflowers and a water hose?

I narrow my eyes at the fence. Challenge accepted. I'll make you proud, Granny. Let's see how the Diamond Family likes dealing with Kennedy 2.0. I press my hands on my hips and look Orlando in the eyes, "Don't you worry about that fence. I'll have a chat with whoever inherited the land from Frank and—"

"His grandson, Luke Diamond. You know, the firefighter," Orlando says.

"Name sounds familiar," I say, wracking my brain for any detail I've heard about him. While Kimbell is a small town, not everyone knows everyone. It's not so strange that I've never met the guy.

The only thing that comes to mind about Luke Diamond is that everyone thinks he's extremely nice and generous.

Or the polar opposite of his grandfather.

In fact, I remember Granny saying Frank had softened once his grandson moved in with him. Let's hope the apple fell extremely far from the tree.

Undeterred, I say, "Convincing Luke won't be a problem. Trust me."

"You're so pretty when you're determined," Orlando says, a sly smile playing at the corners of his lips. "Luke better watch out."

"I'm immune to your flirting, Orlando," I remind him, not even remotely tempted to give him the time of day. After suffering through my sixth breakup in five years months ago, I had to finally admit that my love life is a dumpster fire. I deserve to be called "Kennedy the Dumpee" behind my back. The whole town is right about me.

I suck at love.

It would be easy for me to blame my predicament on my career.

I'm a card-carrying, unapologetic, nerdy accountant.

I run my own accounting firm, Tarkington & Associates, although that's not as glamorous as it sounds. There are no associates. At least not yet. I am the firm's only employee. I'm the go-to accountant for most of the small businesses in town. I work in a beautiful new office overlooking the pristine waters of Lake Lasso and make good money.

But I'm not too busy for relationships like my colleagues.

I have plenty of time to date. Countless hours are available for me to dedicate to cultivating a strong and committed connection with a man.

I also don't have the problem of picking jerks, cheaters, drunkards, narcissists, or commitment-phobes. I have a long line of exes who are amazing and great guys with great personalities, stellar resumes, and good looks. They're all catches.

And they all left me behind to be caught by other women.

Yes, the common denominator of failure is yours truly.

I've been dumped six times in a row, and I never saw it coming.

In fact, I was at that dreamy point in the relationship when I started to believe things were going so well that a ring was in my future. Then the rug would be yanked from under me, and I'd find myself dazed, crushed, and single all over again.

The culprit, I've come to realize, is not my looks.

It's my flawed personality.

And I'm so over trying to make a relationship work anymore.

With each breakup, it chipped away a little more at my soul until I was just numb. I don't care anymore.

I don't care that my exes think I'm gorgeous but boring. Or that I'm a human calculator, spreadsheet lover who lacks spontaneity and loses herself in details no one finds interesting. Trust me, looks are not everything. I have the scars on my broken heart to prove it.

And that's why I decided to give myself a fresh start. One that doesn't involve love or men or trying to be in a relationship. There are plenty of happily single women with no regrets in this world, and I'm determined to become one of them!

"Ouch, that hurts." Orlando clutches an imaginary knife near his heart. "But you've been single for a while now …"

"True, and I plan to stay that way. I'm officially on a relationship hiatus," I announce proudly, clasping my hands in triumph.

"So, why are you moving into this big house? It's a lot for just one person. Could get lonely."

I glance at the towering oak and pine trees that hover near the Tudor house. Dark wood accents contrast against the cream stucco walls. Steep gable points skyward, stretching toward the wisps of clouds drifting overhead. A lump forms in my throat as I take in the leaded glass windows, their panes glinting in the sunlight.

The better question is, why did I take so long to make the move?

Granny passed away two years ago, leaving the land and her home to me, her only grandchild. I've always loved the house, but I couldn't get past my dreams of moving into it with my new husband, where we would live happily ever after and raise our gorgeous but precocious babies. I was determined to wait until that happened, but you blink, and two years have passed, and I'm left with too many regrets.

Not just regrets.

Truth is, my ego is too fragile to keep trying. My confidence is at an all-time low, and I don't think I could survive another rejection.

And I don't need Orlando questioning my decision to move into a house without a family. My happiness doesn't need to be held hostage any longer.

I suck in a deep breath, then respond, "When you think about it, it's a sound financial decision. With the development of the lake houses and modern commercial park at Lake Lasso, property values all over Kimbell have started to skyrocket. Higher property values mean higher taxes. The taxes on this house alone have doubled for the past two years," I explain, a fissure of excitement flowing through me as I think about the thorough analysis I performed. What started as an emotional decision from being tired of waiting for Prince Charming to show up and put a ring on my finger turned into a strategic decision that is a logical move.

"In situations like these, people get spooked and default to selling. They can't see the investment they are sitting on because they can't afford the taxes and are afraid of the IRS. But I ran several financial models on the trajectory of valuation change for the land in this area, probability-weighted, of course, then considering the strain that more visitors would put on our town, the increased needs for infrastructure, and the impact that would have on local tax rates. After that, I extrapolated the likely corresponding increase in rent on my condo as more people are priced out of owning homes and determined ..." my voice falters as I watch Orlando's eyes glaze over. "Long story short, it's cheaper for me to live here than to maintain this place and my apartment at Belvedere on the Lake."

"Makes ... sense," Orlando says, his eyes darting toward his SUV. He scratches the back of his head absently. "Well, I should really be going."

"Of course," I say, not surprised he's bailing. He's no longer looking at me like a delectable piece of eye candy.

The guy can't get out of here fast enough.

"Oh, I forgot to tell you. Your cousin, Vangie, had a gift couriered over here for you. I put it on the coffee table. And Ace Lallo dropped off a trunk that arrived from Austin."

Ace moonlights for me, wrangling a crew to tend to Granny's garden, when he's not at his day job as a maintenance worker for the town. I wonder what could be in the trunk.

"I had him put it in the closet in the foyer," Orlando continues, walking backward toward the driveway. "Keep me posted on how things go with Luke and the fence."

I give him a wave as he drives away.

"Good riddance," I mutter, then make my way to the front entrance of my new home.

Opening the door, my jaw drops as I take in the sleek, minimalist design that seamlessly blends with the Tudor charm. The open-concept living area is bathed in natural light, highlighting the perfect balance of modern functionality and nostalgic touches. Like Granny's collection of glass figurines, tastefully placed between the books lining my custom-built bookcases.

I walk over and grab a little girl with dark brown skin and black hair holding a yellow rose. I remember when Granny let me pick this as her next purchase. I felt so proud to have the responsibility and took it seriously. My heart soared when I saw how much she loved my choice.

That little girl was confident and fearless.

What happened to her?

I place the figurine back on the shelf, then twirl around the living room in a fit of giddiness, like I used to do as a kid. I'm more convinced than ever that this is the right move.

Stopping in the living room, I declare, "Today, I'm reinventing myself. I will be Kennedy 2.0. A woman who seeks out thrilling experiences, goes outside of her comfort zone, and grabs life by the neck. All without needing a man by her side!"

I shake a triumphant fist in the air, then look down at the gift waiting for me from Vangie. She's thoughtful and always knows the perfect gift for every occassion.

Ripping the paper off the thin square, a squeal of delight escapes my lips.

"Yes!" I shout, jumping up and down as I devour the sexy man on the cover of this year's Firefighter Hunks calendar. His name is Enrique, and he's from El Paso. Maybe a trip is in my future …

"No, Kennedy!" I shout, then plop back down on the couch. "Didn't you just say you don't need a man for the brand new you?"

Did I really cave that fast?

I groan as my hand slowly peels back the calendar cover to page six to see the delicious treat for March.

Not needing a man is very different from not admiring one.

Especially sexy ones.

I can reinvent myself and still be open to possibilities … right?

Biting my bottom lip, I fling the calendar open and gasp aloud.

"Oh, my goodness …" I lick my lips slowly as my eyes caress over every inch of the man staring back at me. Tilting my head to the side, I stare into the most devastatingly gorgeous green eyes I've ever seen.

Am I forgetting to breathe?

A caption beside the man's face reads, *"Eyes as green as the March clover and ready to save your day."*

"Wow," I whisper, my eyes dropping to the oil-slicked muscular chest as the man holds a water hose over his shoulder, pointing at the camera. It's an appropriate pose. Every woman with this calendar will need to be hosed down to cool off from looking at him. To the left of his glistening eight-pack abs is an autograph.

I spread the calendar over the coffee table, unable to take my eyes off this man.

I cannot believe it …

Mr. March is my new neighbor—Luke Diamond.

CHAPTER 4

L UKE

~

"SHE'S TRYING TO SUCK YOU BACK INTO HER TOXIC ORBIT and destroy you," Nate rants, stalking around the mulch-landscaped island amid the grassy knoll.

The smell of rain is in the air as slate gray clouds stretch across the sky, matching my somber mood. I drop my leg off the side of the hammock and push, sending it swaying in the breeze.

Nate's rant continues. He's been like this since he arrived ten minutes ago, yanking at his tie to loosen it and tossing his jacket onto the grass.

"You didn't respond to the text, did you?" He stops to glare at me, anger wafting from him.

"Nope," I respond, swaying in the breeze.

"And you're not going to, right?"

That's when I hesitate a fraction too long.

Nate stalks over to me. "Do I need to remind you what happened five years ago? How being entangled with that woman turned your life upside down?"

"Let's not go down that road," I say, although having your life turned upside down can have a bright side. If I hadn't gone through that pain, I never would've found my grandfather. I wouldn't have moved to Kimbell. I wouldn't have the life I love today. Sure, it's different from the fast-paced world of political intrigue and drama that used to fuel me, but I don't miss it. At least, not most days.

Rising from the hammock, I stare at the waters of Diamond Lake behind Nate. The surface reflects the brooding sky like a dark mirror, its surface barely rippling in the gentle breeze.

Nate doesn't take his eyes off me, waiting for an answer to his question.

Clearing my throat, I say, "This is a big deal. It's not like she's the mayor of Houston, Dallas, or even Austin. The fact that her name has gotten that popular across the state to force a runoff means she could have a legitimate shot at being governor—"

"And have you thought about what that could mean for you?" Nate barks the question. "How your name could get dragged through the mud when her opponents dig up dirt on her? You're the dirtiest skeleton in her closet."

My whole body tenses as his words deliver a knock-out blow. I know he's not trying to be mean. He just cares enough to give me a blunt dose of reality.

I fall onto the hammock and close my eyes, heaving a heavy breath. "I'm not going to text her back, and I'm not going to call her. Trust me, I know I should keep a low profile. This is moot if she doesn't win the run-off. If she does win ..."

"You'll have to prepare yourself because it's a bonafide guarantee that the the truth will come out," Nate prophesizes doom and gloom.

I'm not sure I agree with him, but it's too early to get riled up about what could happen. The path to the governor's office is a long and winding one. Madeleine might reach the end of her pursuit sooner than we think.

My best friend finally relaxes enough to sit in the hammock next to mine. Kicking his feet up, he swings back and forth, staring at the sky. "Can you imagine if you were still dating Ciara?"

"No! That would've been a disaster." The words are out of my mouth before I realize it. A shudder ripples through my body, and my eyes fly open.

"An ambitious reporter dating a man who holds an epic secret on a candidate for governor. She would've pried the truth out of you and forced your hand."

"I don't doubt it. But she's out of my life now," I say, a bit unsettled at the thought. If Channel 4 Houston News for You reporter Ciara Thompson gets wind of the truth, I know she'll find her way to my doorstep. I don't know what I'll do if she shows up. How could I, a guy she ghosted, convince her to walk away from a blockbuster story that could put her career on the map? She would probably turn on the charm and try to bend me to her will.

This is one time she wouldn't get the better of me.

"If y'all hadn't already broken up, this definitely would be a deal breaker for both of you."

"There was no breakup, remember," I say, shrugging. "It was just a parting of ways." I use air quotes as I say the last words like Ciara did to me.

Nate laughs out loud. "Leave it to her to put a spin on things so she doesn't look bad. Whatever. I'm glad the parting of ways didn't impact you much." He leans forward to look me over. "Or at all. Guess you really weren't that into her, were you?"

"I was at first," I say, remembering when Ciara and I met after the fire at Elm Street Brewery. There was something so intoxicatingly fresh about her as she interviewed me. I couldn't stop thinking about her. But initial physical attraction can't compensate for lack of chemistry and an uneasy vibe. "But the more we got to know each other, the more things didn't fit."

"The dreaded incompatible goals and desires. Kills a budding relationship every time," Nate says, then swings out of the hammock. "What were you doing at the tax office anyway?"

"What?" I ask, jolted by his change of subject.

"You said she texted you after you left the tax office. What's going on?" Nate raises an eyebrow.

I lean over and jump down from the hammock. "Paying my tax bill late again. It's almost doubled from last year thanks to Zaire's lake houses. They're good for the town, but writing that check is getting harder and harder every year."

Nate falls in step next to me as we walk back toward the house—a charmingly worn single-story cabin with weathered cedar siding. The wraparound porch is casual and welcoming and adorned with mismatched rocking chairs and potted ferns.

"Well, don't ask me for a loan because I'm not giving you one," Nate says.

"And don't offer to give me money because I'm not going to take it," I respond.

It's an infrequent but well-known impasse between the two of us. Having a billionaire as a best friend has complications that must be navigated almost daily. Most people don't have a friend who could wipe out their financial woes with a single check.

But Nate and I got close because it never crossed my mind to expect him to swoop in and help me with money, unlike his other friends. It's probably why I'm the one person he'd write the check for that I'd never accept.

"Guess we're still at a stalemate," Nate says, then waves a hand back toward the orchard. "I bet if you research it a bit, you could make this place pay for itself. I'm sure the orchards produce a lot of fruit and pecans. Might be worth trying to sell your harvest instead of eating it."

"Not a bad idea," I say, glancing at the trees of Gramp's orchard in the distance. The intricate patterned design evokes awe from everyone who sees it. It's a deliberate design that remains harmonious with the wild brush. An alternating pattern of diamonds and circles comprised of fruit trees and nut trees. He grew everything imaginable: figs, peaches, pears, apples, plums, and, of course, Texas pecans.

Gramps claimed the orchard was there when he got the land. He had nothing to do with the orchard or the design that matched our family surname. I don't believe him. He was no stranger to lying if it suited him.

Admitting that the poker-playing, alcohol-swigging ladies' man the town knew him to be also had a hankering for gardening would never happen. It was the kind of thing he'd do on the sly to thumb his nose at the community that made him feel like an outsider.

But the sting dulled over the decades and vanished completely when I arrived in Kimbell. I loved the property from the moment I stepped foot on it. We would pick a different section each day and walk every inch of it while secretly healing from our respective demons. Something about the beauty and quiet of nature settled both our spirits.

I continue, "Much better than selling the land or parts of it to Zaire."

"Is she still on you about that?" Nate balks.

"No more official offers, but she manages to bring it up in any conversation we're in together as a joke that's not a joke."

"Money isn't everything," Nate says.

"That's for sure."

Gramps turned down every offer he'd gotten to buy the property with the same sardonic response, "some things are priceless." That's what he thought about his land. It didn't take me long to adopt his views.

"But starting a farm business would be a lot of work and come with more expenses," I say. "I'd need to do a lot of research and understand all the aspects of it before implementing anything."

Nate shrugs, then says, "Or you can hire someone with experience to help you. When Mya got to town and wanted to start her personal training company, she got Tarkington & Associates to help her. Now, look at how well she's doing. She's got more clients than she knows what to do with."

The velvety-skinned beauty from the billboard pops into my head. The wasted time with Ciara showed me it's been too long since I've had someone special in my life. A person who understands me and appreciates the quiet life I've built here. In my past few relationships, that's been the missing piece ... the one that matters the most to me that never came to fruition.

But I'm not going to stop trying or looking.

"You know much about that company? Who runs it?" I ask, hoping I don't sound too interested. If Nate thought for one second that I had an ulterior motive for asking, he'd be all over me.

"Kennedy Tarkington," Nate says, then whistles under his breath. "She's stunning and smart as a whip. Our accounting team consults with her on complex accounting matters. I hear she's gotten us out of a few jams."

"But you've never met her."

"Nope. That doesn't mean I can't arrange an introduction if you're serious about getting this place to be a revenue generator," Nate offers. "Just let me know."

"Yeah, I will."

And I'm not just saying it.

Deep down, I know crossing paths with the beauty from the billboard is in my future. I'll discover what's behind the pretty face.

CHAPTER 5

K ENNEDY

HOLDING THE FIREFIGHTER HUNKS CALENDAR UP HIGH FOR all of us to see, my cousin Yolanda shakes her head in amazement. Luke Diamond's devilishly handsome face is on display, making my heart flip and flop.

I need another crush like I need a hole in my head.

I'm at the start of my Kennedy 2.0 man-free life of bliss. I can't suffer a setback by letting an attractive man derail all my plans. Yet, all my bravado about facing off with my neighbor and demanding he disable the stupid electrified fence waned once I realized Luke was the man I'd need to convince.

No one should be that freaking handsome.

I catch myself tracing the outline of his jaw with my eyes, imagining how it would feel under my fingertips. Shaking my head, I force the thought away.

"Please put that down," I say, turning from the calendar. The floorboards creak under my feet as I move to the stove, a comforting sound that reminds me of my days with Granny. This house holds so many memories, and now it's mine to fill with new ones. Like tonight when I invited Yolanda and Vangie for my first dinner in the house.

I check my fried chicken. I'm old school. No electric or air fryers for me. All I need is a massive pot with piping hot canola oil. The grease pops and splatters onto the stove as my chicken turns a heavenly shade of brown.

For a moment, I wonder if Luke likes fried chicken. Does he cook? Or is he the type to survive on takeout and protein shakes to maintain that firefighter physique?

Stop it, Kennedy, I scold myself. I can't let my imagination run wild, conjuring up fantasies of Luke that will end like all my past relationships—with me dazed, confused, and alone. I'm determined to prove my happiness isn't tied to being with some man.

If only Yolanda, Vangie, and I had been little girls interested in something other than fairytales of princesses who marry the men of their dreams, maybe this wouldn't be so hard.

Vangie was the first to capture her Prince Charming and happily ever after, only to find out the guy was just a frog. The relationship was a disaster. I'm so glad she's back home where she belongs, away from that fool who duped her.

Yolanda is the most cautious of us, living vicariously through the brides she makes beautiful wedding dresses for. But she's barely let any man get close enough for her to have a chance at happiness. She claims her standards are too high. But Vangie and I think she's scared because she's had a front-row seat to our relationship woes.

And well, my story is lined with finding a bunch of princes who realize I'm the frog in the love story. It sucks, and I'm not in the mood to go through that again. Which is why I'm annoyed I'm feeling those fluttering butterflies every time I look at Luke Diamond's photo in the calendar.

Yolanda says, "What's your problem with the calendar, Kennedy?"

"Have y'all forgotten what I told you about the electrified fence on the property line between my land and my neighbor's?" I look from Yolanda to Vangie and back again. "The fence that was put up by crotchety old Frank Diamond just to annoy my granny. Since he passed away, I have to talk to the person who inherited the land to get the fence turned off."

Vangie and Yolanda look at me with identical masks of confusion.

I point at Luke's photo.

"Oh … Oh!" They say in unison.

"That's a good problem if you ask me," Vangie quips. "Any excuse to talk to that man again is one I'd take. Trust me, I saw him with my naked eyes, and he's so much hotter in person than he is in this calendar."

I exhale loudly. "Luke could be just like his stubborn grandfather. I might be in for a fight to get him to see reason. Him being incredibly hot just complicates matters. I'm trying to avoid hot guys. That's a big part of Kennedy 2.0—avoiding temptation."

Yolanda arches an eyebrow. "There is nothing wrong with window shopping, Kennedy 2.0. You don't have to buy anything."

Vangie nods in agreement. "Plus, this big fight with him that you're gearing up for probably won't happen. He was a sweetie when I met him. Getting to know your neighbor is a good thing. The two of you are the only people living along Abbott Road in the boonies. You need to be on good terms with him in case you need help when a bobcat shows up on your doorstep."

"Are you serious?" My mouth gapes open.

"Bobcat is a stretch. But a deer could kick your door in," Yolanda chimes in.

"Having Luke on speed dial to rescue you from a wild animal is the best emergency plan," Vangie says.

An image flashes through my mind: Luke, axe in hand, heroically facing down a wild animal at my door. His shirt's conveniently missing in this fantasy, and I can practically see those calendar-worthy abs in action. I feel my cheeks heat up and hope my cousins don't notice.

"And who knows if you're even his type," Vangie says, raising an eyebrow. "He might like the petite version of a Tarkington woman instead." She winks, then does a little shimmy around me.

And the ice bath of her words douses the flames of my fantasy. I laugh but it sounds forced to my own ears. She's totally right. I'm all tied up in knots over a picture of a guy who probably isn't attracted to me. And if he is, it wouldn't take him long to bail like all the others once he got to know me better.

Embarrassment sobers me, and I jolt back to reality.

"Who cares who he likes," I announce. "The most important thing is getting that fence turned off so we can have the jacuzzi we've been dreaming about. Am I right?"

"Yes indeed," Yolanda says as she leans in for a high-five. We slap hands, then turn and repeat the move with Vangie.

"Now that's settled, how about the two of you go through that trunk while I finish dinner," I say, pointing at the trunk I dragged into the kitchen from the foyer closet.

Vangie claps her hands excitedly. "Ooh, yes! I love a good mystery. What do you think we'll find in there, Ken?"

I shrug, trying to appear nonchalant despite the curiosity bubbling up inside me. "Could be anything. But I'm guessing it's a bunch of old photos and letters from Granny's childhood."

"Or there could be a treasure map leading to a fortune in gold doubloons," Yolanda adds with a wink.

We all laugh, but as I turn back to the stove to finish up dinner, I can't shake the feeling it's not a coincidence that the trunk was delivered on the same day I moved into Granny's house. There's something important inside, and I'm anxious to find out what it is.

CHAPTER 6

KENNEDY

A SAVORY AROMA FILLS THE KITCHEN AS I JOIN VANGIE AND Yolanda at the dining table. I place the waffle fries between the basket of fried chicken and the bowl of green beans.

But my cousins aren't tempted by the food. Their attention is focused on the contents of the trunk. It's constructed of wood covered in navy blue canvas with camel-colored leather accents around the edges. Looking at it, I can feel the weight of history it carries. We stare into the luxurious blue silk-lined interior filled with chaotic stacks of paper.

"Where did this come from?" Vangie asks, her voice hushed with awe.

I relay how the church in East Austin discovered it in their attic as they prepared to move into a new sanctuary, my words tumbling out faster as excitement builds. This trunk is more than just an old container—it's a direct link to my great-grandfather, Cornelius Butler. To the life the maternal side of my family lived before I was born.

As we begin to sift through the papers, I can't help but feel we're on the brink of uncovering something big.

Yolanda smiles as she grabs some documents from the trunk. "It was really nice of them to track your family down and get this to you. Most people would've sent it to the trash dump." She carefully places a series of papers on the opposite end of the table, away from the food. Each page contains hand-sketched drawings of a garden design with an orchard. I peer at the corners and see the signature of the woman who is my hero, my granny, Alice Butler.

"What do you think this is?" Yolanda asks as I pick up one of the pages. The date is older than I expected.

"Well, if this date is right, Granny drew this before she went to college at Huston-Tillotson and became a horticulturist. This might be her very first garden design." My hands tremble at the potential significance of the work.

"It's stunning," Vangie says.

Yolanda adds, "You got to get this over to Bell Botanical Gardens. Since the Bell Family renamed the visitor center after your granny, I'm sure they'd love to have drawings like this on display to educate people on the history of her work."

"That's a great idea," I say.

"Let's see what other goodies are inside," Vangie says, then pulls out stacks of pages and places one in front of each of us.

As I sift through the papers, each discovery feels like unwrapping a piece of history. There's a faded picture of a stern-looking man I recognize as my great-grandfather from old photo albums Granny had. A yellowed newspaper clipping announces the opening of a "colored-only" school in East Austin. I even find a handwritten recipe for peach cobbler that makes my mouth water just reading it.

"Look at this," Yolanda says, holding up a document. "It's some kind of legal paper."

My heart skips a beat. "What's it say?"

She squints at the faded writing. "I can't quite make it out. Something about Lasso County property taxes?"

A chill runs down my spine.

I reach for another stack of papers, my fingers trembling slightly. One page catches my eye. Lifting it up, I scan the document as a fissure of excitement slides across my skin. It looks like a property deed.

"Oh my goodness ..." I say, flipping to the next page. At the bottom, I see the signatures of my great-grandfather as grantee and Zebediah Abbott as grantor. The document is notarized and signed by a witness.

"What you got there?" Yolanda asks, leaning over.

"Y'all know how my granny always talked about how her family lived in Kimbell, and her dad owned land here that he lost. That's why they moved to East Austin when she was a teenager."

"And when she moved back, she was determined to buy property here to re-establish the family in town," Vangie says. "That's how you got this amazing five-acre property and gorgeous house."

"Well, I think this document proves everything she remembered is true. It's a deed to property here in Kimbell."

"Let me see that," Yolanda says, taking the document from me.

"If that's the deed, how did the Butlers lose the land? Did your granny ever say?" Vangie asks.

"No, she was always vague about it. She talked about how unusual and difficult it was for black families back then to own land and hold onto it. But nothing much more than that."

"Kennedy ..." Yolanda says, looking at me with an intensity that sets the hairs on my neck on edge. "Did you read the description of the property on this deed?"

"Just enough to know it's some land in Kimbell. Why?"

Yolanda says, "'Fifty-five acres of land within Kimbell, Texas contained within the borders of Lake Lasso on the east and Abbott Road on the west.'"

"Well, that sounds a lot like the land you're living on right now," Vangie says with a laugh that falters.

"Fifty-five acres?" My heart pounds, and my breath quickens.

"She bought five acres, so the other fifty ..." Yolanda turns to look at the calendar.

"Is Frank Diamond's land," I say, bolting up from my chair. "He stole the land from my family!"

My heart pounds in my ears as the implications hit me like a tidal wave. I grip the edge of the table, suddenly dizzy. This isn't just about a fence or a jacuzzi anymore. This is about my family's legacy, about righting a wrong that's been festering for generations.

"Kennedy?" Vangie's voice sounds far away. "Are you okay?"

I shake my head, trying to clear it. "I ... I don't know." My voice comes out as a whisper. "If this is true, that land really belonged to my great-grandfather ..." I trail off, overwhelmed by a mix of anger, excitement, and uncertainty.

Yolanda places a hand on my shoulder. "This could change everything."

I nod, my mind racing. Granny's determination to move back here, her insistence on buying this particular piece of land—it all makes sense now. She knew. She must have known or at least suspected.

And now, it's up to me to finish what she started.

A surge of determination courses through me, pushing aside my earlier reservations about confronting Luke. This isn't just about me anymore. It's about honoring Granny's memory and reclaiming my family's rightful place in Kimbell.

"I need to know more," I say, my voice stronger now. "I need to understand exactly what happened. And then ..." I pause, meeting my cousins' concerned gazes. "Then I'm going to do whatever it takes to set things right."

CHAPTER 7

L UKE

~

"I'M SO SORRY YOU'RE ENGAGED TO THIS UNROMANTIC oaf," I say, slipping in between Mya and Ronan at the take-out counter of Baker Bros BBQ. "This is a crappy date night, my friend. Nothing says romance like the aroma of smoky meat, warped wooden walls, and the soothing ambiance of fluorescent lighting."

Ronan gives me a look that lets me know the night isn't his fault, then shakes his head at the cramped back room designated for to-go orders at Kimbell's most famous restaurant. It's not surprising we're the only three in the take-out room on a Friday night. Raucous conversations filter through the thin walls from the main dining room.

Mya drops her face in her hands and inhales a deep breath. "It's all my fault. I got the dates mixed up and thought it was tomorrow night."

"We're on shift at the fire station tomorrow," I say, frowning as I lock eyes with Ronan. He gives me an annoyed look and nods his head again.

"I completely looked at the calendar wrong and was double booked with clients until early evening. When Ronan came to look for me, I realized my mistake. I ruined everything."

"My grand plan was to wine and dine this sexy lady at Resviglio, stuffing her with carbs and dancing the night away. Georgia's off from the hospital and agreed to let the boys have a sleepover. It was supposed to be very romantic," Ronan explains, wrapping his arms around Mya. She leans into his embrace as they exchange a loving glance.

"I promise I'll make it up to you," Mya says, turning in Ronan's arms to kiss him quickly.

As I watch Ronan and Mya together, longing claws at me. I want what he has—someone who lights up at the sight of me, sharing inside jokes and stolen glances across a room. The easy intimacy between them reminds me of the void in my life, a space I've tried too many times to fill, coming close but never finding the right woman to eliminate the emptiness. I can't say I haven't been in love because I have a few times. But I've never been with a woman I looked at like Ronan is looking at Mya.

That's the prize I'm still trying to win. As much as I loved Gramps, I don't want to be him when I'm old and gray. Before I got to Kimbell, he was a recluse with no friends and a steady stream of women who flowed in and out of his life. He admittedly never had a woman he shared a deep and profound love with. He was quick to warn me not to make the same mistake.

A flash of the Tarkington & Associates billboard infiltrates my mind. The beautiful woman with the big brown eyes staring back at me with a playful glint. I picture her curled up on my porch swing, laughing at my terrible jokes, her eyes sparkling in the twilight as we drink wine and gaze at the countless stars dotting the onyx sky.

I don't even know Kennedy Tarkington, yet I'm drawn to her and becoming impatient to figure out why. What started out as an intense physical attraction is shaping into something more. Hearing Nate's glowing assessment of her accounting knowledge and professional success yesterday impressed me. I've always been a sucker for an intelligent woman. While I suspected Kennedy fit the bill, getting a first-hand account from my best friend only fueled my interest in her.

I shake my head slightly, amused by how quickly my thoughts are running away with me.

Mya turns back to me. "I've been a mess trying to juggle all my new clients and plan our wedding. I can't set a date until I find a perfect venue."

"I told her we could get married at Harlow Rose's winery," Ronan says with a shrug.

"No, that place has bad mojo. I heard at the last wedding there the bride left the groom at the altar." Mya looks horrified.

Shaking my thumb toward Ronan, I say, "This guy is quicker than he looks. You wouldn't get far."

"Or we could elope like Darren and Jasmine," Ronan offers.

Mya shakes her head. "If I had a family that loves and adores me like Jasmine does, there's no way I would've gotten married without them there. All I have is Uncle Tony and a few cousins living in Houston. I can't bear to think about getting married without them. We have to get married where all our friends and family can be there. I want to do it somewhere in Kimbell. But you know how popular this area is for weddings. It's a nightmare."

"I see why you're so stressed out," I say.

"Brother, if you know any wedding planners, please let us know. It's the only way Mya and I will get married this year," Ronan says, a pleading hint in his tone.

"I might be able to help." I pull my phone out of my pocket and scroll through the contacts. "Now, she's not a professional, but she has a knack for planning parties and celebrations. In fact, Mrs. Williamson uses her to help with planning the big celebrations in Kimbell, like Founder's Day and the Love Under the Stars event that was just done for Valentine's Day." I stop on the name and then copy the phone number.

When I open the text app, I see the message that is still awaiting a response.

UNKNOWN NUMBER

We need to talk soon -M

I should delete it.

My finger hovers over the button but I don't press it.

I can't bear for it to be gone.

As much as I dread the reconnection, a part of me longs for it.

Maybe I've been waiting for it for all these years.

Nate would tell me this is flirting with disaster, and he's probably right.

I scroll past the text and start a new one to Mya and Ronan, pasting the number into it and pressing send.

"Please tell me you're not suggesting we hire Zora as our wedding planner," Ronan deadpans.

"That's exactly who you need." I flash him a big grin.

Mya asks, "Who's Zora?"

"Another pretty woman named after a famous writer like you," I say, then give her a wink that causes Ronan to look like he wants to punch me in the neck for complimenting his fiancée. To clear things up, I add, "And she's my ex-girlfriend."

She balks. "Luke, you're going to be a groomsman. Do you really want your ex hovering around as my wedding planner? Wouldn't that be awkward for you?"

Ronan chuckles. "Luke doesn't have any jilted or angry exes. In fact, they all have warm and fuzzy feelings for Kimbell's resident good guy. Isn't that right, Luke?"

"There's nothing wrong with being on good terms with your exes. Just because we didn't last doesn't mean we should hate each other," I explain.

Mya's eyes grow wide. "You're friends with … all … of your exes?"

I hesitate. "I'd say ninety-nine percent of them, yes. Plus, it's harder in a small town. I'd have to become a hermit if I wasn't on good terms with them. That's a nasty habit I'm already trying to break."

Mya laughs. "I'm impressed. You're sure you don't mind?"

"Not at all. Tell her I sent you. She might give you a discount," I say, knowing that's exactly what Zora will do.

As I put my phone away, I can't help the wayward thoughts going through my mind. In politics, sharing a contact to help someone out would come with a price—an expectation that the favor would be returned.

But how can I get Mya to help me meet Kennedy?

And should I even try?

CHAPTER 8

L UKE

~

"WHAT ARE YOU GETTING INTO TONIGHT?" RONAN ASKS.

I almost laugh. It can't be this easy, can it?

"Working on a business plan to make my land generate cash to cover the spike in property taxes," I respond, deciding I won't twist this conversation to manipulate one of my closest friends or his fiancée. I blame Madeleine for making me slip back into old ways.

"I can't imagine how hard it is to see all this change happening in the town y'all grew up in. I only visited during the summers as a kid, and I'm kind of mourning how quiet things used to be," Mya says.

I glance out the window, taking in the view of Main Street. Hendrix Jones has moved his auto repair shop into a newly renovated building that sports a fresh coat of paint and bays for more cars, and a trendy coffee shop is due to open next door in a few months. The charm is still here, but there's a new energy buzzing through town.

"I'm not a fan of all this change, but Luke wouldn't know anything about it. He's a newbie to Kimbell," Ronan says.

"Really? I just assumed you grew up here because y'all are all so close," Mya says.

Shoving my hands in my pockets, I fidget as I try to remember how much of the real story I shared when I got here five years ago. It's been so long since I've had to be careful about what I reveal and what I keep a secret. But Nate would tell me I need to get used to doing it again, especially if Madeleine wins the primary run-off in a couple of months.

"I grew up near Dallas, then went to Southern Methodist University. That's how I met and became friends with Nate."

Mya whistles under her breath. "An alum of Southern Millionaires University. Very interesting."

"I was a scholarship kid," I say, the old lies flowing from my lips. "But it didn't hurt to have a billionaire best friend while I was there. It stopped me from being shunned by the rest of them."

"And you came to town after discovering your grandfather lived here, right? The one you never met because he was estranged from your dad," Ronan says.

"That's right. It was the best coincidence in the world that Gramps lived in my best friend's hometown," I say, then add, "I didn't grow up here, but I got here as fast as I could. I love this place."

I can't even share how much it means to me.

Only Nate knows what a dark place I'd sunk to after everything blew up between me and Madeleine. My whole world had been destroyed, and I needed a lifeline to cling to if I was going to survive.

That lifeline turned out to be my grandfather, Frank Diamond.

He took me in without any hesitation.

Never asked me for anything.

Just showered me with all the love and affection I needed to heal from the pain I'd endured. All the while, he shared his love of Kimbell with me, and I fell in love with the place, too. But no place more than the land where we lived near Lake Lasso. It healed the darkness festering within me. For the first time, I felt like I truly belonged somewhere.

After getting a dose of reality from Nate, I realized there's a real chance I could lose the land if I can't afford to pay the increasing property taxes. I need a plan to ensure I don't lose my inheritance from Gramps.

And not just because he wanted me to have it.

Because the land is my home. It's where I belong. The place where I found myself after feeling utterly lost.

"So, you're going to open up a new business on your property?" Mya asks.

"The property will be the business," I say, then give them the rundown on the ideas Nate and I discussed.

"My boys would love to trample all over that orchard and pick fresh fruit and pecans. They'd probably compete for who could fill their baskets up with the most, which would cost me a lot of money," Ronan says.

"I think it's fantastic idea. Definitely one that locals and tourists would enjoy," Mya agrees.

"But it's going to require work to get set up. I spent most of today researching everything it would take, but I have a long night ahead of me. I took a break to grab dinner, then I'll finish the rough draft of the business plan."

Mya holds up her hands. "Let me stop you there. You gave us a recommendation for a wedding planner. Now, I'm going to return the favor and give you a recommendation to help set up your new business. Kennedy Tarkington."

Excitement buzzes through me, and I feel like I've tossed back a few tequila shots even though I know I'm stone-cold sober. Things worked out without any manipulation. It has to be a sign.

"Kennedy the Dumpee," Ronan says.

Mya glares at him.

"People call her that?" I ask, unable to hide my curiosity.

"Only behind her back," Ronan says, a sheepish look on his face as he dodges a swinging punch from Mya.

"Let's just say Kennedy has been unlucky in love for several years," Mya explains.

"Dumped six straight times and counting," Ronan adds. "The streak started with Dillon Crockett."

"Dillon, who got me to do the Firefighter Hunks calendar?" The words are out of my mouth before I can stop them. Dillon's not a bad guy, but he does have a sleazy, used car salesman vibe to him.

Ronan nods, then says, "And Maxwell Jones was the last guy to run for the hills. He's a great guy. Teacher. Upstanding. If you ask me, the common denominator isn't the men. There's something wrong with that woman."

"There is nothing wrong with Kennedy," Mya admonishes. "Stop spreading unfounded gossip." She turns to me. "Do not listen to him. Kennedy's personal life is irrelevant for what you need. She has an excellent mind for business matters and can help with your business plan."

My phone buzzes in my hand, and I glance down at the screen.

Why do I feel like I just won the lottery as I stare at the ten digits in the text?

The only downside is I'm on shift at the fire station tomorrow and have to wait over twenty-four hours before I can call the dark beauty.

But I have a feeling she'll be more than worth the wait.

"Luke, your order is ready."

I squeeze past Mya and Ronan with their confused faces and grab the plastic bag filled with two Styrofoam containers of my favorites. Shrugging, I say, "It helps to call your order in when you're on the way over." Laughing, I wave goodbye to them and head out the door.

CHAPTER 9

ENNEDY

IDENTICAL.

They are identical.

I stare at the document on the counter of the Lasso County records office and scratch my head.

How in the world can this be possible?

"You can take that copy," the woman behind the counter says, sweat beading along her hairline as she smooths away frazzled strands. Irritation oozes from her words as she gives me a disgusted look. "It's after hours. I really need to lock up and get home."

"Of course," I say, grabbing the copy of the deed to the fifty-five acres of property between Abbott Road and Lake Lasso. Stuffing the pages into my purse, I give her a warm smile. "I really appreciate you digging this out of the warehouse. I didn't know that historical records hadn't been scanned into the online database yet."

She ignores me and walks toward the door.

I don't blame her.

After doing as much research as I could on the property at the library, I didn't give her much choice after I arrived.

The online records for the land have already been updated to reflect Luke Diamond as the property's owner. There were no scanned copies of the documents before he received his inheritance. Comparing the deed from the trunk to the original deed that Frank Diamond had would require a trip to the Lasso County Records office.

I was determined not to leave empty-handed.

Shifting into full-blown Kennedy mode, I deftly reminded the staff of state laws and statutes on public records and the County's duty to provide information to the public upon request. Then, I made it clear I wasn't leaving until the deed was found.

The clerk had no choice but to spend the past four hours in the warehouse going through disorganized and mislabeled boxes until she found what I was looking for.

Pushing through the glass door, I open my umbrella as dreary rain drizzles from the sky. I trudge down the wide pedestrian walkway of Main Street in Downtown Kimbell toward the town center.

Anxious thoughts crowd my mind.

Frank Diamond's deed is identical to my version, except in two critical ways: the grantee is Frank Diamond instead of Cornelius Butler, and the signature line has Frank's scrawling script instead of my great-grandfather's.

Otherwise, the documents are identical.

It just doesn't make sense.

My breath catches for a moment as the realization sinks in. I pause mid-step, blinking rapidly as I process the implications. A slight tremor runs through me, my mind racing with questions and possibilities.

It's almost like someone constructed a perfect forgery of the original deed to pass it off as the real thing. And by somebody, every fiber of my being believes Frank Diamond did this to my great-grandfather. I'm just not sure how to prove it.

Grabbing my phone, I scroll through the contacts until I find the number of Kimbell's planner of community events, keeper of every minute detail of Kimbell history and folklore and resident gossip. Tapping the talk button, I don't have to wait long before it's answered.

"Kennedy, how are you, dear?" Mrs. Williamson asks, her tone warm and inviting.

"I'm good," I say, unsure of the best way to broach the topic to get the information I want but not wanting to beat around the bush. "What do you know about Granny's old neighbor, Frank Diamond?

Mrs. Williamson groans. "Besides the scandal of how he was found dead in bed with a woman half his age?"

I almost drop my phone, but manage not to gasp aloud.

"Sorry, that was wrong of me. But honey, Frank was no friend of your grandmother's. He was always doing things to vex and harass Alice. A paranoid old fool who thought she was trying to take more of his land than he sold to her, which she had no way of doing. But that's what happens when you get property in a shady way."

"Shady way?"

"Yes, dear. Frank was a con artist and grifter who first blew into town around sixty years ago when he showed up with a deed for the Abbott land. Rumors swirled that he cheated the land out of Zebediah Abbott in a poker game. Mr. Abbott was a notorious gambler. Foolish man with inept card skills. He was always selling off things for money to gamble with. Ultimately, his addiction caused the family to go bankrupt, and they moved away in disgrace."

"Frank Diamond didn't buy the land from the Abbotts?"

"Well, no one knows for sure. Frank was rude and stubborn, insisting that the deed was enough and how he got it was irrelevant. But those rumors followed him until he died a couple of years ago. Of course, back then, no one wanted the property by the lake, and it wasn't worth nearly what it is today."

A germ of a theory forms in my mind. "Did anyone ever challenge his ownership?"

"Not that I ever heard about. But the Abbotts confirmed they no longer owned the land."

"Because it was now owned by Frank Diamond?"

"Well … from the rumors, that was never explicitly confirmed or denied by the Abbotts," Mrs. Williamson says. "Why are you so interested in Frank?"

"Well, he put up an electric fence on the border of our property that's stopping me from having some renovations done …" I say.

"Oh, you won't have any problems now that Luke owns the land. Do you need his cell phone number? I'll text it to you. I'm sure he'll have no issue with turning that fence off. Luke has such a generous soul, the opposite of his grumpy grandfather. And he's quite handsome. Have you seen the firefighter hunks calendar?" Mrs. Williamson giggles like a schoolgirl. "I bought two. One for work and one for home."

I stifle a laugh, imagining Mrs. Williamson flipping through the calendar pages with a mischievous glint in her eye. It's both endearing and slightly mortifying to think she and I shared the same thoughts about Luke as we drooled over his photo.

"Thanks for the number. I'll let you know how things go with Luke," I say, ending the call. My thoughts immediately turn to the information she shared, fueling the theory blazing in my mind.

Rumors persisted that Frank Diamond cheated the Abbotts out of their land, but what if that family wasn't the only one he cheated? What if my great-grandfather bought the land from the Abbotts only to have Frank Diamond steal it? The fact that there are no stories about the Abbotts confirming Frank Diamond as the land's new owner could support my views.

I pause and take a deep breath, then glance to the left to see the take-out door for Baker Bros BBQ. I inhale the heavenly scent of smoked meat and turn toward the door. There's nothing better to fuel intense analysis than a pulled pork plate. Whenever I'm stressed and anxious, it's the perfect antidote to calm me and help me to think more clearly. Whoever said that food shouldn't be used for comfort clearly was misguided.

Stepping underneath the awning, I close my umbrella and reach for the door just as it opens.

I freeze as I stare into Dillon Crockett's dark eyes. The man who started my regrettable string of broken hearts.

"Kennedy ..." Dillon says my name as if it's a treasure on his lips. A smile curves his face as he steps back to let me inside. "It's so good to see you."

Is it? But I decide to be cordial. I won't remind him how he abandoned our relationship to make a fortune for himself unencumbered by a girlfriend who didn't match his spontaneous spirit.

"I'm surprised to see you. What brings you back to town?" I ask, squeezing past him to enter the small to-go room.

"Planning some events in town for the Firefighter Hunks calendar," Dillon says, following me inside. "You look beautiful, Kennedy. The years have been more than good to you."

I ignore his compliment. The last thing I need is Dillon giving me the attention I wanted years ago. Too little. Too late. "You're involved in that calendar? How?"

"My company created it. It's what put me on the right road financially after mom cut me off," he says with more admiration than malice.

"You weren't cut off from your trust fund. She just delayed when you'd get access to it," I remind him. "Have you gone to see her yet?"

Dillon looks embarrassed. "Not yet."

"I didn't think so. She would've mentioned it to me."

"You still visit my mother? Even after she moved into Oakbrook?"

"Of course. Just because you and I broke up doesn't mean I couldn't continue to be close to your mother. She doesn't have many people in town who care about her anymore," I say, deciding not to indict him and his siblings for moving out of town and leaving Mrs. Crockett alone. "We still get together for tea once a week."

"That's great. I didn't get it back then, but her actions helped me mature. There's no way I would've become the man I am today if I had access to my money. I've changed a lot over the years. More than you know," Dillon says, stepping into my personal space.

"We've all changed in five years." I look at his handsome face but feel none of the old sparks that used to overwhelm me.

"I'll be around for the next couple of weeks," Dillon says, then pauses as if gauging my reaction.

My face remains passive. My heart's not racing. How many times did I fantasize about a moment like this? One where I'd get a second chance at a love I thought was so important.

But with Dillon in front of me, angling for a reconnection, I find I don't want it. I'm Kennedy 2.0, and I don't need him anymore.

CHAPTER 10

K ENNEDY

~

FIFTEEN MINUTES LATER, I CRADLE MY BELOVED BBQ dinner like a precious baby as I cross Main Street and head toward Bell Park. The rain has transitioned from a light drizzle to a wispy mist. I tuck my umbrella in my purse and give up on taming my wild hair as it floats against my shoulders.

Dusk settles across the massive expanse of trees. Twinkling streetlamps illuminate the park. Wet dew clings to the blades of grass. Not surprisingly, the park is deserted from the rain, which suits me fine. I meander through the open gates to the entrance.

If this deed truly is what I think, it could change everything.

And if the orchards sketched by Granny are on the property, then one of her first designs and an essential part of her history is there. A critical piece of her legacy that must be preserved, no matter what. I can't help but smile at the thought, knowing she's smiling just as big from heaven at the possibility.

But at the same time, guilt teeters on the edge of my mind.

Luke Diamond lives on that land. He has no clue it might not be his.

My triumph would be his unexpected tragedy.

The last thing I want to do is hurt someone else, but what other choice do I have. I need to find out the truth.

Zigzagging across the lush grass, I clench my stomach as it rumbles loudly. The smoky, savory smell of the meat causes my mouth to water. I can't wait to dig into the delicious sandwich and plot my next moves. First on the list is a trip to my favorite lawyer and friend, Lance Bassett. He'll know the legal steps necessary to help me authenticate—

A yelp escapes my mouth as pain radiates in my left foot. I stumble forward, tripping on a slick tree root jutting from the ground. My steps grow uncoordinated as the damp grass looms closer and closer to my face. I do the one thing I didn't want to do and release the bag containing my precious pulled pork sandwich. Time slows as the Styrofoam container crashes into the ground. My pulled pork sandwich leaps from the opening, sending delicious meat tumbling across the lawn, along with my side of creamy potato salad. I watch helplessly as I brace myself for the inevitable impact with the hard ground.

I really don't want to knock out a tooth, so I twist at the last minute as the world around me tilts dangerously.

"Whoa there, falling for me already?" A deep, rich baritone sends shivers down my spine as a pair of taut, muscular arms envelop and lift me into the air, saving me from the devastating crash landing. My unexpected savior cradles me like a toddler. Instinctively, my arms fling around the broad neck of my rescuer, and I inhale a deep breath of his cologne. My heart slams like a jackhammer against my rib cage as my gaze collides with the most gorgeous emerald green eyes I've ever seen. Well, actually, I'd looked at those eyes earlier today, but boy, are they more impressive in person.

Eyes as green as the March clover and ready to save your day.

"Luke … Diamond," My voice is a breathy whisper.

Recognition dawns in those beautiful orbs as a sexy half-smile plays on his lips. "So, Kennedy Tarkington knows who I am. You okay?" He tightens his grip on my hips as my body presses into the rippled muscles of his chest.

My head bobs up and down as a response since my voice isn't responding to my brain's communication cues. Am I short-circuiting because the calendar photo of Luke Diamond pales in comparison to the magnificent man holding me in his arms? He exudes a movie star aura with his chiseled cheekbones, strong jawline, and alluring lips that beg to be kissed. His hair is damp from the rain but still stylish. Wearing a black t-shirt and jeans, the simplicity of his wardrobe heightens his handsomeness. He's a man who knows exactly how to showcase his best qualities and leave a trail of swooning women in his wake. A bonafide knight in casual armor.

I hate to admit it, but I'm feeling pretty swoony at the moment.

"That tree root tried to kill me," I say as my brain connects with my mouth again to allow intelligible speech.

"Sneaky roots." He chuckles. "Always waiting to trip unsuspecting beautiful women."

I inhale a sharp breath.

Wait.

Did he call me beautiful?

No, couldn't have.

Luke continues, "Lucky for you, I'm in the saving lives business. It's in the Kimbell Firefighter Handbook. No way I was letting that tree take you out … like it did your dinner." His brows furrow as he glances down at the wreckage that was my BBQ feast.

"My dinner never had a chance," I say, with more sadness than I intended. I needed that sandwich.

Luke's eyes sparkle with mischief. "Fate works in mysterious ways." He turns slowly toward the benches. Two styrofoam containers rest on one of them. "I was just about to enjoy my BBQ dinner over there. I have two pulled pork sandwiches and don't mind sharing."

I hesitate, feeling like a troll, knowing I have a deed in my purse that could change Luke's life as he knows it, yet still wanting to take him up on his offer … once he puts me down.

Wait.

Luke Diamond is still holding me in his arms?

What is happening?

I stifle my smile and say, "Shouldn't you put me down first before offering me half your dinner?"

"What?" Luke looks confused and it's the most adorable expression. Reality dawns on him.

Instead of lowering me to the ground immediately, his sexy grin grows bigger as if he's contemplating whether releasing me is the right move or not.

"Luke Diamond," I say, dropping my arms from his neck. "You can put me down now."

He chuckles. "If you insist."

I immediately regret pushing the issue as he sets me down gently on my feet. His warm hands linger on my waist for a moment before pulling away.

"You should take me up on my offer. Pulled pork sandwiches are the best food for fuel when you have to work through a complicated issue."

"Oh, I totally agree! Something about the smoky flavor and spicy barbecue sauce really gets the brain churning through options and possibilities," I say, then stop as amusement plays across his face.

"You had the same plan?" Luke asks, tilting that sexy face toward me in mock surprise. He glances down at the ground. "Yep, that's a pulled pork sandwich, for sure."

"Now it's food for the squirrels."

"I guess if a sneaky tree root had to trip you up, it happened at the right time and place. Like I said, I have two pulled pork sandwiches over there." He takes a deep breath. I see signs of something weighing heavily in his eyes for the first time. The emerald green has shifted to darker, holding a hint of insecurity that is totally irresistible.

Luke's gaze settles on me. The tension dissipates from his face. "Actually, it's good that we ran into each other. We can eat the sandwiches and swap stories about our complicated problems. Who knows? We might be able to help each other out."

"Trust me, you won't want to share your dinner with me once you know the problem I came here to work through," I mutter, then bend down to grab the remnants of my dinner to throw in the trash.

"Try me." Luke squats next to me and picks up most of my ruined meal.

"I'm the last person you should help."

"How about you let me be the judge of that."

"Stop it, okay!" I yell. "Stop being nice to me."

His frown deepens, making him infinitely more handsome. Who knew a scowl could be more attractive than a smile?

Luke asks, "Why?"

I clench my eyes shut and shove my hand into my purse. Grabbing the deed, I yank it out and thrust it against his chest. "The land your grandfather gave to you when he passed away."

His gorgeous green eyes narrow.

"It really belongs to … me."

CHAPTER II

L UKE

~

THIS IS DEFINITELY NOT THE KENNEDY TARKINGTON FROM
the billboard.

The three-dimensional version, live and breathing, in front of me puts that picture to shame. I wrack my brain for a woman more beautiful than her and come up empty. Not surprisingly, since I've been admiring her from afar for weeks now.

And that's probably why I cradled her in my arms like a bride carried by her groom. We're the furthest thing from a couple, but I'm not one to believe in coincidences. Her phone number is burning a hole in my cell phone, demanding I call her, and then she shows up in Bell Park out of the blue? I couldn't have planned it better if I tried.

Which I absolutely did not.

I had every intention of finishing my business plan alone, under the soft glow of lights at Bell Park, until I saw her. She was power walking across the grass, holding a take-out bag like it was the most precious thing on earth.

The disaster about to happen was obvious to me. The grass was slick and damp from the rain that had only stopped a few minutes earlier. Several yards away, the gnarly roots of the old oak tree peeked through the lawn. But Kennedy looked deep in thought. She never saw the danger.

If I hadn't acted quickly, she would've face-planted onto the ground, bruised that gorgeous face, and probably knocked out a tooth or two. I did what any competent firefighter would do and rescued her from imminent disaster.

But as I stared down into those dark chocolate brown eyes, I doubt even a banged-up, snaggle-toothed Kennedy would've stopped her from being … breathtaking.

Yes, that's the word I'm looking for.

Breathtaking.

All thoughts of business plans, tax bills, and the text I got yesterday vanished from my mind and were replaced with … her.

Black loose curls frame her fresh face, devoid of makeup, because, frankly, she doesn't need any. There was no mistaking the bonafide banging curves of her body as I held her against my chest for her protection, of course.

I literally saved her from an emergency room visit—

"Luke Diamond! Did you hear what I said?" Her words crash through my thoughts.

I glance down at the paper in my hand and scan the title. "Yeah, of course. You own some land, and this is the deed for it."

"You were not listening to me," Kennedy says, snapping a finger once, then twice in front of me. A perturbed and slightly concerned expression settles on her face.

The honest answer is I was too distracted by her, but I can't tell her that. I give Kennedy a long stare. In fact, I can't seem to tear my eyes away from her as she studies me in return. My curiosity is piqued by this woman.

What is it about Kennedy Tarkington that's turning my mind into mush?

I can't let her think I'm a befuddled, brainless fool.

Time to get my act together and impress this woman.

Clearing my throat, I admit, "Okay, maybe I didn't quite catch what you said. What does this deed to your land have to do with me?" I hand the document back to her.

She turns the paper toward me and slides a hand under one sentence detailing the property description. Her finger drops to the bottom of the worn, yellowed pages where two signatures are scrawled in black ink. The document is very familiar to me. I've seen it dozens of times, but there's something wrong with this version.

She draws a circle around the name listed as the grantee with her nail.

"This is … wrong," I say, then snatch the paper back and read the document. My gaze bounces to all the key elements of what looks like the deed to the land I live on. But this isn't the real deed. I got a copy after my grandfather passed away to change his name to mine after he put in his will that I was to have the land, not my father.

I run a hand through my hair, then return the deed to Kennedy. I feel bad about bursting her bubble, but she has to know the document she has is fake. No one owns my land but me.

A sympathetic smile spreads across my lips as I say, "I don't know what that paper is supposed to be, but I can assure you it's not a valid legal document. I have the deed to the fifty acres my grandfather gave me. It's filed with the county records. No forgery changes that."

Kennedy lowers her arms as her hands rest on her hips in defiance.

I cringe inwardly at my choice of words which had the unintended effect of drawing a battle line.

"I think the real question you should be asking is who has the forged deed and who has the real deed. This document was discovered in a trunk owned by my great-grandfather. According to this deed, the land belongs to him. Perhaps it was your cad of a grandfather who forged your deed and stole land from my great-grandfather," Kennedy says, her voice coming in a quick staccato punctuated by heavy breaths. She's getting worked up about this, and so am I.

Did she really just disparage my grandfather?

A man she probably never met and couldn't possibly know how caring and kind he was despite his reputation in town.

I take a step back, stuffing my clenched fists into my pockets. "My grandfather withstood ridicule and scrutiny when he moved here to claim his property. He withstood every challenge to his ownership of the land and came out on top. The land is mine. Period."

"His signature is not on this deed," Kennedy presses, stalking toward me as she closes the distance between us. "Cornelius Butler owned this land. Father of my grandmother, Alice Butler, your grandfather's neighbor. Now, it makes sense why she wanted to own part of that property. It's because she grew up living there. It was my family's land, and I will get it back one way or another!"

I suck in a breath as her words slam into me. She's too distracting. I need to focus on these ridiculous claims she's making. I know she's a smart woman, but she's not thinking clearly.

"The real deed for the land is filed with the county records department," I force the words through gritted teeth.

"I know that. I have a copy of it, too. Strange that it's identical to the one signed by my great-grandfather."

The rain-cooled air has turned warm, sticky, and oppressive. I swipe at the sweat beading along my arms and avoid Kennedy's intense, imploring, gorgeous brown eyes.

"Perhaps that's because whoever forged that document wanted to make it look authentic. Seriously, how do you even know that's your great-grandfather's signature. Did you compare it to any other documents he signed? Is there any proof that your family owned any land in Kimbell other than stories y'all passed down to each other?" I scoff and roll my eyes. "That's not enough and you know it. Especially when my grandfather lived on this land for over sixty years, unchallenged by anyone, and has a deed filed for the property with the county."

I turn away from her and walk toward the food on the park bench. "There's some explanation for that document, but it's not that you or your family own my land."

"This deed could be the real one. You could have the fake!" I hear her steps stomping across the mushy lawn, then tapping against the stone as she walks around to face me.

"Do you hear yourself?" I ask. "Could be? You're not even sure that what you have is real." A heavy sigh escapes my lips as I try to get my breathing under control. I'm not sure if it's the ridiculous suggestion or the close proximity of this woman that has my heart racing.

"It's notarized and signed by witnesses," Kennedy insists.

"So is the deed filed with the county that's signed by my grandfather." I cross my arms over my chest.

Kennedy's face turns to exquisite stone. Nostrils flaring in the cutest and most frustrating way, she says, "Right, the deed to the land he won in a poker game. Who knows if that's really true or if he used it as a cover for swindling land out of my great-grandfather!"

"Who told you that?" The vein in my neck ticks and throbs at her insinuation. I swallow hard, then step toward her. My jaw clenches. I force myself to relax. I know I'm right, and she's wrong. There's no point in getting all riled up.

Calming myself, I rest a hand gently on her shoulder and say, "Those are just unfounded rumors that haunted my grandfather the entire time he lived here. He earned the money in a poker game but bought the land fair and square from the Abbotts. That's the real story."

She glares at my hand as if it's something heinous, then jerks her shoulder away. A flash of uncertainty crosses her face, then quickly disappears. It's replaced by something scarier. A stunning, thousand-watt smile that does nothing to hide the anger and determination brewing in those smoldering coffee-brown eyes.

She mirrors my stance, crossing her arms over her exquisitely shaped chest. "You know what, you're exactly right. I wasn't expecting to see you so soon after discovering this deed, so I haven't had a chance to validate what I know in my heart is true. But when I do, you'll have no choice but to deal with me."

"Come on, Kennedy." I step toward her, then stop. I'm not sure I can trust myself to behave in my best interest when she's standing there looking so pretty. "Do you really want to waste time with this?"

She laughs, then grabs her purse from the grass. "I'll see you in court."

My mouth drops open as she spins around on the lawn and walks off like a model on the runway.

Despite myself, I enjoy the view as I hope like hell that she's wrong.

CHAPTER 12

L UKE

~

HOW CAN THE WOMAN TRYING TO STEAL MY LAND ACTUALLY make me forget that she's the enemy?

I remind myself to breathe as she lingers in my view, partially obscured by her lawyer. But she's not hidden enough for me to miss that she's dressed in a tailored charcoal pantsuit with a white silk blouse—the epitome of professional sexy. Her glossy dark hair is pulled back in a sleek twist, with a few loose tendrils framing her face. Smoky eyeshadow makes her brown eyes smolder, and her crimson lipstick is bold against her deep brown skin.

I should not think about kissing those cupid bow lips.

That should be the last thing on my mind.

Thankfully, the voice of my lawyer, Olivia Garnet, jolts me back from the fantasy.

"With all due respect, Judge Barnes, the deed presented by Ms.

Tarkington lacks authentication. We have a deposition from the clerk at the records office indicating that Ms. Tarkington arrived and would not leave until she was given a copy of the original deed on file," Olivia says, a hint of condescension in her tone. "We only have her word, and that of two family members who would obviously do anything for her, that she found the alleged deed in a trunk, as opposed to creating it on Photoshop herself. At this point, her claims are baseless until that deed is validated by an expert. That should be the only point considered in this temporary injunction ruling."

"Are you accusing me of faking this document? You have some nerve!" Kennedy bolts up from her chair, finger pointed at Olivia, who looks even more amused.

"That's a more likely scenario than my grandfather faking it over sixty years ago," I retort, shaking my head. "Seriously, I don't understand how someone as smart as you can be so blind about this. That deed you have is too suspicious to hold up in a kids' game of pretend, let alone a court of law."

Kennedy shifts from my lawyer to me. "Condescension isn't a good look on you. It's bad for your 'good boy' brand around town. There is no indication that my deed is fake, and I have no problem getting an expert to prove that." She looks Olivia up and down. "We can even use whatever expert you suggest, Ms. Garnet."

"The only thing an expert is going to confirm is that you're delusional if you think you have any claim to my property." My jaw clenches.

"Delusional? You're the one who's been living a lie, thinking you had a right to that land when it was never truly yours to begin with." Kennedy's voice rises in pitch.

I throw up my hands. "I've had enough of your baseless accusations. If your family owned my land, why didn't your grandmother raise this issue years ago? Why did she buy land from my grandfather instead of just suing him for what was rightfully hers? She didn't for a reason, and you know it. Trying to get my land now, when she never did, is pathetic."

"How dare you!" Kennedy is practically shouting now. "You have no idea what this means to me, to my family. My great-grandfather left Kimbell a broken man, disillusioned and disheartened from losing his property. My grandmother left behind her very first horticultural masterpiece on that land. The inspiration that propelled her to pursue her career in garden design. Critical pieces of my family are on that land. Historically significant treasures important to Kimbell are on that land. It must be preserved and protected by the family that truly owns it. My family. Me. I won't rest until it's in my hands."

"Well, get ready for a lifetime of restless nights because that land is mine. My grandfather was ridiculed and ostracized for purchasing the land from a gambler. He endured decades of being an outsider in this town, determined to hold on to his land, regardless of what people thought about how he got it. He nurtured and protected that land, refusing to sell it. It's a veritable nature preserve because my grandfather kept it that way. He wanted nothing more than for it to stay in our family, and it will. The land is mine. No fraudulent deed is going to take it from me." My tone is pure ice.

Kennedy physically recoils as if I've slapped her. "Are you calling me a fraudster? That's your family's modus operandi, not mine. Your days of living on stolen land are numbered."

Some kind of way, we've faced off with mere inches separating us, breaths coming fast, eyes locked in a battle of wills. The tension crackles between us like a live wire.

"You're going to regret this," I say in a low, menacing tone. "I promise you that."

"The only thing I regret is that I have to waste one more second of my time dealing with you," Kennedy shoots back. "But it will all be worth it when I walk out of here victorious."

The judge bangs her gavel, the sound cutting through our crackling antagonism. "Enough! Both of you sit down. Now."

Kennedy glares at me, sending a trail of heat burning against my skin. I'm sure I'm red as a tomato, glaring back at her.

Judge Barnes says, "Olivia, Lance. I need both of you to keep your clients under control. We don't have time for emotional outbursts. It's counterproductive to what we need to accomplish here." Her gaze darts from Kennedy to me and back again. "I understand this is emotional for both of you, but attacking each other will not help the situation. You're here for one reason. To address the request for a temporary injunction filed by Ms. Tarkington. There will be no decision on who owns the land today. That will happen in a separate hearing after both sides have had ample time to gather evidence to support their positions."

Kennedy looks like she wants to scratch my eyes out. I decide to be the bigger person, since one of us has to take the high road and give her a tight smile. "Please, let's sit."

Wrong move as it elicits an exaggerated eye roll.

But she complies after pulling her chair as far away from mine as possible. After she's settled into the chair, she crosses one long leg over the other. I take a seat on the opposite side. Olivia and Lance don't budge as they remain in the center before the judge.

The lawyers spend the next thirty minutes talking through the evidence and responding to the judge's questions on behalf of Kennedy and me. I stew in silence, rubbing my temples to temper the ache, growing stronger by the minute.

Time slows as I wait for Judge Barnes to communicate the only conclusion that makes sense—Kennedy is crazy for trying to take my land, and her evidence is flimsy and fraudulent. I swear, if I never see Kennedy Tarkington again, it would be too soon.

The judge studies our documents for what feels like hours.

Removing her glasses, she looks at me.

My heart sinks.

"In the matter of the temporary injunction on the fifty acres of land between Abbott Road and Lake Lasso," Judge Barnes says, then rests her elbows on her desk. "I rule that all aspects of the property that existed at the time of the original deeds be shared between Luke Diamond and Kennedy Tarkington."

"What?" I jump up from my seat. Olivia grips my hand, tugging at me. I shake my head. "You can't do this. Judge Barnes, this is ridiculous."

Olivia pulls on my arm harder. "Sit down."

Something about her tone tells me I need to comply. I don't bother to look at Kennedy. I'm sure she's gloating, but that's not an image I want trapped in my head. Easing back into my chair, I try to focus as the dull ache transitions into a full-blown jackhammer unleashed in my brain.

"All access to the property must be shared, and no changes can be made to the land until the final ruling of ownership is made," Judge Barnes concludes. She rifles through several documents, then says, "Luke, this means you'll need to give Kennedy full access to the land and all the buildings on the property, including your home."

"I don't understand," I say, still reeling.

Judge Barnes's voice softens. "The temporary injunction effectively makes you and Kennedy joint owners of the property."

"Joint owners?" Kennedy asks. "I have to share this property with him? How on earth will that work? And what can I do to make sure he doesn't do anything to harm the orchards that my grandmother designed on the property?"

I bristle at her line of questioning. "Why would I do anything to harm orchards that my grandfather took care of for decades? When I moved here, those orchards were his pride and joy. We worked together to make sure they stayed healthy."

Kennedy looks at me, her face a mask of an emotion I can't read. "You did?"

"It's not just your family's legacy that needs to be protected. The Diamonds may not be as big and important as the Butlers or the Tarkington's with all their contributions to Kimbell and Lasso County. But our traditions are important, too. They're worth protecting."

"There is another option," Judge Barnes says.

"What is it?" Kennedy and I ask in unison.

"Both of you can be barred from accessing the land until ownership is established."

"That doesn't work for me," I say.

"No. I don't like that either. I want to see the orchards. I want to see the land."

"Then the two of you will need to work together to determine how to share it temporarily."

Judge Barnes bangs her gavel.

CHAPTER 13

K ENNEDY

~

G RAVEL CRUNCHES UNDER MY STEPS AS I WALK TOWARD THE sleek, modern structure with reclaimed wood walls and expansive solar panels gleaming on the roof. I stare at the cranes towering underneath the blanketed gray sky as construction workers crowd nearly every part of the building, hammering, welding, and maneuvering materials into place with practiced precision. The air is filled with the sharp scent of fresh-cut wood and metallic tang of welding fumes. The Bell Family raised millions to create a center that honors my grandmother for her decades-long commitment as the Head Gardener of Bell Botanical Gardens.

A smile spreads across my face at the thought of the thousands of people who will walk the halls after it opens, learning about Granny's storied career, taking classes, and participating in community events in the building that bears her name.

Clutching my purse, I groan as my cell phone buzzes from inside.

I don't need to take it out to know who is sending me yet another text.

I've ignored all of them.

LANCE

> Why didn't you move in with Luke last night???
> Call me.

> This is a legal strategy only. Pack your bags
> and get over there.

> Still waiting on your call. Please move in
> TODAY.

> Seriously, staying away weakens your case. It's
> temporary. Just do it, okay.

> If you want to get your land back, you need to
> do this.

I grab my phone and then decide to ignore it.

It's not that I don't understand why Lance wants me to move in with Luke. I must show the judge I'm serious about believing the land is rightfully mine. Staking a claim to my temporary fifty percent ownership is the best way to do it.

Doesn't matter that I just partially renovated and moved into Granny's magnificent Tudor house days ago. I have to abandon my new home and play house with Luke to prove to the court that I genuinely believe my deed is valid.

It's preposterous.

However, with two contradictory deeds, Lance believes the judge will ultimately base her decision on circumstantial evidence *and* behaviors. That means going overboard to present myself as what I am —a woman desperate to right a wrong and reclaim land that belongs to my family.

Still, I'm not sure I want to go so far as to move in with Luke Diamond.

Ignoring that he's stupid handsome, sexy, and a hero, he's also rude, condescending, and hates me.

Seriously, the guy is nice to everyone in town but me.

For good reason, I suppose.

It makes for a toxic situation between us.

Why would I want to subject myself to being around him more than I have to?

I open my purse, stare at Granny's sketches, and have my answer.

Exhaling, I close my purse and walk past construction workers eating lunch under a towering oak tree. I enter the half-constructed facility and scan for someone who looks like the boss. Exposed beams and sheetrock surround me, with plastic sheets billowing in the breeze from cutouts where windows will be installed. My eyes settle on a man wearing a crisp business shirt stained with sweat. He holds a clipboard under his arm and has a dire look of concern etched across his face.

I approach him slowly, waiting for his conversation to end before speaking. Clearing my throat, I say, "Hi, I'm Kennedy Tarkington, Alice Butler's granddaughter. I was hoping to talk to the head curator responsible for the content inside the center. Can you tell me where that person is?

The man swipes at the sweat beading on his forehead. Frowning, he replies, "We don't have a curator anymore. Boss fired him."

"Fired … the curator. Why?" I ask, taken aback.

"Because he was incompetent, that's why." A booming voice with a heavy drawl fills the space. David Bell, patriarch of the Bell Family and Granny's old boss, walks toward me. His imposing frame is clad in a custom-tailored navy suit and cowboy boots. A shock of silver hair peeks from under his Stetson. His tanned, weathered face breaks into an easy grin beneath piercing blue eyes. He exudes the confidence of a man accustomed to getting his way.

"How are you, Kennedy?" He yanks me forward and pulls me into a bear hug that is oddly comforting.

"I think I'm good," I say, then step back from his embrace. "But firing your curator when the center is only months away from opening is risky, don't you think?"

"Alice would've fired him a long time ago. We're over budget and behind schedule, but I just signed a contract with the perfect person to get things back on track." David gives me a big smile. "No way we're delaying the opening of the Alice Butler Center for Horticultural Excellence at Bell Botanical Gardens. You'd rip me a new one if we were late."

"I'm not that bad," I say, smothering my typical response to vigorously defend myself.

"Bad? No! Persistent, determined, and full of righteous conviction? Absolutely. You came to every board meeting for over a year demanding that we recognize your grandmother's contributions to the gardens."

"I went to seven board meetings within a year, and I gave passionate pleas," I counter, raising an eyebrow.

"We all knew you were right. We just had to ensure we could get funding before agreeing to your demands," David says, then steers me toward a hallway in the building. "Have you gotten a tour of the place?"

"Not yet," I say, falling into step next to him. The smell of fresh paint and new carpeting fills the air as workers bustle around us. "Who's this miracle worker who's going to step in to do the curation of the exhibits and content?"

"Mary Jones," David says, obviously impressed with snagging the curator of the two major museums in Lasso County to work for the center.

"Good choice," I say, thinking of the woman I once believed would be my future mother-in-law. Her youngest son, Maxwell Jones, was the last in my string of six straight relationship dumpings. Our breakup happened at the county fair, of all places. Maxwell chose the top of the Ferris wheel to tell me it was over, leaving us stuck in awkward silence for three more rotations before we could exit. To this day, I can't look at a Ferris wheel without feeling a mix of nausea and embarrassment.

But my past failings no longer matter.

Kennedy 2.0 is on hiatus from men. I'm focusing on self-care and happiness without a romantic relationship.

David asks, "What did you want to talk to the curator about?"

"Well, I received a trunk from a church in East Austin where my great-grandfather was a deacon long ago. It has a lot of mementos and family documents from the Butler side of my family. Inside, I found these sketches that Granny did as a teenager. I think this is one of the first garden designs she ever made. I'm hoping they can be part of the exhibitions on my grandmother's career," I explain.

"Of course, darling," David says, then levels me with a curious stare. "I heard you also found a deed in that trunk that challenges Luke's ownership of the land he got from his grandfather."

"Look, I know your son and Luke are very close," I say, although the crash course on the epic bromance between Nate Bell and Luke Diamond was relayed to me by Lance in the week leading up to the hearing. Neither guy was ever in my circle of friends, and I didn't know much about them. "I'm sure Luke is like family to you. I can't imagine what you think about all of this."

"You're right. Luke is family. But so was Alice, and that means you are, too. There's nothing that the Bell Family wouldn't do for Luke or you. Right now, the best thing we can do is be Switzerland while y'all work out this dispute." David leads me through another maze of hallways until we emerge in a wide-open area with a soaring atrium designed to house living plant exhibits. The gray rain clouds cast gloomy shadows over the vast space that will soon be filled with lush greenery.

Relief settles within me. The idea that I'm fighting a man backed by the Bell billions was daunting. "I appreciate that. We've only had one hearing, and everything has become more stressful, complicated, and harder than I ever realized."

"Legal disputes always are. They can bring out the worst in even the best of people like you and Luke."

"I'm being pushed to do things I never would've fathomed. Things

I'm not comfortable with and I don't agree with, just to better position myself for the twists this case could take. It's so hard, and I hate it," I confess, wringing my hands.

"But when the outcome is important, shouldn't you be willing to do whatever it takes to get the right result? Even the hard stuff? One thing I know for sure is that Alice never backed down from a challenge just because it would be hard or uncomfortable. I don't think she taught you to take the easy road either," David says, leading me through a series of state-of-the-art lecture halls. Boxes of new electronics and digital displays line the floors, waiting to be installed.

"Of course not." I turn to face David. "I'm convinced that if she had known this deed existed before she passed away, nothing would've stopped her from challenging Frank's ownership. But all she had were memories of her father being distressed over losing the land. What could she do with that?"

"Nothing. But now that you have what could be proof, you have a duty to do what she can't." David places a hand on my shoulder.

"You think I should do whatever it takes—"

"I think if you're not going to give this everything you have, then why bother starting," He interjects, eyes stern.

"Not bad advice," I concede with a small smile as I contemplate what I'll bring to move into the house with Luke.

CHAPTER 14

L UKE

~

M Y CELL PHONE BUZZES ON THE PASSENGER SEAT AS I DRIVE
home after my shift ends. It was a busy night with a rash of medical
emergencies. All I want to do is lay in my own bed and get rest.

Taking my eyes off the road for a second, I read the text message.

UNKNOWN NUMBER

I'm still waiting on your call. -M

I resist the urge to chuck the phone out the window.

Speeding down the narrow gravel road, I take a sharp right toward
the driveway in front of my modest one-story ranch-style home.

During my last conversation with Madeleine years ago, I made it
clear there was no future for us. Not after her lies and betrayal. How
could she think I would let her back into my life? And using Herbert to
make the initial contact was a cowardly move. Talking to her now

would do nothing more than dredge up a lot of old hurt I've spent the last five years putting behind me—

I slam on my brakes, then yank the steering wheel hard toward the left to avoid hitting a car parked in my driveway. My truck whips around in a dizzying circle, tearing up the grass in the lawn before coming to a rocking stop. I beat my hands on the dashboard, then glare at the vehicle of the unexpected visitor.

Why can't people in this town call before they drop by?

Then, I remind myself that this open-door policy was one of the things I found endearing when I first moved here. The casual closeness where everyone treats you like family, even from the first moment you meet them.

I inhale a deep breath and force my ire away.

Whoever timed their visit to be here after my shift must need my help and I'm going to give it to them. A not-so-random act of kindness could be what I need to halt the gloomy mood threatening to ruin my day. Putting the truck in park, I grab my cell phone and jump out. Jogging over to the car, I slow before I approach the door. There's no one inside. Tension claws along my neck as I scan the property for a sign of someone waiting in the shadows. The low, dark gray clouds blanket the sky, casting shadows from the towering pine and oak trees littering the front yard.

I close my eyes and inhale a sharp breath.

The car could belong to Herbert. I wouldn't put it past him to hunt me down. Well, if he made the trip to Kimbell, it's a wasted one.

Returning to my truck, I crank the engine and pull into my garage. Lowering the garage door, I enter the house through the kitchen. My mind is made up that I'm not answering the door whenever he comes back to knock on it.

I navigate the dark hallway from the garage without turning on the lights. As I turn toward the living room, my breath quickens, and my heart skips a beat, then almost stops entirely.

Kennedy Tarkington is standing in my house by the fireplace.

She doesn't notice me as she runs her hand along the mantle, pausing to lift one of the pictures. It's Gramps and me in front of Diamond Lake near the house. We were soaking wet from a spontaneous swimming race when the old man claimed he could beat me. Never one to back down from a challenge, I gave him a head start and plunged into the clear, tepid waters. I was never more proud to see his dogged determination as I waited on the banks of the lake for him to finish. It didn't matter that I beat him by a couple of minutes. The exhilaration on his face that I took the challenge seriously was all he wanted—a free gift from me to him. Afterward, I whipped out my phone and took a selfie of us. It's one of my favorite memories with Gramps.

Placing the photo back on the mantle, she turns and walks back to the couch. She sits cross-legged in the middle and reaches for my favorite SMU coffee mug on the side table. The smell of peppermint tea lingers in the air as she takes a sip.

The thoughts slamming into my mind are not what I expect.

Kennedy has let herself into my home without discussing it with me, and she absolutely looks like ... she belongs here.

Like coming home to find Kennedy waiting for me is the most natural and perfect thing in the world.

I push away the thoughts before they take root and get me in trouble. She's not here because she wants to see me. This is a takeover. A declaration that she's claiming my house and my land as her own, and she wants everyone in town to know it.

Pushing away from the wall, I storm into the room. "What are you doing in my house?" I demand, my voice harsh.

Kennedy jumps, sloshing tea on the woven rug beneath the coffee table. Her stunning chocolate eyes stare at me wide with shock.

"Luke ... you're home," she sputters, her gaze slowly caressing me from head to toe and back to my face. I feel a momentary satisfaction that perhaps she's just as attracted to me as I am to her, and I love that it rattles her. I'm used to getting gawked at around town, especially when I'm dressed in the casual firefighter gear of a black t-shirt and black cargo pants. Ladies love this look.

She continues, "I mean, I didn't hear your truck pull up—"

"I don't need to warn you that I've returned to my home. But maybe you should've warned me that you would be here. A simple text would've sufficed."

My words hit her like well-timed blows.

"How long have you been here?" I stalk into the room. "Long enough to make yourself comfortable with my things, I see."

She looks genuinely sorry, but that's not enough for me.

"I got here this morning. I was going to wait in the car, but the wind started blowing really hard, and I have a key, so—"

"You decided it was well within your rights to let yourself in." I throw up my hands, then turn away from her. Swiveling back around, I point a finger at her. "You just couldn't help yourself. Wanted to see what the house you're trying to take from me looks like on the inside. Decided to make yourself at home. Drinking my tea out of my favorite coffee mug." My anger is rising faster than I can control. It's not like me to lose my cool with anyone, but Kennedy is triggering me in ways I don't understand. I cross the room and snatch the mug from her hands.

Wrong move.

My mind goes blank as I get a whiff of her intoxicating perfume.

She's too close, pulling me like a moth to a flame.

I stumble backward. "Don't get used to this. The injunction is temporary. You won't keep half my land, and you definitely won't take it from me because there's no proof of something that isn't true. This may be hard to hear, but the Butlers don't own this land. It's Diamond land. Always has been. Always will be."

Kennedy rises gracefully from the sofa like some ballerina, holding her hands up in surrender. "Let me start over. First, I want to apologize for disrespecting you. I shouldn't have come inside before you got home." She takes a deep breath. "This situation is hard. There are things that I'm committed to do to make sure the judge knows I'm serious about my claim to this land. Things I'd rather not do, and I know you hate me for it. But it's not about you or me. It's about what happened decades before we were born. I have to find out the truth."

"Sometimes, when you hear hooves, it's horses, not zebras," I say, shaking my head.

"What does that mean?"

"The truth is usually the most obvious answer. This land has been in my family for over sixty years. My grandfather owned it, and now I do. That's the truth you're trying to find."

"That's the truth you hope I find," she retorts. Her eyebrow raises, and she tilts her head at the perfect angle to showcase just how pretty she is. But a fire in her gaze tells me I just crossed another line. "Because you can't bear to think that your grandfather could've been the mastermind behind stealing land that belonged to my family. It's called confirmation bias and doesn't make it the truth. Those deeds are identical, which means one is fake, and one is real. There's a reason I found that deed in the trunk. It wasn't to go on a wild goose chase for something that doesn't belong to me. I will find the proof that this land is owned by my family. I won't apologize for taking back what rightly belongs to us."

"I guess they don't teach counting chickens before they hatch in accounting school," I mutter.

She rolls her eyes and says, "You can take all the potshots at me that you like. It's not going to change anything. We are co-owners of this land, temporarily, and we need to figure out how to make this work until the final ruling."

Why does she have to be so reasonable? Now, she's the one taking the higher road? I take a deep breath.

"All of that could've been discussed over the phone. You didn't have to ambush me."

"Fine, you're right." She looks uncomfortable as she reaches for her giant purse. "The truth is, I was dead set against coming here until I remembered there's something I need to see on this land." She pulls out papers and thrusts them toward me.

"The last time you handed me papers, it didn't work out well for me," I say, but reach for them. I glance down. They're drawings of a place I've visited hundreds of times.

"Where did you get these?" I remember the first time Gramps took me to see the orchards. He was beaming with pride. Over the years, I'd pitch in and help him maintain the trees. His meticulous care gave us more fresh fruit and nuts than we could ever eat. The production could be a way to help me earn enough money to keep up with the rising taxes on the property if I could finish off my business plan. The same one I thought Kennedy could help me with before she swooped in and staked a claim on the land for herself.

"That's my Granny's signature. Alice Butler," Kennedy explains, pointing to the scrawling cursive writing on the bottom corner of the pages. "Based on the dates, these orchards are the first garden Granny ever designed. Maybe it was even what convinced her to pursue a career in horticulture. Who knows?"

"She never told you about this?" I hand the documents back to her.

"No, she didn't like to talk about the land her dad lost or its impact on the family. I never pushed her because I didn't see the point. Now, I'm regretting that," Kennedy says. "You mentioned taking care of the orchards at the hearing and I got so excited that they really exist. They're still here after all these years. I really want to see them. I was hoping you'd tell me how to get to them."

"So, you're only here to see the orchards ..."

"I didn't say that." Kennedy looks away. "Lance insists that I move in here until the final hearing."

"Thanks for your honesty," I say, then walk toward the door. "Given the judge's ruling, there's nothing I can do to stop you, is there?"

"No, but you don't have to do anything else to help me. You can refuse to show me the orchards. I probably couldn't find them without you. Fifty acres is massive. I wouldn't know where to start—"

"I'll take you to the orchards."

Maybe this is the not-so-random act of kindness I need to do.

CHAPTER 15

K ENNEDY

~

HONESTLY, I'M NOT IN BAD SHAPE. I WORK OUT JUST
enough to not feel like a slob, but hiking across the land behind Luke
to get to the orchards tests every ounce of my endurance. I wonder for
a moment if we're taking the longest route to get there, but then I
remember Luke wants to minimize the time he has to spend with me.
He hates me for good reason.

"Can you slow down?" I call out, falling further behind him.

Luke turns around but continues to walk backward through the
brush with the same ease that he walked forward. His luminous green
eyes turn a shade darker before my eyes, sending a tingle along my
skin. "You can't keep up because you're wearing those ridiculous
sandals and a dress that …" His words falter, and I swear he's pausing
to enjoy the view.

The view that would be me?

No, I must be misreading things.

They call it projecting when you transcribe your feelings onto other people. Namely, my insane attraction to Luke Diamond hasn't died off like I'd expected. The man is an obstacle to finding out the truth about land that could belong to my family. Add that fact to our nasty exchanges and he should be instantly ugly in my eyes.

But those broad shoulders and bulging biceps in that fitted black firefighter t-shirt that's doing a poor job of hiding those ripped chest muscles are making it hard for me to forget that I shouldn't be swooning over Luke Diamond. He definitely deserved to be Mr. March in the firefighter calendar. In fact, they could've given him a few more months, too.

I point a finger at him. "Don't even say I told you so." Against my better judgment, I hike up my dress and jog through the swaying weeds to close the distance between us. A mist fills the air, a not so subtle reminder of the rain expected this afternoon. Maybe I should've waited, but I couldn't be sure Luke's generosity would last that long.

"I won't," he calls over his shoulder. "But you'd find it much easier if you'd accepted the overalls and rubber boots I offered you."

I scoff. "I'll have you know that I've walked through plenty of fields in my life, and I don't need to be dressed like a farmer to do it."

"But have you ever done that dressed like a model on one of those fancy runways in New York?" Luke turns slightly, his gaze trailing down my body and back up.

"Point taken," I say, as my skin flushes with heat from the look in his eyes. So, maybe he finds me as attractive as I find him. That would even the playing field—we loathe each other but find each other attractive. What's the harm in that?

I don't even allow myself to answer that question.

I narrowly avoided stepping into several fire ant beds as we trek through calf-high brush. I silently pray I don't step on a snake, then gaze at the landscape enveloping me. Even under the dark, ominous gray clouds smothering the sky and the heavy rain in the air, the land is stunning.

I understand why he wouldn't want to part with it.

"You were the one who insisted on coming out here right when the thunderstorms are moving over the hill country. My plan is to get you to the orchards and back before those clouds unleash a deluge of rain on our heads," Luke says, the edge of annoyance returning to his voice. "So, country girl, how about you do a better job keeping up."

"Explain this to me," I say, pushing my legs faster until lactic acid burns in my muscles. I'm determined to match Luke stride for stride as I catch up and walk alongside him.

"What?"

"How is it that you're known for being such a nice guy who helps everybody whenever they need anything, but I'm stuck with this brooding, rude, and sour version of you?" I ask, not caring if I push his buttons. I'm sweltering under the suffocating rain clouds. With every step, my mood dips, and I wish I'd come out here to find the orchards alone.

"I'm nice to people who are nice to me," Luke says. "Not people who are trying to steal my land."

"The issue is not with you and me. All I'm trying to do is solve the mystery of the two deeds. Figure out which one is real. You should want to figure that out, too. This isn't personal."

"Don't tell me it's not personal. You wouldn't be hiking miles across this property to see the orchards when monsoon rain is coming if it wasn't personal," Luke snaps back, then stops abruptly. "Let me explain to you how personal this really is."

I bite my bottom lip as a few drops of rain plop against my face.

Luke points to a nearby clearing. "Over there is where Gramps and I used to sit and talk for hours after I came to town. He'd tell me stories about his life, and I'd share my dreams for the future. Those talks convinced me to move to Kimbell for good." He then gestures toward a distant structure surrounded by a copse of trees. "And that's the barn we built together, just the two of us. It was our special project, a way to bond and create something lasting. Gramps wanted to buy mini ponies and raise them out here." He pauses abruptly and takes a deep breath. "We didn't get a chance to do that."

I don't have to ask why. His grandfather passed away before they could see the dream to completion. I know how that feels. "Granny helped me build a patio garden for my apartment before she passed. We were going to plant chili peppers, tomatoes, and basil so I could make a spicy arrabbiata sauce better than my dad's." Tears prick my eyes.

"Going to? Did you ever plant them?" He looks genuinely interested.

"No. I finally threw it away when I moved a couple of weeks ago."

Luke sighs, then rakes his hand through his blond hair. "I get that you want a chance to preserve your grandmother's legacy. But hers isn't the only legacy that this land holds. My grandfather endured ridicule and derision for decades living here … alone. No one accepted him until I came. He told me that finally meeting his only grandson changed his life for the better. And you know what, he did the same for me. I finally had family that made me feel like I truly belonged."

I'm struck speechless by his vulnerability.

The insights into his life that I never could have expected, hiding behind his good-guy image. I have too many questions, but I know better than to ask any of them.

Luke and I aren't friends.

We are in a heated battle over land. If the situation was different between us, I'd wrap him in my arms and give him a tight hug. Comfort from the woman who is going to take his land and all the amazing memories he has is the last thing Luke needs.

"Come on, it's right after that hill," Luke says, then trudges forward but at a much slower pace. As much as I yearn to get back the land that rightfully belongs to my family, I can't help but feel a pang of guilt at the thought of taking this away from him.

When we reach the top, I gasp. "It's beautiful." The intricate alternating pattern of fruit trees in a diamond shape separated by nut trees in a circular shape stretches for as far as I can see. It must have taken months to plant the entire garden and decades later, the trees are blossoming and mature.

"There was a quicker way, but not one that would give you this view," Luke says, stepping back to allow me to gaze at the splendor. "Gramps and I always took this route to the orchards. I swear it never gets old. Never ceases to amaze when we get to the crest. It was his favorite part of his land, hands down."

"This is a dream come true," I say, trying to take it all in. "She was so gifted. Do you see that?" I point to the ornamental grass. "It's a rare species she uses to create a border along the pathways weaving between the trees. The way it sways in the wind and gives movement and direction to the orchard. That's become her signature element, included in all the gardens she's designed. It's at the Bell Botanical Gardens, and in the private gardens, she was commissioned to design for rich people's homes all across the country. And she discovered this when she was a teenager. I wonder if she ever came back to see what had become of her first work."

"I doubt it. Gramps didn't roll out the welcome mat to the folks in town. That she was his only neighbor wouldn't have changed that."

"It's sad, though. Of all the parts of the land I've seen, it's clear that he put a lot of effort into keeping the orchards up."

"This area and the lake are the only two parts he cared about. The rest, he let nature take its course."

"Lake Lasso?"

A sly smile spreads on his face. "Diamond Lake. It's a freshwater lake completely contained within the property. Water so still like a mirror, reflecting all of nature around it. You should probably see it, too. Just not today."

I'm touched by Luke's willingness to share more of the land with me, even under these strained circumstances. A glimpse of the good guy everyone in town raves about is finally starting to peek through.

"I had no idea there was a second lake on the property."

Luke nods. "It's a hidden gem. Pun intended."

I give him an exaggerated eye roll.

"Gramps and I went fishing there on lazy Sunday afternoons. There's nothing quite like the tranquility of that place."

I smile, imagining Luke sitting alongside his grandfather, fishing poles in hand, bonding over the simple joys of nature. It's a side of him I hadn't considered, making my heart ache in a way I didn't expect.

Luke reaches a hand toward me. "Ready to go down and see it up close?"

I glance down at the steep descent of the hill, then look at Luke's outstretched hand. Placing mine in his, the warmth and strength envelop me, and I feel safe and at peace.

"Yes," I say. "I'm ready."

CHAPTER 16

L UKE

~

I GLANCE DOWN AT KENNEDY'S HAND. I'M STRUCK BY THE warm, softness of her skin. Her hold is strong and trusting as if she knows I would protect her despite the circumstances that have brought us together.

Rain drizzles around us as we step gingerly down the hill. The cutest frown of concentration graces her face. She's absolutely not dressed for this trek to the orchards, wearing a shirt dress with a sash tied around her waist that accentuates her hourglass figure. I kick myself for not doing more to dissuade her, but I doubt she would have listened to me. Probably would've accused me of making excuses to go against the temporary injunction, which I would never do.

I may be the only person in Kimbell who understands exactly how she feels. The orchards were one of the places Gramps and I visited the most, our go-to location to talk and catch up under the canopy of the mature trees, surrounded by the sweet smell of fruit in the air. Finding out that her grandmother could be the reason we had this area to enjoy was humbling.

As much as I doubt her deed is authentic, I can't help but wonder about the sketches of the orchard. It seems too strange for it to be a coincidence that they match the layout of the trees on my property. I can't help but wonder what that could reveal about the history of the land.

It's a stretch to believe a young Alice Butler would've trespassed to create something this magnificent on property she didn't own. I also think it's unlikely Gramps paid her to do this. So what answer does that leave? Who knows? What I do know is that Kennedy deserves to see the orchards, regardless.

"You okay?" I ask as she moves slowly through the brush. The hill is riddled with potholes and ant beds, which I carefully navigate her around.

"I think so. Just don't let go," she says, a softness in her voice.

"I won't," I whisper as we navigate to the bottom of the hill. The shrub lined pathway stretches ahead, guiding us through the orchards.

"I may be biased, but this is stunning. The layout of the trees are abstract but work in perfect harmony with the nature around it," Kennedy says, staring at the orchard in awe.

"You're biased, and I completely agree with you," I say, reaching up to pluck a plum from the tree. I turn it over and over in my hands, looking for blemishes. Satisfied there aren't any, I rub it against my damp t-shirt and hand it to her.

She smiles. "I love plums."

"Of all the fruit grown out here, the plums are the best." I turn away from her, disturbed by how the blissful look on her face is affecting me. Her grandmother's legacy could be these orchards, but the entire fifty acres are a legacy left to me from Gramps. When I was at my lowest, finding him and this property renewed me. Moving to Kimbell to be near him was the best thing I could've ever done. I don't have any regrets.

As I turn back around, Kennedy is biting into the plum. A sensual act that makes me forget to breathe. How in the world is she eating fruit in such a sexy way?

"Come on, let's head toward the pecan trees." I leave her behind with the spell she's trying to cast on me.

The soft thud of her sandals against the damp earth grows louder as she catches up.

"Luke …"

"Yeah," I say, but I don't trust myself to look at her.

"Thank you for bringing me out here. I know this isn't easy for you," Kennedy says. "But it means the world to me. I would visit Granny at Bell Botanical Gardens all the time. She'd explain to me the changes she planned to make and why. There was an art and a science to her work. She was so passionate and dedicated to bringing nature to the world in a way that showcased its beauty."

"I researched the trees after Gramps showed them to me the first time. He was always worried about taking care of them. Turns out everything he'd done was good for the area. It's why they are still here."

Kennedy presses a hand against the bark and closes her eyes as if communicating silently with the pecan tree. "I'm glad he took good care of them. Honestly, I was scared I'd come all this way only to find stumps where the orchards used to be."

"You think I would've done something to them?"

"Of course not!" Her hand touches my forearm gently, and I believe her. "Just wasn't sure if they'd been kept up or neglected."

"I'm surprised you didn't bring your cousin to see it. The one who works at the tax office," I say.

"Vangie? Well, she's my cousin from my dad's side. Yolanda, who owns the bridal shop downtown, is also my cousin from my dad's side. All three of us grew up more like best friends and sisters than cousins. They wouldn't have hesitated to be with me if I'd asked. But this is something that I was comfortable doing on my own."

"What about your mom?" Curiosity is getting the better of me now that Kennedy is opening up. It's nice to have a normal conversation with her, not laced with animosity.

She shakes her head quickly. "Mom lives in Chelsea, you know, in New York City. Even if she was in town, I don't think she'd be as excited as I am about all this. She and Granny had a falling out. That's why Granny cut her out of her will."

"Seriously? She didn't want her own daughter to have anything?"

"Well, Granny didn't like the position my mom put me in when she decided to cheat on my dad with an artist passing through town. But if you ask my mom, it was love at first sight, and I was old enough to handle my parents splitting apart."

"That's an interesting position ..." I know all about cheating mothers. How much more do Kennedy and I have in common?

"Granny thought so, too. She thought it was selfish of my mom not to wait two years until I graduated before blowing our family apart. She never forgave her for doing that."

"How did you feel about it?"

"I was sixteen and could clearly see that my parents' relationship was hanging on by a thread. My dad loved my mom to death, but she was so restless about our life. Itching to move on to something ... different. I wasn't shocked when she told me she'd asked Daddy for a divorce," Kennedy says, contemplative. "But that put me in the tough position of choosing which parent I would stay with. Mom was moving to New York to be with her new man and wanted me to come. Daddy was staying behind in Kimbell, heartbroken. My decision was a no-brainer."

"It was?" I'm confused since the obvious answer is that a teenage girl would stay with her mother. I'm pretty sure Kennedy didn't move to New York.

"Didn't I tell you I was sixteen? There was no way I was leaving all my friends behind to start a new high school on the East Coast when I'd be graduating in two years." She looks mortified. "And New York at that. I might as well be going to school on Mars for as different as it is from here in so many ways. That was a no-go. Plus, Daddy needed me more," Kennedy explains without any hint of animosity toward her mother.

I wish I could look back on my situation and feel the same way. But she wasn't as directly impacted by her mother's indiscretions as I was.

"I can't imagine that your mom took that well. She had to be hurt that you didn't want to stay with her."

"For sure, but we worked through it and never stopped being close. Our relationship didn't change much. The conversations we'd have in person were now over the phone, and I'd fly up to NYC a few times a year to hang out with her." Kennedy turns and looks at me, a question in her gaze. "And that's how I ended up getting everything Granny owned. What's your story? How are you the sole heir to Frank Diamond's land instead of your father?"

"My story isn't too different from yours."

"Seriously? Your granddad had a falling out with your father?"

I nod. "And it was caused by my cheating mother."

"You're joking!" Kennedy grips my arms, staring at me intently.

"Would I really joke about something like this?" I inhale a deep breath. "I was a lot younger than you when all this happened. Gramps disapproved of how my parents handled my mother's transgression, which caused a rift between him and my dad. That rift stopped me from meeting my grandfather until I was in my mid-twenties."

"Wow, that's uncanny. So eventually, you found him, and y'all were able to build a close relationship with each other."

"The closest. Even though I didn't get much time with him, it feels like he packed in a lifetime of memories to last me now that he's gone. People think he was cold and unfeeling, a mean man. To me, he was caring, generous and protective. Everything I needed when I needed it the most."

"Kind of like how Granny swooped in to be a mother figure for me when my mom was fifteen hundred miles away." She tosses her devoured plum core onto the ground. "Too often, people take family for granted. Don't realize how important it is until the person is gone. I'm glad you got the time you did with your grandfather."

"And I'm glad you got the time with your grandmother—" My words are nearly drowned out by a booming thunder that rumbles the ground.

Kennedy squeals, then peers up to the sky through the branches. A flash of light brightens the sky, blinding me. She reaches for me, and I pull her close. A crash of lightning strikes a pine tree near the edge of the orchard.

"Oh God!" Kennedy screams as the bolt splits the tree in half and crashes to the ground.

"Come on, we need to get to the barn ... now."

CHAPTER 17

KENNEDY

"I SHOULD CARRY YOU," LUKE ANNOUNCES.

Laughter bursts from my lips. "Carry me? You can't be ... serious."

The wind blows fiercely, and the rain slashes to the ground at a sharp angle, flooding the plain around the orchard. From where we stand, the barn is about the length of a football field away.

The stern look on his face tells me he's more than serious. He's convinced it's the right thing to do. "It wouldn't be the first time. I saved you from face-planting in Bell Park, remember?"

I swallow hard, memories slamming into my mind. Luke holding me in his arms is entirely different from carrying me as he runs a hundred yards to the barn. I can't deny I wouldn't mind knowing what it would feel like to be carried by Mr. March. It's the stuff Hollywood romance movies are made of. Given my current love drought, that's not the kind of experience I can handle. I can't be sure I'd keep it in the proper perspective instead of letting my fantasies run wild.

I shake my head and give him what I hope is an equally determined stare. "You're not carrying me. It's faster if we both run. We're wasting time even discussing this."

Luke presses his hands on his hips, superman style, and says, "The field is flooded. Underneath all that water are bugs, ants, maybe even snakes. We both know you're not dressed for this. Those shoes won't survive or help you move as fast as you need to."

Mirroring his pose, I say, "I can handle it. Trust me, this isn't my first thunderstorm or run in the rain. Put your hero cape away, and let's get to the barn."

"You're infuriating, you know that?" He yanks my hand and gives me an emerald glare, warning me not to resist. I don't bother, realizing that's the compromise he's forcing me to take whether I like it or not.

Luke gives me a sly grin. "Fair warning: if you have trouble keeping up, I'm throwing you over my shoulder."

My heart does a stupid flip, then flop.

Get a grip, Kennedy.

I respond, "I'll keep up."

He tugs me forward, and we burst forth into the pelting rain. I can barely see in front of me as I struggle to keep up with Luke's powerful strides. We're halfway to the barn when my sandals get sucked into the mud. I stumble out of them but don't lose pace with Luke. My feet pound against the slimy, muddy terrain.

Luke releases my hand and pushes through the barn door. I stumble forward, close behind him, and collapse on a stack of baled hay near the door. Heaving breaths, I grip the hay and flip over on my back. Swiping the rain from my face, I grimace as the hay sticks pierce and poke me through my wet dress.

"Well, that was fun," I mutter, rising slightly to watch Luke as he closes the door. He turns, and his gaze lingers on me, a mix of concern and something more intense, like embers smoldering beneath the surface.

"What is it?" I ask, panicked, thinking maybe a water moccasin or other swamp insect is stuck to my body.

Luke crosses the distance and sits next to me. His body is so close that his heat warms my skin.

"Your hair was straight," Luke says, a glimmer of wonder in his eyes. "And now it's curly."

A long, 4C wavy strand flops over my face as if on cue. Luke reaches a finger out slowly, tracing along the curl pattern until his finger is hovering near my lips. I hold my breath, not knowing what stupid thing I'd do if he dared to trace my mouth next.

Luckily, he snaps out of his momentary trance and pulls his hand away.

"You've seen women with natural hair before," I say, suddenly self-conscious about my unruly curls. I'm disappointed that my two-day-old silk press is ruined, but it's not uncommon during the spring.

"Just never saw it change like that right before my eyes." A soft smile plays at the corners of his mouth. "It's magic."

"More like a nightmare. I'll have to wash it and flat iron it again tonight," I say, tugging the curly strands behind my ears. "I'm sure I look a mess."

"That's impossible." Luke rises from the haystack and glances at my mud-crusted feet. I'm instantly embarrassed and wonder if I should've let him carry me instead of insisting on being so independent. "And you lost your shoes like I said you would."

"Stop being a know-it-all." I curl my legs backward, trying to hide them from view. "Okay, hero. When the rain stops, you can go find them for me."

"In the meantime, let's get you cleaned up." He jogs away.

I force my eyes away from him and take in my surroundings. The barn's interior is unexpectedly posh—polished hardwood floors and a sturdy wooden staircase leading to a spacious loft. Exposed beams stretch across the vaulted ceiling, their rough-hewn texture contrasting with the minimal chic furnishings below. Across from the stacked bales of hay are four leather bean bags arranged in a cozy sitting area, illuminated by the soft, diffused light filtering through the rain-splattered windows.

Along the walls, tasteful rustic decor—antique farm tools, vintage lanterns, and sepia-toned photographs—pays homage to the barn's agricultural roots. The loft above houses what appears to be a small living space, complete with a bed and a writing desk, offering a bird's-eye view of the inviting room below.

Luke returns with a blanket, towels, two granola bars, and four bottles of water. Stacking the items on the floor, he wraps the blanket around my shoulders. "That should help get you dry and warm." He shakes a finger at me. "Only one of those granola bars is for you. Don't think about eating both of them."

I roll my eyes and grab a bottle of water, ignoring the granola bar I'm in no mood to eat. I take a swig just as Luke kneels before me.

"Wait, what are you doing?" I sputter, water spraying from my mouth.

"I'm not going to let you track mud through my barn," Luke says with a hint of disdain. He cradles my feet in one large, powerful hand and pours water slowly over them.

With gentle, methodical strokes, he washes away the grime, his fingertips grazing my skin and sending shivers racing up my spine. He takes his time, thoroughly cleansing each foot with a tenderness that steals my breath. As he works, he glances up at me through his lashes, a small, intimate smile tugging at his lips. The moment feels charged, the air between us electric with unspoken tension, and I find myself unable to look away, transfixed by the unexpected intimacy of his touch.

I part my lips, a question forming on my tongue, but the words evaporate as Luke's hands still. His gaze locks with mine, the intensity in his eyes sending my heart into a frenzy. For a breathless moment, we remain frozen, caught in the gravity of the unspoken emotions swirling between us.

Then, as if remembering himself, Luke clears his throat and returns his attention to my feet. "Almost done," he murmurs, his voice husky.

With a few final swipes of the towel, he ensures all traces of mud are gone. The spell broken, he sits back on his heels, a satisfied smile on his face. "There, all clean."

I flex my toes, marveling at the care he's taken with such a simple task. "You must be the world's best boyfriend."

Luke's emerald gaze sears a trail of heat up my body until his eyes lock onto mine. "What makes you say that?"

I fight back a grimace and inwardly curse my loose lips. Taking a deep breath, I say, "If this is how you treat someone you hate, I can't imagine how wonderful you are to someone you love."

His eyes dance with amusement, shifting from a deep emerald to a light moss. "I don't hate you Kennedy. What we're going through is tough, but like you said, we'll figure out the mystery of the two deeds. In time, there won't be any hard feelings between us."

"I hope you're right," I say, and I mean it. If the land belongs to Luke, it won't be difficult for me to return to how things were before. He and his grandfather made sure Granny's orchard was maintained. I could pitch my idea about the educational hikes to the property to him and still have a shot of them being incorporated into the programs at the new center. I couldn't ask for anything more.

But if the land belongs to me, Luke will be devastated. I can't imagine how he would ever get past losing it or forgive me for taking it away. I shift a bit on the hay, uncomfortable with the thought.

"As for your other comment, you'll have to ask my exes about that." He pulls thick socks from his back pocket and puts them on my feet. "I'm not so sure."

I frown, remembering the latest gossip about Luke. "Why wouldn't I ask your current girlfriend, Ciara Thompson?" My voice sounds strained to my ears as I fight back an unexpected wave of envy.

Luke's head falls back, and he groans loudly. "Ciara and I never got off the ground to be a couple. She's too busy making a name for herself as a world-class reporter to waste time with a relationship."

I detect more than a hint of anger in his tone, a bitterness I didn't expect from the town's resident good guy. "She broke up with you?"

He shakes his head. "We weren't a couple, so we didn't have to break up. But I was the one who suggested we stop pretending that we were trying to become one. She agreed."

"You seem pissed about that."

He looks surprised, the anger dissipating from his face. "A little, but not for the reasons you probably think."

"Oh, so you're a mind reader now?"

"You think I'm mad because she chose her career over me." His words hang in the air.

I reluctantly shrug my agreement.

"I'm more upset because she lied. She led me to believe she would carve out some time to explore a relationship when she knew she wouldn't. I never got to know her well enough for things to work out between us. But I also wasted months with her, trying to see if they could. Can't get that time back."

"You weren't dating other women while you were with Ciara?"

"Some guys do that. I never have. I like to give a woman my full attention to see what could be."

"Maybe those months weren't wasted. The delay could've been preparing you for—"

"The next best thing?" Luke finishes my sentence. "You could be right. I need someone here, in Kimbell. A woman I can see every day, except when I'm on shift, of course. Relationships need quality time and you're more likely to get that if you're not working around someone's busy schedule. I want to be with a woman who likes it if I pop in on her at work. I want her to feel free to show up at my house unexpectedly ..."

His words trail off as my eyebrows shoot up to the top of my head. I warn myself to keep my cool. He's absolutely not talking about me. It was just a generic example.

Clearing my throat, I say, "But you had that before, right? With Ginger."

"Ginger was a while ago. Zora was my last serious relationship." He looks up as the rain batters the barn roof. The sound is ominous, matching the shift in his mood. Who knew Luke had this side to him? "She broke up with me."

I give a mock gasp. "Why on earth would she do that?"

"She gave me an ultimatum about marriage, and I had to be honest," Luke says, eyes narrowed. "I told her I needed more time to make that kind of commitment. My answer wasn't what she wanted to hear. Maybe she wanted me to chase after her with a ring, but I think she did the right thing."

"You weren't ready for marriage?"

"In my heart, although I loved her, I knew she wasn't my partner for life." He laughs under his breath, but it's without mirth. "I must sound like a troll."

"You sound honest, which many women struggle to appreciate when they really should," I say, reflecting on my failed relationships. As blindsided as I was by all six of them, I never questioned the guy's conclusions. I respected that their feelings were, unfortunately, different from mine.

"Sounds like you're speaking from experience," Luke says.

"You know I am." I roll my eyes. "I'm Kennedy the dumpee, remember."

"All losing streaks come to an end, you know," Luke says, tickling the bottom of my foot.

I giggle and jerk my foot away. "You think so?"

His answer lies somewhere in the sparks dancing in his eyes. Is Luke casting some spell on me? And would I care if he is?

"Rain stopped."

"What?" I'm jolted back to reality, noticing the silence ringing in the barn.

"We can head back now." Luke rises to his feet. "I'll go get your shoes."

"Okay," I say, then close my eyes.

I remind myself that none of this is what my imagination is tricking me into thinking. Nothing is happening between me and Luke Diamond.

CHAPTER 18

L UKE

~

I SWEAR IT TOOK EVERY OUNCE OF WILLPOWER TO STOP myself from staring at Kennedy the entire walk back to the house. Her dress clung to her banging figure like a wet t-shirt, leaving nothing to the imagination. The view is seared in my brain, and I have no plans to forget what I saw. Ever.

"That took a dog's age," Kennedy says, stepping onto the porch. She squeezes excess water from her dress onto the wooden planks. "I feel so gross. I need a shower bad. Then I need to do something with this hair." She grabs chunks of her thick, curly tresses in both hands and makes a face that's adorable.

"Are your suitcases in your car?" I ask.

Her mouth gapes open, then shuts.

"It's okay. You planned to move in with me today, right?"

"Right."

"So how about I show you to your room? While you get cleaned up, I'll pull your car into the garage and bring your stuff inside."

She raises her hands. "I didn't bring much. I swear. This arrangement should only be for a couple of weeks. One way or the other, we will get to the truth soon. I don't want the lawsuit to be drawn out."

"Neither do I," I say, but I'm not entirely convinced. Having Kennedy under my roof reignites my initial interest in her when she was just the woman on the billboard. Honestly, it's a long shot that she'll come up with any evidence that will cause the judge to rule in her favor. Doesn't matter whether she shows her commitment to her belief that the land belongs to her by living here.

Why shouldn't I take advantage of this time? See if there's something to that pull I felt for her before she tripped into my life and tried to take my land.

She wipes her feet on the mat outside the front door and waits for me.

"It's open. Go inside and get your car keys," I say, selfishly constructing a way to sneak another glance at those curves.

Kennedy sways sensually as she enters my house, and I'm hit again by that sense of her belonging here. But not because this land is hers. Maybe because I'm hers. Or will be hers. And she'll be mine.

I clench my eyes shut.

Slow down, Luke.

You need to get to know Kennedy and not just go by her looks.

But isn't that what happened today?

In less than twenty-four hours, I learned more about Kennedy than I did about Ciara in over six months. The shared experiences with our grandparents and similarities with our cheating moms made me feel a connection to her I never expected. Seeing how differently she responded to similar shocking revelations struck a chord with me. Her ability to handle it better than I had impressed me. Especially since she was much younger when the truth came out than I was.

In fact, when I think about Kennedy, there's a long list building on the plus side and only one pesky item on the minus side.

"Here they are," Kennedy says, breaking through my thoughts. "But I thought you were going to show me to my room first."

I take the keys from her, careful not to touch her hand. I've done enough touching of Kennedy's body today to drive me insane for the rest of the night.

"Follow me." I move past her and enter the house. Passing the study, I maneuver through the great room, taking a right to head through the kitchen and dining room before pushing open the double doors that lead to the game room and the two bedrooms. "Now, this place is nowhere near as fancy as your grandmother's Tudor House."

"It's nice and homey," Kennedy says.

I steer her around the air hockey table and past the arcade games to the hallway on the other side. Taking a left, I stop outside the bedroom door. "You can sleep in here." I turn on the lights. "The first set of doors over there are to the closet, and the door next to it is the bathroom."

"And your bedroom is on the opposite side of the house?" Kennedy asks.

"My bedroom is right there." I point down the hall to the room twenty feet from hers.

"You didn't move into the master suite after …"

"I couldn't. Still can't." I rub the back of my neck and suck in a breath. "That was Gramps's side of the house, and this side was mine."

"You're okay with sharing your side of the house with me?"

"It's the only option." My words are final. No one is disturbing Gramps's old room. I haven't changed a thing over there. I'm not ready to. Not yet.

Seemingly satisfied with my answer, she says, "Well, I'm about to disappear for several hours. You get a break from me."

"Several hours?"

"Doing my hair is a three-hour process, and that's after I let myself soak in the shower for an hour to wash away this grime," she says, her face pinched with disgust.

"So, I won't see you again until … dinner time?"

"I'm not going to be a burden, Luke—"

"A guest in my home won't fend for her own meals. Even one that is legally imposed on me," I say, shutting down her resistance. "Any food off limits?"

She shakes her head.

"I'm a pretty good cook, so you don't have to worry about starving around me," I say, my mind already cycling through options of my best dishes to impress her. Which I shouldn't care about, but for some reason, I do. It's time to put some distance between me and the lovely Kennedy Tarkington. Jangling the keys, I say, "I'll go get your things."

CHAPTER 19

K ENNEDY

"How are you up so early?" Luke stumbles into the kitchen, groping along the counter until he's in front of the coffee maker. He grabs an SMU mug from the cabinet, slams it into the slot of the machine, and presses the buttons like he's going to pound them off.

A low hum fills the air, followed by the smell of freshly brewed coffee. Luke yawns, stretching his arms over his head. I glimpse the eight-pack abs that made him one of the most famous men in the Firefighter Hunk calendar and almost drop the wooden spoon onto the floor.

Luke levels me with a bewildered stare. "Or did you forget that we stayed up til two in the morning?"

"I didn't forget." I focus my attention on the food bubbling within the cast iron skillet. There's no way I could forget the conversation with Luke last night. It was easy, effortless, and fun, without any lingering tension from the lawsuit. "I just wanted to prove that you're not the only one with chef-caliber cooking skills."

"Is that so?" Luke says. The coffee maker sputters to a stop, and he grabs the mug and takes a long sip. It seems to invigorate him. "I wonder what kind of magic we'd make if we tackled a meal together?"

"Maybe we should find out for dinner tonight."

"Good idea. We'll have to brainstorm some ideas before you go to work."

"I'm not going. It's the in-between season for me. Just finished up the company annual financial statements for my business clients, but the tax returns for my individual clients haven't picked up yet. I can take a day off and not miss anything."

"You're going to stick around and hang out with me?" He asks, looking at me over the rim of his coffee mug as he takes another sip.

"I thought I'd explore more of the property. Go see Diamond Lake and whatever else is out there. Don't feel like you have to show me around—"

"I don't mind. God ... what are you cooking? It smells divine," Luke says, closing the gap between us.

"Chilaquiles with chorizo and eggs."

"Is it almost done?"

I flip the mixture a couple more times, satisfied that it's as close to perfection as I will get it. "Yes, it's ready."

Luke grabs two spoons from a drawer and then pushes it closed with his hip. "Come on, let's have breakfast on the back porch."

"Don't we need plates? Napkins?" I say, wondering how I'll carry the scalding hot cast iron skillet and all the things Luke forgot to grab.

"Nope," Luke says with a devilish grin. "I reckon you'll eat about a quarter of that skillet. I'll polish off the rest. I need a lot of fuel to keep this going." He gives me a wink.

"God forbid I do anything to stand in the way of you keeping that body going," I mutter, but my voice isn't quiet enough based on the sexy grin that spreads across his face.

He grabs a trivet. "After you."

I lead the way onto the back porch, placing the skillet on the small table between the two rocking chairs. Easing down onto one, I gaze out at the sun's golden rays, peeking through the haze of storm clouds. It looks like it's going to be a beautiful spring day.

Turning to dig into the chilaquiles, I laugh at Luke, who has already devoured about a quarter of the dish. "You weren't lying, were you?"

He shakes his head, looking like an adorable kid who got caught with his hand in the cookie jar.

"This is the best breakfast I've ever had in my life. Don't tell Gwen," Luke says, leaning back on his chair.

Digging in, I take a bite and am quite pleased with myself. I dare say Daddy would be mightily impressed. It's almost as good as his version, which he prefers to make with brisket instead of chorizo.

"Imagine us, sitting like this, having a civilized conversation," I say as guilt claws at me over what I did before cooking breakfast.

"Your surprise move-in definitely ticked me off … at first. But I'm alright with it now."

"Well, I have a confession to make." I lay my spoon down.

"This must be serious if you're taking a break from breakfast." He chuckles.

"You gave me a partial tour of the house last night. This morning, I gave myself a self-guided tour of the rest." I pause, studying his face for any signs of anger. I'm surprised when I'm greeted with just a look of curiosity.

"So, you saw Gramps's suite," he says, then rocks gently in the chair. "Did you look through all the rooms, bedroom, closet, bathroom, and reading nook?"

"I did."

"What did you think?

"I think you're insane for not moving into that room. It's by far the most magnificent part of this house. The private porch and the tree swing a few feet away where you can sit out there and see Diamond Lake. What's not to love?"

"I never said I didn't love the space. It's just been hard for me to wrap my head around taking Gramps's room. It feels like it's still his."

"You think that's what he wanted for you when he gave you this house? For you to only live in half of it?" I scoff. "If I were him, I'd be pretty ticked off at you right about now."

"You think I'm wasting my inheritance, huh?"

"Absolutely," I say, then take another bite of the chilaquiles before Luke devours the whole skillet. "Let's break it down. The furniture has to go. You need to bring in some that reflect you and your style. Take down the wallpaper. It's hideous."

Luke laughs. "Tell me about it."

"Give it a fresh paint job, maybe some hard wood floors instead of carpet, and that room will feel like it's always been yours."

"Is that what you did with the Tudor house? Renovated and made it your own."

I nod my head. "And I believe it's what Granny wanted me to do. I didn't know Frank Diamond, but I'm sure he had the same wish for you."

"Funny, when I first came to town, he wanted me to take his room. Thought I'd have better use of it with the ladies than he did." Luke laughs. "Gramps could be such a perv sometimes. He was always in my business trying to figure out if I was getting lucky." He moves his fingers in air quotes.

"From what I hear, your grandfather got lucky quite a bit. It's a shame that's what took him out," I say, reflecting on the tidbit Mrs. Williamson shared with me in her rant about how wretched Frank Diamond was.

"At least he went happy," Luke says with a rueful smile.

"Did he bring women home while you were here? That must have been awkward."

"No!" Luke grimaces. "Absolutely not. He made sure I was either on shift or with whoever my girlfriend was at the time. If I was home, it was just me and him."

"Zora was your last relationship, right?" I ask.

He nods. "Yours?"

"A little over a year ago with Maxwell Jones," I say, waiting for the tightness to grip my chest. I'm pleasantly surprised when it doesn't come.

"He seems like a good guy. Surprised y'all didn't work out."

"He is a great guy. Amazing actually. We just stumbled upon some clear dealbreakers … for him," I say. Usually, I avoid talking about my failed relationships, but with Luke, it feels easier than ever. "When I care about someone, I have this tendency to nerd out and get really into the details when they have a problem. I do everything in my power to fix it for them because I don't want them struggling if I can make it go away."

"I take it he didn't like that much."

"He never said the exact words, but I think he started to feel emasculated by how much I tried to takeover and fix … things," I say, then shut my mouth. The last thing I need to do is blab Maxwell's private issues with Luke.

"Well, I don't have that problem. Trust me, I'd still be one hundred percent man even if a pretty lady wanted to swoop in, nerd out, and help me fix my problem." Luke raises an eyebrow like an invitation.

He's obviously not talking hypothetically. I say, "You did mention you were dealing with a challenge when we saw each other in Bell Park—"

"When I saved you from busting your face open, yes."

"I thanked you for that."

"I just remember you demanding that I put you down."

Laughter erupts from my mouth. "What is it with you and wanting to carry me?"

He shrugs and gives me a second wink. "You're soft and cuddly. What's not to like?"

I erupt into laughter. "You make me sound like a teddy bear or something." I swat at his arm, impressed by the rock-solid feel of his muscles. I'd forgotten how sculpted his body is. I force myself to forget how attractive Luke is and turn my attention to helping him. It's the least I can do. I take one last bite of the breakfast, my stomach full for foolishly trying to keep up with Luke, then say, "Tell me your problem."

CHAPTER 20

K ENNEDY

Over the next half hour, he lays out the issue of increasing property taxes due to the skyrocketing valuation of property around the lake, which I'm very familiar with. Then he segues into his discussions with Nate about setting up a business to sell the produce and nuts from the orchard. He doesn't want to be a direct seller, preferring to hand that off to small local grocery and candy stores.

"What do you think?" Luke asks, and he seems genuinely eager for my perspective. Despite myself, I feel satisfied and gratified to have my thoughts and opinions held in high esteem by a guy who is—

What ... Kennedy?

I need to get a grip.

Luke and I are not on a stupid date. I'm here for one reason only. To prove to the court that I wholeheartedly believe this land and its contents belong to the Butlers, not the Diamonds.

If that's true, why do these moments with Luke feel like so much more?

"It's a good start …"

"But you see flaws in my approach?"

"More in your analysis. While I'm in love with the orchards because of Granny, they aren't big in the grand scheme of what stores would purchase."

"I guess you should know, with your dad running the best grocery store in town."

"You can sell most of what you produce to my dad and other stores beyond Lasso County, but it's not going to produce the kind of revenues you need to cover the uptick in maintenance for producing fruit and nuts for sale or the taxes."

Luke's shoulders slump, and he looks off into the distance.

I grip his arm and shake him.

He turns back toward me. "Tell me that was the bad news, and you're going to follow it up with the good."

I bounce on the rocking chair with excitement. "You're thinking too small. With the beauty of this land being as close to how nature intended it, that's your selling point. With as many people moving to town for the new lakehouses and commercial developments, they also come here for what we have that they are lacking."

"Small town peace and quiet."

"Exactly. They will flock to experience this if you open up the land for tourism. People can walk along a guided path through unspoiled nature, maybe visit some mini ponies."

"That's good."

"They'll have baskets where they will pay you much more than any grocery store to do all the work for you and pick fruit to take home. You can set up tables by the lakefront and allow picnics. Maybe even reach out to some food trucks to sell food to the guests. That's how you turn a profit here," I say, then rattle on. "Most orchard farms typically welcome around five to ten thousand folks a year, taking into consideration the slower seasons. A reasonable target for you would be turning a healthy profit in as soon as two years. The going rate of entry is around ten bucks, but you'll make most of your money from the extras you sell. You'll have to keep a close eye on expenses though because ..." my voice trails off, and I close my eyes.

Here I go again, nerding out in front of a guy and turning him off. When will I learn?

"Hey, why did you stop?"

I open my eyes and Luke is staring at me.

My heart aches for how attracted I am to this man, and not just because of his physical beauty, which is definitely stunning. He's so much more than the two-dimensional goody-two-shoes everyone talks about. He's a guy with flaws balanced with self-awareness. I can talk to him for hours, and he is passionate about his views. And that temper is something I never expected, rearing its head when he forgets to keep it in check. Even good guys are allowed to be annoyed.

He's all of that, and I ... like him.

Worst of all, I want him to like me.

"Sorry, I nerded out on you. I'm sure you weren't expecting that level of detail—"

"It's perfect. I'm in awe of how quickly you cycle through analysis off the top of your head. It's brilliant, actually. I should've been taking notes, but I didn't want to miss anything you were saying."

"Stop it, Luke," I bolt up from the rocking chair and walk to the edge of the porch. My heart pounds in my chest, and I'm two seconds from passing out.

"What's wrong?" Luke is next to me in an instant. His hand presses against the small of my back. "Do you feel ill?"

More like lovesick. But I can't tell him that.

"No, I just ... don't know what to make of ... this. You hated me, and now, it's like you—"

"It's like I really like you." His voice drops deeper as he says the words.

"And what's worse is that I want you to like me." I take the chance and turn to look into those emerald orbs.

A mischievous glint dances in his eyes.

"Kennedy," Luke says my name in a way that sends my heart soaring. "I really like you."

"Oh ... okay ... so what does that mean?"

His arm slips around my waist. "I hope it means I can do what I've wanted since I found you in my living room yesterday morning."

"What's ... that?"

"Kiss you," Luke says, his gaze dropping to my lips.

"Luke ... are you sure?"

He moves closer to me. "Never been surer."

I swallow past the lump in my throat. "Then do it."

CHAPTER 21

KENNEDY

THIS COULD BE MY LIFE.

Yes, those are the thoughts going through my head as I navigate through the darkened rooms of the house, making my way to the garage. If there's one thing I've learned about Luke, he's not a morning person. While I'm up at five, he's stumbling awake closer to nine. That's the only reason I don't knock on his bedroom door to say goodbye before heading off to work. He starts his shift at the fire station today, and after spending another late night talking for hours on the back porch, I know he needs his rest.

As I walk through the kitchen, I grab a banana and a container of orange juice, then open the door that leads to the garage. Easing it closed behind me, I turn and …

Scream.

The sound rattles and echoes through the cavernous space as my brain struggles to comprehend that it's not an axe murderer standing in front of me.

It's … Luke.

He's already dressed for his shift in a navy t-shirt that hugs his muscles and fitted dark cargo pants.

"You scared the life out of me!" I squeal, then push his broad shoulders. He doesn't budge. Not even an inch as a sexy smile plays at the corner of his mouth.

"I knew it."

"You knew what?"

"You'd sneak out of the house this morning without saying goodbye. Rob me of a last kiss before I have to suffer through twenty-four hours without you," Luke says, crossing his arms over his chest. He's still smiling, but I detect a hint of hurt in his dark green eyes. Like he might really be upset with me.

"After we stayed up so late, I didn't want to disturb you."

"Lame excuse."

"It's not lame. I was being considerate." I reach for his face, caressing his cheek gently. His eyes soften as he steps closer to me.

"I'm surprised you're up so early."

"Couldn't sleep."

"Why?"

He stares at me in response, an intense gaze that reels me in and provides a better answer than any words could ever. He tilts his head toward my car. A brown paper bag rests on the hood.

"I made you breakfast. Overnight oats with granola, raspberries, and honey. Much more filling than that banana."

"You are the sweetest, most perfect man in the world," I say.

"So, you kind of like me."

"I like you a lot."

"I miss you already."

"It's only twenty-four hours, Luke."

"Feels like an eternity."

"How about I give you a good memory to focus on until we see each other again tomorrow?"

"Would you please?" He bites his bottom lip in the cutest way.

Any nervousness I might have felt about kissing Luke melts away as he looks at me like I'm the most beautiful woman in the world. Rising on my tiptoes, I drape my arms around his neck. Before I can make my move, Luke's lips are on mine. His touch feather-light yet blazing with heat. My skin flushes as I melt into him and his irresistible force. The kiss grows deeper as we take our time exploring each other. I cling to him as if he's going to slip away like a dream, but somehow, I know Luke isn't going anywhere. He's proven over and over that the only place he wants to be is right here with me.

I'm breathless as I break away from the kiss. A hint of my lip gloss shimmers on his mouth, and I slowly wipe it away. Freely touching him like this has goosebumps peppering my skin. The passion in his eyes doesn't help, either.

"I really need to get to work," I say, hating being apart from him.

Adopting a sad puppy dog face, he nods. "I'll stop by your office when I get off of shift tomorrow and bring breakfast."

"That sounds perfect." I maneuver around him and flee to my car before we end up kissing the morning away in the garage.

CHAPTER 22

ENNEDY

I DRIVE TO WORK ON CLOUD NINE AND SETTLE INTO MY
office.

Then pandemonium erupts.

I log in to my accounting software.

Warning messages glare back at me about dozens of client contracts that have been declined.

I scroll through the list and see long-time clients who I've performed their personal tax returns for years. There's no way they didn't renew their contracts. It has to be some kind of glitch. After spending hours on the phone with the help desk trying to figure out the problem, I'm flummoxed, annoyed, and in need of a double espresso from the coffee house a few doors down.

I lean back in my chair, frustration rising. Closing my eyes, I take a deep breath and can almost feel Luke's lips tickling my neck with kisses like he did last night underneath the stars. We sat in the tree swing looking out toward Diamond Lake after cooking dinner together. It was the most romantic moment I've experienced in my life. And all this with a man I'm technically not dating.

How in the world is this my life?

And should I even let myself enjoy this?

We were very open and honest about the future impacts of the lawsuit and what that could mean for the feelings growing between us. Neither of us can predict how we will feel when there is a final ruling, especially if there is a clear loser.

Still, I was relieved when Luke suggested that we not let that stop us from delving deeper into getting to know each other. The more I learn about Luke, the more I wonder if he's the guy I've been waiting on all this time. Things with him feels so effortless and comfortable. Not that we see eye-to-eye on everything, because we don't. We've had our fair share of debates over the past two days. But while we passionately defend our positions, it never leads to anger or resentment. Only a deeper interest and … connection.

My main problem is that every issue that has caused my six previous breakups doesn't seem to bother Luke … at all.

It's like he accepts me for me, the good and the bad. I don't have to stifle or temper any part of my personality with him, and it's liberating.

My eyes fling open.

"Focus Kennedy. Now is not the time to pine over Luke Diamond. You need to get this computer glitch fixed." I push back from my desk and stand up.

I know exactly who can help me. Kincaid Real Estate is at the end of the office park. I can ask Zaire's assistant, Simona, for Wiley's number. He's a wiz at fixing IT-related problems. Grabbing my purse, I head to the door. As I reach for the handle, it swings open abruptly. I stumble back, startled.

"Oh, I'm glad I caught you before you left," Nelly Wheeler says, her usually warm eyes cold and hard as she stares at me. Her lips are pressed into a thin line. I can practically feel the disapproval radiating off her. This is not the same woman I spend hours pouring through her shoebox of receipts with as we do her taxes.

I take a step back, a knot forming in my stomach. "Come on in, Nelly. You know I always have time for you."

Nelly doesn't move from the doorway. Her stance is rigid, unyielding. "Yes darling, I know. That's why this is very difficult for me."

"What is?" Tension grips the air between us.

"You're fired. I'm going to let Eric Watson do my taxes this year," Nelly says. Her words hit me like a physical blow.

I blink rapidly, trying to process what I'm hearing. Nelly was one of my first clients. She convinced all her kids to use my services, including Wheeler Chesterton and his gym—one of my biggest accounts.

"I don't understand. Why are you firing me? What did I do?"

"You know exactly what you did with that inconsiderate lawsuit against Luke Diamond." Nelly's voice rises. "That sweet man has done nothing but bring joy, hope, and charity to this town. He's willing to give the shirt off his back to anyone, and here you are, trying to swoop in and take his inheritance. Luke will be homeless if you get your way, and that's just not right—"

I hold up my hands. "Nelly, there's much more to the lawsuit than you think. We have identical deeds. I'm just trying to get to the truth—"

"No," Nelly cuts me off sharply. "You're trying to take Luke's property away from him. Now, that grandfather of his was no saint, but Luke is not a chip off that block. He's the opposite of that miserable old fart in every way, and everyone in this town adores him, including me. That's why we are going to do everything in our power to stop you."

A chill runs down my spine. "What do you mean by 'we'?"

Nelly's eyes glitter with determination. "There's a grassroots effort to stop you, Kennedy. The town is pulling together to encourage you to drop your lawsuit and let things go back to the way they've been. No matter what those old documents say, Luke doesn't deserve to lose everything after all the good seed he's sown in this town since moving here." Her eyes narrow and she leans in closer to make her point. "We figured if you started to lose business, you wouldn't have enough money to continue with the lawsuit."

"Are you serious?" I ask, dizzy with shock.

"As a heart attack," she snaps back as if insulted. "We are boycotting you, young lady. Once you come to your senses, we'll all come back. But until then, I have to stand with Luke and not use your services."

Nelly gives me a haughty tip of her head, then turns on her heels. As she marches away, she tosses over her shoulder, "I hope you make the right choice, Kennedy. For your own sake."

CHAPTER 23

L UKE

~

Her words ring in my ears.

Not my imagination.

Not the fantasies that have been playing in my head.

This is the invitation I've been hoping for …

But now that I have the green light, I find myself pausing to savor this moment.

My first kiss with Kennedy Tarkington.

The woman who charged into my life with her infuriating claims and dogged determination has become who I've spent the last two days laughing, joking, teasing, flirting, and opening up with in ways I never expected. An undeniable attraction simmers underneath the surface between us. It's more than physical. We connect on a much deeper level that just works. I can't explain it, and I'm not going to try to figure it out.

What I need to do is kiss this exquisite woman before she comes to her senses and pushes me away.

Stepping closer, I caress her face and stare into her mahogany orbs. I stroke the edges of her soft lips and dip my head toward her. Our mouths are close—our cautious breaths mingling in the small space between us. I breathe her in, then press my lips to hers.

And it's like the movies … fireworks explode within me.

Kennedy responds instantly, her arms wrapping around my waist as time and space disappear. We lose ourselves in the most sensational kiss. I can't get enough of her sweet lips. I'm intoxicated by the emotions triggered by this intimacy that exceeds everything I ever imagined. I deepen the kiss, shifting to hold her against me.

I swear, I never want this moment to end.

If I could stand here kissing Kennedy for the rest of my life …

I want Kennedy in my life.

The slow tug of her breaking the kiss and pulling away from me makes me moan in protest. I give her space but don't entirely release her from my grasp.

Kennedy grins at me as she touches her lips gingerly. "Wow … I'm not sure where that came from, but it was—"

"Amazing," I complete the sentence for her.

"Luke! Did you hear me?" My head jerks around to see Ronan staring at me with a frown. Darren, Wiley, and Nate sit in their usual spots at the table in the break room at the fire station. Their faces reflect various stages of amusement.

"Sorry, I was … umm … lost in my thoughts," I say, dragging a hand down my jaw. I've been on shift for less than four hours, and I'm already zoning out into memories of the kiss that started many kisses with Kennedy yesterday.

"Right, Captain Obvious," Wiley says with a chuckle. "And what's with that goofy smile? What are you thinking about?"

I feel Nate's gaze.

"More like … who, right Luke?" Nate prods, poking me in the arm. "Have things changed with your rooming with the enemy situation?"

"Rooming with the enemy?" Darren repeats, then leans forward. "What have I missed?"

My jaw tightens as Nate updates Darren, Wiley, and Ronan on Lance Bassett's legal strategy to strengthen Kennedy's odds in the land dispute. He also mentions how she unexpectedly appeared at my doorstep two days ago to claim her temporary fifty percent ownership by moving in with me.

"Wait a minute," Wiley says, raising his hands as he leans his chair back on two legs. A feat of impressive balance none of us can copy. "You've been sharing your house with Kennedy the Dumpee? She's freaking gorgeous!"

"Tell me about it," I mutter, then glare at my best friend. When I called him frustrated about the situation, I swore him to secrecy. The last thing I wanted was the aftermath of the lawsuit to dominate our conversations when we got back on shift.

"You have no poker face, so you might as well tell us what's going on with you and Kennedy," Ronan laughs. "It's pretty clear you don't see her as the enemy anymore."

"It's worse than that," I say.

Nate shoves me. "What could possibly be worse than starting to have sympathy for the woman trying to take your inheritance from you? Luke, you really are too nice for your own good. She could be there to snoop around the house for evidence to use against you."

"She wouldn't do that. Kennedy is a straight shooter. If she wanted to go through Gramps's things, she'd be upfront about it," I say.

"Sounds like you've gotten to know Kennedy quite well," Darren says.

Wiley glances at Darren, a bright smile spreading across his face. "So, Luke. How well have you gotten to know Kennedy?"

"Fine. You know what? Y'all are going to nag me until I spill the details, so I might as well just tell you," I say, my voice rising.

They stare at me in expectation.

"We ... kissed."

The room erupts with reactions. Wiley falls over in his chair, then races around the room with his hand over his mouth. Ronan's mouth gapes open as he stares at the ceiling. Darren shakes his head, looking bewildered.

And my best friend Nate looks like the cat who ate the canary.

Is it possible he sensed this could happen?

I wouldn't be surprised.

Still, I pinch my mouth shut so I won't tell them how we spent the rest of the night on a stay-at-home date, making dinner together and sharing more kisses. The connection between us was magnetic. Neither of us resisted it. But we couldn't ignore the elephant in the room—the lawsuit.

Luckily, Kennedy and I were on the same page about taking things slow and focusing on getting to know each other better. We agreed not to discuss dating until after the lawsuit is over.

Who knows how she'll feel when she realizes the evidence she needs doesn't exist? Losing the lawsuit could be closure for her or a huge blow.

In the meantime, we agreed to avoid labels and live in the moment.

We're roommates who hang out. Nothing more. Yet.

Darren lets out a heavy exhale. "Luke, do you have feelings for Kennedy? Like real relationship vibing, chemistry out of this world, she could be the woman for me kind of feelings for her?"

"Yeah, I do." The words are out before I can stop them. "But I know it doesn't make sense. Just because she's suing me doesn't mean I don't see what an amazing person she is."

A smug smile spreads across Nate's face, but he doesn't utter a word.

"Amazing person? Are you talking about … Kennedy?" Erin's voice wafts into the break room.

Our attention snaps to our receptionist standing in the doorway. I don't think she heard everything I said, but who knows? I exchange a look with Nate and get a subtle nod. He'll help me find out and do damage control if needed.

Erin fidgets with the ring on her finger, twisting it around and around. "Oh, Luke. We should've known you wouldn't be mad at Kennedy for suing you. But the town ... is." She frowns. "I think you better get over to Bell Park."

CHAPTER 24

K ENNEDY

∼

I STAND FROZEN IN THE DOORWAY, WATCHING NELLY'S retreating figure. The implications of what just happened wash over me in waves, each threatening to knock me off my feet. I need my cousins. Now.

Jamming my hand into my purse, I pull out my cell phone and call them on speed dial, three-way.

"Hey, have y'all heard anything about—"

"The town boycotting you," Yolanda says, then sighs. "Just got wind of it this morning. Apparently, it's something Ivy Paul organized over the past few days. People are really getting behind it."

My stomach drops. "No, no, no. This can't be happening."

Vangie yells, "These crazy small-town kooks! Why shouldn't you try to figure out if that property is yours? What business is it of theirs anyway? Why do they even care?"

"Because the person I'm suing is the town's resident good-guy." My voice trembles as I speak, and I dab at the tears stinging my eyes. "When I got to work this morning, I saw many of my client contracts had been declined. I thought it was a fluke. Then Nelly Wheeler came to my office and ripped me a new one for even daring to sue Luke."

"Definitely not a fluke," Yolanda says, her voice soft and concerned. "A couple of ladies came into my shop this morning and gave me the scoop. Ivy has street teams telling all your clients to pause their services with you until you drop the lawsuit or Luke wins, whichever comes first."

"Oh God," I whisper and clutch the desk for support.

"This is awful! How dare they mess with your livelihood like this," Vangie screeches. I can hear her pacing back and forth in her cube at the tax office.

"Can you imagine what they would do if they knew I forced my way into Luke's house after getting temporary ownership of half the land?" I shudder to think of how that would set them off.

"You'd be tarred and feathered," Yolanda says.

Vangie adds, "Or branded with a scarlet letter and chased through the streets."

"Look, I'm sure all of this will blow over soon," Yolanda says, but her tone lacks confidence and conviction.

"I'm not so sure about that," I say, as depression swallows me whole. "I wholeheartedly believe the land belongs to my family. I won't drop the lawsuit."

Luke is the only person who has the right to try to hurt me like this, but he hasn't. In fact, even as Luke and I got closer, he never once pressured me about the lawsuit or tried to change my mind.

"And you definitely shouldn't. Tarkington girls do not bow down to town bullies! I'm going to march right over to that rally in Bell Park and tell them," Vangie says, her voice rising with indignation.

"What ... rally?" I can barely get the words out.

"Vange! We said we weren't going to tell her about that," Yolanda admonishes through gritted teeth.

My heart races, and I feel lightheaded. "There's a rally? Against me?" My mouth goes dry. I struggle to breathe. "Never mind, I have to go," I say, putting two and two together to equal Kennedy the Dumpee has been canceled by her hometown.

"No, wait, Kennedy. Let us meet you somewhere. You shouldn't be alone right now," Yolanda pleads, voice thick with worry.

Tears run unchecked down my face. "I'll call y'all later."

I hang up before they can protest further. The weight of the town's rejection crashes over me, leaving me gasping for air.

My pain intensifies as the realization strikes me. The only thing I can do to stop the rally from becoming a witch hunt is the last thing I want to do.

But I'm going to do it anyway.

Grabbing my keys, I head out the door.

CHAPTER 25

L UKE

~

IN A FLASH, I'M ACROSS THE ROOM, STANDING MERE INCHES from our receptionist. "Why? What's happening at the park?"

"There's a rally going on. Turn out is bigger than anybody expected," Erin says, twisting the bottom of her t-shirt into a tight spiral.

"What does the rally have to do with Kennedy?" I ask, growing impatient for information.

"It's actually a rally for you." She smiles broadly.

"Why do I need a rally?"

"Because you're being sued," Erin says as if I'm daft, then adds with a hint of disdain, "by Kennedy."

Nate stalks over. "What exactly is the point of this rally, Erin?"

"To gather support for a boycott on Kennedy's business," Erin looks down at the floor.

"Why would anyone want to do that?" Ronan asks.

"Because the lawsuit hurts Luke. We don't want you to lose your land, and we want to do everything we can to help," Erin explains.

I run my hands through my hair, trying to fathom what I'm hearing. "The lawsuit isn't personal. It's not about me or Kennedy. She found a deed that looks like it's identical to mine. The lawsuit expedites getting to the truth of why two deeds exist."

Erin rests her hands on her ample hips. "Her deed is obviously a fake, and she should've realized that. We don't like that she's wasting your time with this lawsuit," she says, defiance in her eyes. "Since lawyers cost money, people around town thought the best way to get her to drop the case was to hit her in the pocketbook. Take away her business."

"Y'all can't do that to Kennedy. It's cruel. She's brilliant at her job, and everyone knows it," I say.

Erin waves a hand dismissively. "It's just temporary until she drops the lawsuit. I thought you'd be touched by the support ... until I overheard what you said about, you know ..."

"I gotta get over there," I say.

"We all should go," Ronan says, then turns to Erin. "We won't be far, so call or come get us if we need to head out on a call."

"Will do," Erin says, reaching for my hand and squeezing it. "There's nothing against her. We just want to support you. That's all."

I shake my head and pull away.

Minutes later, we're standing in Bell Park behind almost a hundred townsfolk, chanting a rehearsed refrain—"Accounts are red, lawsuits are blue, Kennedy back off, or we'll boycott you."

Ivy Paul holds the microphone, beaming as she raises a hand to silence the chants. She paces across the stage as she speaks to the crowd. "By a show of hands, how many of you have stories of Luke helping you?" All the hands in the crowd shoot up in the air.

Wiley appears at my side, leaning in to whisper, "If Ivy is behind this, then Kennedy is in big trouble. That woman has been jonesing for you for years."

"No, she hasn't. She's nice to all the customers," I say, frowning as I glare at him.

Ivy continues, "Some of us have multiple stories that we could tell. We've already heard some amazing ones today during this rally. Luke has always been the first person to do whatever is needed to help others, and now he needs our help! Kennedy is trying to steal his land from him. We can't let her!"

"No! No! No!" The crowd chants.

"Flyers contain details of all of Kennedy's clients. If you're one of them, we ask that you get another accountant to do the business until she drops the lawsuit. If you know people on her client list who aren't here, please reach out and get their support to do the same," Ivy says.

"Unbelievable," Darren says, moving forward to stand on the opposite side of me.

"Now, let's all hope Kennedy comes to her senses and responds to phase one because none of us want to do phase two. It's not her daddy's fault that she was misguided enough to pursue this ridiculous lawsuit. But as a last resort, we will boycott Earls Grocery, too. Are we all in agreement?"

Yeahs ring out from the crowd.

"I'm putting a stop to this," I say, then jog toward the makeshift stage.

Ivy turns to see me coming. Her face lights up. "Luke, you're here. We didn't want to bother you since you were on shift today, but we'd love to hear you say a few words. Isn't that right, everybody?"

The roar of the crowd grows louder.

Ivy hands the mic to me. "We are one hundred percent behind you. We'll get Kennedy to stop this stupid lawsuit."

"Kennedy Tarkington's lawsuit is not stupid," I say into the microphone. Murmurs spread through the crowd, then die down as all attention turns to me. "And she doesn't deserve any of this. I want it to stop. Now. Seriously. Do not do anything to hurt Kennedy. Don't torch her social media. Don't disrupt her business. Don't try to punish her for filing the lawsuit." I gaze at the shocked faces in the crowd. All people I recognize and love. Ivy was right that I've shared many moments with all these people. "Come on, y'all know me. Do you really think this is something I'd ever want you to do? Does it fit in with the kind of man I am?"

Hushed whispers ripple through the crowd.

"This is not how I'd ever want anyone to be treated. The thing I have always loved about Kimbell is that it is a place that embraces everyone. We rally around each other and support each other. But we also embrace a diversity of ideas, thoughts, and opinions. We don't lash out or try to hurt people when someone does something we don't like. The people in this town have always sought understanding, not derision. I don't want to be the cause of that kind of change. It's not the Kimbell that I know and love."

"You're right, Luke," Ace Lallo speaks from the crowd. "Maybe we got carried away trying to help you. It's only because you've done so much for all of us."

"This is not a situation where I need help. This will play out in the courts. We all know how fair Judge Barnes is. She's not going to make a final decision that isn't backed by sound evidence. Right now, Kennedy doesn't have any real evidence. The likelihood that she's going to win this lawsuit is tiny. So why would y'all make things worse for her now when she'll have that to deal with in the future?"

Shame spreads through the crowd, and apologies ring out.

"I'm grateful that so many of you care enough to support me, but this is absolutely not how to do it." I drop the mic and jump off the stage, leaving the chaos behind.

"You did good, brother," Ronan says.

"Now I need a favor," I say, hoping that Ronan, my friend, will override Ronan, my boss, and bend the rules this one time.

"You can take your lunch break offsite," Ronan says, unable to hide his concern. "Back in one hour. No exceptions, got it."

"Got it."

CHAPTER 26

L UKE

~

I TURN ONTO THE COUNTY ROAD ON TWO WHEELS, glancing in my side mirror to see the billboard of Kennedy's beautiful face reflected in it. I'm thankful no one has had the bright idea to vandalize it in their misguided support of me.

There's no way she hasn't heard about the smear campaign against her. Clients are leaving in droves, and my heart aches for the pain she must be feeling.

It's strange but after spending the past two days with her, I instinctively know what she would do next. That's how close we've gotten. How connected I feel to her. This kind of pressure would never make her drop the lawsuit. Finding out the truth about the ownership means too much to her and her family legacy.

But the pressure would make her drop ... me.

Us.

The us we agreed to put on hold, then proceeded to act like we hadn't.

Yeah, she would run, not walk, away from us because deep down, she doesn't believe anything between us could survive the lawsuit.

I grip the steering wheel tighter and press the accelerator to the floor. The fields of grass blaze by in a blur.

She's probably right.

But I'm too stubborn to not try because she's turned on something in me I didn't realize had been turned off. I've never felt this alive with anyone.

Turning onto Abbott Road, I hope I'm not too late.

She could already be gone.

When I turn into the driveway, relief slams into me. Her car is parked next to the front porch.

Jerking my truck to a stop, I jump out, not bothering to close the door, and race into the house. The sound is low, but I can definitely tell she's crying. A mix of worry and frustration washes over me.

I rush to her bedroom, pausing at the door.

Kennedy is beautiful.

But it's more than that.

It's the feeling that settles over me every time I see her in my house. The feeling that she's meant to be here with me. The house isn't going to be the same if she leaves.

With her back to me, she's yanking clothes off the hangers from the closet and stuffing them into an oversized suitcase on the floor. Her movements are quick and decisive, filling the compartment at lightning speed. Each drop of clothing into the void is like a knife to my heart.

"Kennedy ..." my voice is low and strained.

She doesn't hear or notice.

Swiping angrily at the tears coursing down her face, she sniffles as she extricates her things from the room. Reaching for the last dress, a frilly number in pale blue I'm sure looks amazing on her, she snatches it from the hanger and turns to toss it into the suitcase, but I grab the other end.

She looks up at me with shock, then sadness and resignation. "This town loves you. It's sweet if I wasn't the one being canceled." She gives me a sad smile, then releases her hold on the dress.

I hold onto it.

She continues, "I'm going home. I think it's better if your fans don't find out I took over half your house. Who knows what diabolical plan they'll put in motion if they knew about this."

"They're not going to do anything else to you," I say, then toss the dress onto the bed and grab her hands in mine. "I stopped the rally in the park. I told them not to boycott you—"

"No!" Kennedy rips her hands from mine, anger flashing in her eyes. "What you told them, and I quote, is, 'Right now, Kennedy doesn't have any real evidence. The likelihood that she's going to win this lawsuit is tiny. So why would y'all make things worse for her now when she's going to have that to deal with in the future?'"

My words are like stones thrown back in my face. I don't have to imagine how it sounded to Kennedy. The look on her face says it all.

"Videos of your good deed in the park are all over social media." She stomps away from me. "So, if you thought I had a better chance of the judge ruling in my favor, then what? You'd be okay with them torching my career and my business?" Her tone burns with sarcasm.

"I'm not going to fight with you."

"I want an answer."

"You already know the answer. Every part of me hates what they did to you. That they thought I'd ever want anyone treated this way is ridiculous. It's worse because they don't know how close we've become. All I want to do is protect you from this madness."

"I do not understand you. If the whole town knew about this, they'd think you're insane!" She jerks strands of her loose curls behind her ears. "Or better, they'd think this is another shining example of what a great guy you are and how Kennedy is the big bad bore trying to make you homeless." She rages as fresh tears fall down her face.

My heart aches for her. But words are not enough. I can't tell her what I want to do. I just need to do it. I close the distance between us and pull her into my arms. She pushes back, resisting with half-hearted shoves until she stops. I wrap her tight in my arms, cradling her head against my chest as her tears flow more freely, dampening my shirt.

"This really sucks," she says between muffled cries.

I kiss the top of her head, and my heart skips a beat when she winds her arms around my waist and holds me back.

"You cannot be this good," Kennedy continues.

"I'm not," I admit. In fact, the thoughts going through my mind about Ivy Paul and her band of mean girls are ones I shouldn't be thinking. Tactics of sabotage from my political days come to mind, ways to destroy them without being caught. And there's only one reason I'm having this strong reaction. "You don't deserve any of this. You're a good person who wants to get to the truth."

She pulls back a few inches to stare at me. Her expression pleads for a reprieve from the onslaught of nastiness she endured today. Pressing my forehead against hers, I continue, "You have to know that's the only reason I can be around you after you had the audacity to sue me. You didn't need to go to such extremes to get my attention, though. That billboard had already put you on my radar."

"My billboard?" Kennedy raises her eyebrows. "You saw it?"

"I always take the scenic route into Downtown Kimbell. My commute got even better when that stunning face arrived to smile down at me."

"So while I was drooling over your calendar picture …"

"I was drooling over your billboard."

Kennedy pulls away from me, and I instantly miss her warmth. "This isn't going to get any easier, Luke."

"We don't do easy. Not with each other. Nothing about this situation is easy, yet here we are on the cusp of something significant."

"Something we agreed to put on hold until after the lawsuit."

Annoyance claws at me as she insists on bringing up the one thing in our way.

"We should put things on hold starting now." She turns her back on me, focusing on trying to zip her overstuffed luggage.

"Yeah, that doesn't work for me."

Kennedy laughs, then turns and sits on the luggage. "Luke, my relationship track record is garbage. I'm Kennedy the Dumpee, remember?"

"You just hadn't met the right guy."

"And you're supposed to be him?"

"I could be, who knows? There are no guarantees, but I want a chance."

"The likelihood that we would last longer than any of my other relationships is lower than me winning the lawsuit for this land."

"So, not zero?" I raise an eyebrow at her.

She laughs. "You're crazy."

"No, I'm falling for you, and I want more than anything to know that when I land, you're right there next to me feeling the same way."

"We've already crash-landed and burned." She drops her head in her hands.

"That's that smell?"

Kennedy bursts out laughing. I pull her up from the luggage.

She looks unsure. "Happened kind of fast, don't you think?"

"Nope, we're just efficient." I lean in slowly, hesitating just long enough in case she wants to pull away. But she doesn't. Our lips meet softly and tenderly, then intensity growing with each second. Every nerve in my body is alive, every sense heightened by her sweet mouth. It's electric yet tender. Time stands still as we lose ourselves in this moment of pure bliss. I'm struck by how natural this feels and how perfectly we fit together. I feel like she's mine.

And that's enough for me to give her what I know she needs.

"Is there anything I can say to get you to stay?" I ask.

She shakes her head.

"But we're good?"

"So good that you better show up at my office tomorrow with breakfast after your shift is over like you promised," Kennedy says.

As if I would miss any chance to be with her.

"Yes, ma'am."

CHAPTER 27

K ENNEDY

"Daddy!" I slam the door and stalk into the living room, throwing my purse onto the worn sofa that's seen better years. "Where are you? I have news!"

Looking around the home I grew up in, I'm comforted that it hasn't changed. The old grandfather clock in the hallway steadily ticking. The faded wallpaper in the entryway, peeling slightly at the corners. The television stand overflowing with framed photos of us and nearly every member of our extended family.

It's a stark contrast to the rest of my life.

Over the past weeks, Luke and I have gotten closer than I could've imagined. Moving out of his house didn't stall anything between us. In fact, we've slipped into a routine of secretly hanging out with each other most nights. Given my reputation as Kennedy the Dumpee and the ongoing lawsuit that set the town ablaze, I'm thankful we're off the radar and not the focus of town gossip.

Earl Tarkington pokes his head out of the kitchen. "Give me one second, Sugabean." Then he disappears again. But that was enough time to see he was wearing his "Kiss Me, I'm the Cook" apron covered in food stains.

Resting my hands on my hips, I debate whether to storm into the kitchen or wait for him to come out. These days, my dad only cooks when he's happy—like ecstatic about something in his life, and he can't help but celebrate by making an intricate, delicious meal. The exploding popularity of the grocery store has him working almost round-the-clock with no time to do what he loves.

In fact, it's strange he's home this early and is using this free time to cook instead of taking a nap after a long, hard day. I sniff the air, immediately recognizing the decadent and rich meal he's preparing. Now I know something is really going on.

Eyes narrowing, I yell toward the kitchen. "Are you making beef wellington?"

Daddy emerges from the kitchen, his gaze not meeting mine as he motions for me to sit on the couch. "What's your good news, Sugabean?" His fingers drum an anxious rhythm on his thigh.

"Answer my question first."

"Yes, I'm making beef wellington ..."

"On a random Tuesday night. What's up?" I demand.

A soft voice floats in the air. "He did it for me." Mom wheels into the room, her chair gliding smoothly over the hardwood floor. The accident that paralyzed her lower body happened years before I was born, but it never dimmed her spirit. She navigates her world with grace and determination, the same way she guided me through childhood.

"Mom, what are you doing here?" I ask, then turn to glower at Daddy. "Did you tell her?"

"Your mom has a right to know," Daddy says, a sheepish look on his face.

"I never said I wasn't going to tell her. I just wanted to find out if there was anything to tell first. You promised you wouldn't say anything until we knew the date of the final hearing." I'm practically screaming as Daddy goes to stand near Mom. They look like a unified team, ready to face off against their wayward adult daughter. Of all the times for them to be aligned on an issue, I never thought it would be this.

"Ken, stop talking like I'm not in the room," Mom says.

"You didn't have to come all this way, Mom. You know about the deed. I didn't tell you about the lawsuit or the temporary ruling because Lance doesn't think we have strong enough evidence yet. Timmy Quinn is investigating, but he hasn't found anything useful. No date has been set for the final hearing. That's the latest."

"That is not all your Mom needs to know about," Daddy says, then rests a hand on Mom's shoulder. He loves being close to her again, even though we all know he doesn't have a chance to rekindle their relationship. Mom is still happily in love with her second husband and sports the gold wedding band to prove it.

Daddy continues, "I ran into Simona Ivanov at the store yesterday."

"Zaire's assistant? What does she have to do with anything?" I ask.

"She told me that those fifty acres are worth millions of dollars. That's a game changer, and you know it. That's why you were keeping it to yourself."

I raise a hand to stop his tirade. "In my defense, knowing what's happening around Lake Lasso from all of Zaire's developments, I presumed that the land had a high value." I pause, then hold up a finger as my dad is almost about to interrupt me. "But ... but ... I never requested an official valuation to know how much it's worth because if we win this lawsuit, we cannot sell the land. Granny's orchards dominate the center of the property. There's no way to carve it up and sell it that wouldn't destroy one of the first gardens she ever created. I can't allow that."

"It's not just your decision to make. Your mother has a right to weigh in on that decision since she's technically the rightful heir of that land. Not you, Sugabean."

I bristle at the truth.

Despite all the conversations that Granny had with me and Mom asserting her desire that I get everything that belonged to her, my grandmother died without a will or life insurance. Mom kept Granny's wishes when all I was inheriting was a savings account depleted by the funeral and paying off the mortgage Granny had on her home. Nothing was left to pay for the ongoing maintenance of the intricate gardens on Granny's property. I spent thousands a month out of my own pocket. My mother had no interest in the land.

But that was before five acres could become fifty-five.

Taking a deep breath, I say, "There's no guarantee the deed is valid. I don't know how this is going to turn out."

"I'm not here for the land, Ken. I told your father that," Mom says, reaching a hand toward me. "My mother made it crystal clear what her wishes were. Even millions of dollars' worth of land isn't enough for me to go back on that. If the deed is valid, the land is yours. I'll sign whatever is necessary to clear up any legal concerns."

"Are you sure about that?" Daddy asks. From the plea in his tone, I realize his ulterior motive. If Mom did want to stake her claim to the land, that could entice her to move back to Kimbell. And if she wanted to move back, her husband may or may not want to come with her. Either way, having her close would give Dad another shot at getting the woman who still owns his heart.

It's sweet if I wasn't so upset that he used my situation in his little plan.

"Of course, I'm sure, Earl. I'm here to support my daughter, not take the land from her," Mom says, squeezing my hand. "I can't imagine how hard this has been for you. The bond that you and my mother shared was extraordinary. Finding her very first work must have been bittersweet. It makes sense that preserving the orchards would become your top priority. The best way of doing that is if you own the land."

"Mom, I..." I start, then falter. A mix of emotions swirls within me —gratitude for her support, guilt for doubting her, and a renewed sense of purpose. "I didn't realize how much I needed to hear that until now."

"I want you to do what makes you happy." Mom reaches out, gently tucking a stray strand of hair behind my ear. Her eyes search my face with a knowing look. "I came down here because Earl let slip another piece of info that you never mentioned on our calls."

I glare at my father.

"Oops!" He gives a wide-eyed look of panic, then shrugs. "I think I need to go check on dinner."

"Yes, run! Coward!" I call after him.

"What is this about the town boycotting you and holding rallies to try to destroy your business? You never told me that, Ken." My mom frowns, obviously concerned.

"That's what I came over to update Daddy about. Everything is back to normal," I say with a bright smile. "Luke and I visited all the clients who planned to boycott me and got them to work with me again."

"Luke Diamond, the man you're suing, did that for you?"

"Took a couple of weeks, but we convinced them all." My smile gets brighter, if that's even possible. The fact that Luke took it upon himself to help me without revealing his real intimate feelings for me to the entire town went above and beyond what I expected. It was the kindest thing he could've done and meant the world to me.

Mom pats the sofa next to her wheelchair. I sit dutifully, just like I did as a little girl.

"You're falling for Luke Diamond," Mom announces.

"What?" A nervous giggle bubbles from my mouth. "No, of course not," I say, trying to lie but knowing she's not buying what I'm selling. Still, how can I explain my relationship with Luke to my mother? It doesn't make sense when I say it out loud. It only makes sense to us. That's the reason I haven't given Vangie or Yolanda details either. "Luke is a great guy. Very charitable. He felt bad that people targeted me because of him. That's all. He wants the lawsuit to be handled fairly through the judicial system, not in the court of public opinion."

"I see ..." Mom's expression remains neutral, but I can see the wheels turning behind her eyes. This feeling that she's seeing right through my defenses unnerves me. "And how's your dating life? It's been years since you and Maxwell broke up."

"What does my dating life have to do with anything?" I balk, and the strained giggle erupts from me again. "You know, I'm doing the Kennedy 2.0 thing. I'm not thinking about guys right now. I'm settling into my new home and focused on the lawsuit. That's all."

"You're lying."

"Mom!"

"When was the last time you went on a date?"

"I ... haven't been on a date in a while." My answer isn't exactly a lie because Luke and I don't define what we are doing as dating since it's a secret. We call them get-to-know-you sessions, which look, feel, and sound like dates but are definitely not.

"From what I can tell, in the past two weeks, you've probably spent more time with Luke than with any other man in a long time," Mom explains. "But Luke wants that land as much and maybe more than you do. All of this niceness could be a tactic to help him get details about your case so he and his lawyer can figure out how to defend against them. Don't read anything more into his friendliness than that. You're still on opposite sides of a significant issue to both of you."

"I'm not reading too much into anything with Luke!" I screech, my voice rising as my mom's words strike a chord that sounds way too clear to my ears. Cheeks flushing with embarrassment, I rise from the couch and put distance between us.

I know how Luke feels about me. His feelings are just as strong as mine and developed despite the lawsuit hanging over our heads. That has to mean something. Doesn't it?

My past experiences scream otherwise.

Haven't I gone down this same road six times before? Had the same feelings for Dillon, Maxwell and all the rest? The unwavering belief that things would work out … and they didn't. What makes me think this will be any different with Luke? He's really into me now, but there's no guarantee his feelings won't change.

I force myself to calm down. "Look, Luke is a great guy. He's super nice and super sweet. He's gone out of his way to not make me feel like a pariah for pursuing this lawsuit, which I appreciate. That's it."

"Okay," Mom raises her hands in mock surrender. "I just don't want you to be confused by his actions. Keep your perspective and focus on finding out the truth about the land. That's really the only thing that matters."

"Absolutely," I say, but I'm not so sure anymore.

CHAPTER 28

L UKE

~

Draping a towel around my shoulders, I maneuver through the state-of-the-art equipment on the second floor of Chesterton's Gym toward the line of rowing machines. The impromptu workout is definitely not what I want to be doing tonight. It's the perfect substitute to work off my frustration from the first night in weeks that I've been off shift and not with Kennedy.

I had already picked up takeout and was ready to spend the night at her place binging old Kung-Fu movies we both love when I got the text from her.

KENNEDY

Don't be mad at me.

LUKE

Not making that promise. What did you do?

It's not what I did, but what I'm going to do …

Spit it out woman

My mom's in town unexpectedly. Going to have dinner with her and Daddy tonight, so will miss seeing you.

I stared at my phone, forcing my anger away. Of all the times for her mom to come into town. I'm at the point where I don't want to share Kennedy with anyone, which is difficult because we're still dating in secret, which is easier to do than either of us expected. We are neighbors, after all, and Abbott Road is far from Downtown Kimbell and most other neighborhoods in town. We're practically on the other side of the lake by ourselves. There are no prying eyes to stop us from seeing each other as much as we want to, which suits me just fine.

So, I'm not thrilled her mom timed this visit on a night when I'm not working at the fire station. Then, guilt kicked in, and I felt bad for not wanting to share Kennedy with the two people who were the reason why she exists.

KENNEDY

Luke? You there???

LUKE

Yeah, no big deal. Have fun tonight and I'll see you tomorrow?

Absolutely. Thanks.

Since Gramps passed away, I'd become comfortable being alone in the house, but Kennedy has changed everything. Staring at the walls, I knew I needed to get out and do something.

An hour later, I'm here at the gym, about to engage in a treacherous workout of an hour on the rowing machine, followed by boxing on the heavy bag. After a couple of hours of intense activity, I'll be too tired to miss her.

Settling into the rowing machine, my phone buzzes in my pocket. I smile as I whip it out to see what Kennedy is texting.

Except the text isn't from Kennedy.

My jaw clenches as I place the phone in the cubbyhole of the machine face down. Another text from Madeleine I have no intention of responding to—

"Whoa, I'd hate to be the person who sent that text. If they could see your reaction, they probably wouldn't text you again."

I glance up into the face of Dillon Crockett.

Kennedy's ex-boyfriend.

The one who started her string of six successive breakups that landed her the moniker Kennedy the Dumpee.

I should be upset that he hurt her. But she and I might not have found our way to each other if he hadn't.

Plus, he's also the guy who produces the Firefighter Hunks calendar.

As much as I want to ignore him, I can't.

Laughing off his comment, I say, "Not that deep, Dillon. What's going on? Surprised to see you in Kimbell." I slip my feet into the straps of the rowing machine, punch the screen to increase the resistance, and then start my workout. My muscles strain from the exertion, and it's the distraction I need.

Dillon leans over the machine and levels me with a conspiratorial look. "I've been here for a few weeks working on a new idea I finalized earlier this morning. It's fortuitous that I ran into you."

"I'm not doing the calendar again," I say, shutting down any thoughts the guy might have on the subject. As much as the extra money would help with my taxes and knowing that fifty percent of the proceeds are given to charity, Kennedy made me promise not to show my goodies in print—her words, not mine—ever again.

"Luke! You're one of the top reasons why the calendar is so successful. Have you seen the comments about you on the social media pages for the calendar?" Dillon asks, his eyes wild with excitement.

"Nope. I'm not into any of that," I say, feeling no pressure to change my mind. "I'm sure you'll have a line of firefighters wanting to be part of the next calendar—"

"Yeah, but the more popular we get, the more I have to be really picky. Can't let any old dad-body disaster with more body hair than muscles in it anymore. It would hurt the bottom line and all the charities that count on the donations from the sales."

I shrug. That's Dillon's problem. Not mine. My only focus is keeping my girl happy … well, the woman who will be mine after the lawsuit is over.

"But I'm not even focused on next year's calendar. I have a better plan to raise money for the communities and put more money in the pockets of the models like you—"

"I'm not doing it, Dillon."

"Come on, hear me out. I've just inked a deal to do a series of companion date auctions in the hometowns of our four most popular models from the calendar," Dillon says, his tone shifting into used car salesman mode.

How in the world did Kennedy ever fall for this schmuck?

I don't see how they had anything in common. She's too good for this guy. I barely pay attention as he lays out the details of the date auctions, the format, and the estimated proceeds.

"The first one is going to be in the hometown of our most popular model." Dillon raises an eyebrow and pauses for dramatic effect.

"Am I supposed to know who that is?"

"It's you, dude! The Baker triplets just agreed to shut down their restaurant on a Saturday night to hold the auction. I put the tickets up for sale this morning, and they're already selling like crazy. You'll be paid well. Half the money bid will go to charities picked by the firefighters. It's a win-win. You've got to be part of it," Dillon insists.

I grip the handles of the rowing machine tighter, exerting extreme force to propel my body forward and backward. There's no way I'm letting any woman buy a date with me when the only woman I want to be with is Kennedy.

"I'll pass," I say, wishing Dillon would go away. And by away, I mean far away from Kimbell and back to wherever he was living before.

"You don't understand, Luke. This date auction only works if you're in it. I've gotten eight models to come to town, but for the Hill Country, you are the draw. We'll get only half the sales if you're not in it."

"He'll do it." I recognize my best friend's voice from behind me.

Slowing down, I turn to glare at Nate. His expression is one I can't read, which concerns me. Usually, I know exactly what Nate is thinking based on his demeanor and expressions.

"I'm not doing a date auction," I say, putting more force in my words. "I'm not going on a date with someone I'm not interested in."

"Who says you won't be interested in the woman? There are gorgeous women all over the Hill Country. You might be pleasantly surprised," Dillon presses, then looks eagerly at Nate for support.

"You'll do it because the Kimbell Community Center lost its application for grant funding and refuses to take a donation from my family. Without it, there won't be summer camps for the less fortunate kids in town and no daily meals. The money donated from your spot in the calendar won't cover the entire summer. They need more," Nate says.

If there's anyone who knows how to twist my arm in the right way, it's Nate Bell. Still, I don't like the idea of another woman bidding on a date with me. What is Kennedy going to think about that? I can't do this without talking to her, at least.

"Look, I'm not agreeing to anything. But I will think about it," I say, hoping that's a suitable compromise.

Nate turns to Dillon. "Sign him up. He'll be there."

"Nate!" My voice rises as my irritation grows.

He ignores me. "Good seeing you, Dillon."

The guy gives me a triumphant grin, then heads across the gym.

"What was that about?" I demand.

Nate hands me his phone.

I stare at the screen and feel like I've been sucker punched.

I can't quite breathe as I stare at the digital flyer.

"No, this can't ... happen."

"It is happening. My dad is holding a fundraiser for Madeleine Rice right here in Kimbell. I'm guessing that's why she's been so insistent in trying to reach out to you lately," Nate says.

"I don't want her to come to town. Can't you stop your dad? I can't believe he would back her for governor."

"David Bell is only interested in money, not politics. A fundraiser for Madeleine will bring in some heavy hitters who have been on our target client list for a while. It's business. I can't interfere," Nate explains without apology.

"I have to call her back. Tell her not to do this. Not to come here," I say, shoving the phone back at Nate.

"No, you don't."

"She'll expect to see me when she comes to Kimbell. She'll orchestrate a way to get me to that fundraiser—"

"Which won't work because you already have plans," Nate says smugly. "You'll be doing a charity date auction fundraiser that night. Not something she would force you to cancel just to meet up with her. Also, not something she'd ever attend just to see you again."

I slump back against the rowing machine. "Oh."

The pieces of my best friend's master plan come together in my head.

"Yeah. Thank me later," Nate says, then heads off to the treadmills.

CHAPTER 29

L UKE

~

PULLING INTO THE PARKING LOT OF GWEN'S COUNTRY Cafe, I saunter toward the entrance and open the door, walking inside. Ivy Paul stands near the hostess stand, scribbling furiously on paper. Her straight blond locks are in a messy bun on her head, with tendrils cascading around her face. She wears a frown of exasperation as if the morning has already been a nightmare.

"Morning, Ivy," I say.

Her head jerks up, and she looks at me with surprise. "Luke! You're … here."

"Yeah … I'm here." A smile tugs at my lips as I look around at the near-empty restaurant. When my attorney called to set up a breakfast meeting, I knew the brief lull between the morning rush and the afternoon lunch crowd would be the perfect time. "Last I checked, this place still has the best breakfast in town."

"I'm glad you still feel that way," Ivy says, blinking her eyes rapidly.

Is she about to cry?

"Of course I do," I say, growing concerned.

"It's just that you haven't come in for breakfast since I organized the rally at Bell Park," Ivy says, swiping at a wayward strand of her hair.

"You mean when you gathered the town together to boycott Kennedy," I say, a slight edge in my tone. Kennedy was devastated by how quickly the town turned on her in an attempt to support me. Seeing her in pain ripped at my soul. I did everything in my power to make things right again for her. I was thankful it didn't take too long to unwind the damage Ivy caused.

"Sorry about that. I had the best intentions, but it wasn't the right move to support you. I totally get it now," Ivy says, then looks away. "But then you stopped coming in for breakfast. Even on the days you got off shift at the fire station. I told Mama you were so disappointed in me that you might never come here again."

In all that time, the thought of holding a grudge against Ivy or the restaurant never crossed my mind. The only thing that mattered was putting a smile back on Kennedy's face.

"Don't be silly," I say, assuaging her concerns. "I've just been preoccupied with ..."

My thoughts instantly go to why I haven't grabbed breakfast from Gwen's Country Cafe—mornings filled with sharing home-cooked breakfast with Kennedy on my back porch.

Cooking together has become our favorite thing to do. Combine that with wanting to see her every day, and we stumbled upon a pattern of meeting up before she goes to work. I sucked it up and rose with the roosters since she insists on getting to work at an ungodly hour.

But seeing the sunrise on her beautiful face each morning is worth it.

"I'm sure dealing with the lawsuit is stressful," Ivy says, then smiles sweetly. "That's why I was surprised to see you on the flyer for the date auction."

"Flyer for the date auction?" I push down my annoyance. Leave it to Dillon Crockett to jump on promoting the event after Nate insisted I participate. It's the right move, considering Madeleine will be in town the same night. Still, I thought I'd have more time to talk to Kennedy before advertisements went up around town.

Ivy whips her cell phone from her apron and shows me the social media ad. A cropped version of my photo from the calendar is displayed underneath the caption: "St. Patrick's Day may be over, but you can still get lucky! Win a date with Kimbell's own ... Luke!"

I groan under my breath.

"All the ladies are scrambling to get their tickets. But I'm planning to be the lucky one," Ivy says, then blushes bright red. "I'm working a few extra shifts to get more tips to bid on you."

"That's ... really sweet. Thanks," I say, wondering if the guys have been right about Ivy all along. "Part of the proceeds from the auction will go to support a local charity, most likely the Kimbell Community Center."

"That's nice," Ivy says, then clears her throat. "You know, I'm really different outside of the restaurant. Maybe if we spend some alone time together, you'll see that I'm a really interesting woman. Someone who you might want to spend a little more time with—"

"Luke Diamond," a sultry, commanding voice interrupts Ivy.

I turn around and see a petite woman, a few inches shy of five feet tall, with shimmering bronze skin and piercing black eyes. She wraps her arms around me in a firm hug.

"Hey, Olivia," I say, grateful for the interruption. My attorney, Olivia Garnet, is a powerhouse despite her diminutive frame.

I turn back to Ivy, who looks dismayed. "Can we get a table for two? Somewhere discreet."

Ivy's tone is clipped. "Of course. Right this way."

She leads us to a table away from the prying eyes of the last remnants of the breakfast crowd.

Ivy slaps the menus down on the table and stomps away.

"Ex-girlfriend?" Olivia asks.

I shake my head. "No, not at all."

She chuckles under her breath. "So, she's angling for a shot. Probably going to make her move at the date auction. Watch out."

"I'm sure you didn't arrange this meeting to discuss the date auction. What's going on?"

Olivia's face turns serious. "Got a call from Judge Barnes's office. She's scheduled the final hearing for Monday."

"That's short notice, isn't it?" A sickening feeling erupts in my gut. I don't know if I've done enough to prove to Kennedy that we deserve a shot at a real relationship regardless of the outcome of the lawsuit. I hope I have, but a big part of me knows losing the case could sour Kennedy's feelings for me if I haven't convinced her that the connection between us is the real deal.

Olivia frowns. "This fits perfectly with the strategy we've discussed. A quick hearing works in your favor, especially since I have good intel that Timmy Quinn hasn't found any additional evidence that could bolster Kennedy's case."

"So, in four days, I'll have my land back," I say, but the only thing on my mind is what that will mean for me and Kennedy.

"If I was a betting woman, which I'm not, I'd be pushing all my chips in on you," Olivia says with a smug smile.

Ivy stomps back to our table, placing two cups of water in front of us. "What can I get you?"

Olivia frowns as she looks at the menu. "Is the oatmeal made of steel-cut oats?"

"No," Ivy says.

"Okay. How about the omelet? Can I get that with egg whites only?"

"Only egg whites …" Ivy looks horrified.

"No yolks," Olivia reiterates as if up to the challenge. "Add spinach and mushrooms. No cheese."

"Are you lactose intolerant?" Ivy's tone softens.

"No, I'm not," Olivia says, then glances at me.

I remain quiet. There's no point in telling my lawyer that no one comes to Gwen's Country Cafe for a healthy breakfast.

"And I'd like turkey bacon."

"Bacon comes from pigs," Ivy says.

"But there's … " Olivia gives up, closing the menu. "Just the omelet and water."

Ivy scribbles on the notepad and then walks away.

"Luke, she didn't even take your order." Olivia is appalled.

I break into a huge grin. "Gwen, the owner of the place, will just send out something she thinks I'll like. Stops me from getting in a rut and ordering the same thing every day."

"Interesting," Olivia says, but I don't believe she thinks it is. She shifts back into lawyer mode. "While we have much to be confident about, I have devised a backup plan just in case."

"What's the plan?" I ask, although no part of me believes we'll need one.

"The deed signed by Mr. Butler was found in a trunk with other important documents and heirlooms of the Butler family. That was a point highlighted by Lance to help authenticate the deed and Mr. Butler's signature."

"I remember that," I say, nodding my head. "The trunk had been in some church in Austin where Kennedy's great-grandfather served as a deacon. The contents indicated that it was a place he stored things of importance."

"And based on that assumption, which again, Lance Bassett introduced, it's doubtful that Mr. Butler was unaware of the deed in his possession," Olivia says, looking pleased with herself.

"I don't understand how that helps us."

"Mr. Butler had a deed in his possession that would've allowed him to contest the ownership of the land, but he never did," Olivia said. "The man had decades to do it and chose not to."

Leaning back in my chair, I understand where Olivia is heading. "If the deed was valid, why wouldn't he have challenged my grandfather's ownership of the property?"

Olivia raises her hands in a "don't know" shrug. "That's exactly what I'm going to argue. Alice Butler may have thought there was no proof of the land that her father owned, but her dad knew exactly where the deed was."

"You think he knew his deed didn't entitle him to the land? Why would he have moved onto the property if that's the case?"

"If I had to guess, I'd say he never paid the Abbotts for the land. So, when someone else came with a deed for the same property, he had no choice but to leave because he knew he hadn't held up his end of the contract," Olivia explains. "But like I said, that's a guess. The good thing is that we don't have to prove it. We need to introduce enough doubt that Judge Barnes feels there isn't enough proof that the land irrefutably belongs to the Butler Family."

"Wow ... " I know Kennedy isn't going to like this information, but it makes a lot of sense. "And the fact that my grandfather took three years before he made his way to Kimbell to claim his land could've made Mr. Butler think no one would find out he hadn't paid the Abbotts for it."

"Speculation, but yes," Olivia nods. "I have to reiterate that this is just a guess. The important thing is there are enough points to be made that would cause Judge Barnes to delay her ruling if it looks like things aren't going in our favor."

Ivy returns with our food and places it on the table. Olivia's pale white omelet looks utterly outmatched next to the decadent Belgian waffle overflowing with berries and whipped cream in front of me. Her eyes get big, and I detect a hint of longing for my food that she'd never admit.

Swiping a strawberry through the freshly made cream, I pop it in my mouth and ask, "Do you believe we'll need to bring any of this up?"

Olivia looks incredulous. "No. I predict that you will once again be the sole owner of the land by Monday afternoon."

Her words should make me feel better.
They don't.
All I can think is that I only have four days left with Kennedy.
After that, I'm not sure she'll ever want to see me again.

CHAPTER 30

K ENNEDY

"WHEN IS THIS RAIN GOING TO STOP?" YOLANDA complains, shaking her umbrella on the wet sidewalk while I open the Elevation Cupcake door.

Gloomy slate-gray clouds dump sheets of rain on us. Malaise snakes its way through my veins. After spending glorious sunny weeks doing my favorite things—accounting work by day and time with Luke at night—my fairytale life has ended.

It's no coincidence the call from Lance coincided with the shift in weather, plunging me into a mood that only one thing can fix—sugary confections from the best bakery in town.

"Feels like never," I pout, then follow her inside. Vangie waves at us from a table in the corner. She stands as we approach, and I walk into her open arms. She hugs me tight, then pulls back, searching my face.

"What's the bad news?" Vangie asks, then looks at Yolanda, who gives her an almost imperceptible shrug.

"No, ma'am," I say, shaking my head. "Dessert first, then we catch up."

My cousins follow me to the glass case lined with every imaginable variety of decadent desserts. Ignoring the gorgeous cupcakes, which are always dry and uninspired in flavor, I focus on the pastries, truffles, pecan myrtles, and chocolate tarts. But my eyes are drawn to a new item I've never seen here before.

"Hey Brianna, are those macarons?" I ask, glancing up at the long-time worker at the shop.

She nods enthusiastically. "The latest inspiration from Raven's trip to Paris last month. They are absolutely divine. I swear she nailed the recipe. Perfectly crisp on the outside and soft on the inside. I have to stop myself from eating all our inventory." She laughs under her breath, but the guilty look in her eyes makes me think she's already been warned by the owner about that.

"I love macarons!" Yolanda says, her voice dipping an octave lower as she swoons beside me. "Can we get a dozen?"

Vangie nods her head enthusiastically, and I'm already in. We pick four flavors each, then return to the table by the window while Brianna arranges them artfully on a plate for us. I drop my head in my hands and stare at the rain streaming down the fogged window.

"Kennedy! You are scaring me. Like completely about to freak me out," Vangie says, interrupting my racing thoughts. "What in the world is going on? Why did you send us the SOS text?"

"I've been hiding something from both of you," I say, then inhale a sharp breath.

They lean forward, gazes full of worry and fear.

"Remember a few weeks ago when the whole town was boycotting me at the same time that I had moved in with Luke for those two days?" I hesitate. Telling my best friends in the whole world what I've been up to and about the call from Lance could give me a dose of reality I'm not ready for. But maybe it's the wake-up call I need.

They remain quiet, refusing to give me any opportunity to delay by interrupting my story. I hate that they know me so well.

Brianna approaches and places the plate between us. We each grab a macaron. I choose the salted caramel. Tapping the cookies together like clinking wine glasses, we simultaneously take a bite. It tastes like heaven on my tongue and feels soft and decadent on my lips.

Like kissing Luke.

I know I shouldn't have but I've gotten too comfortable with him in my life. Technically, we're not dating. We're not a couple. We're just two people who hang out basically every night, then return to our respective homes and do the same thing the next night. The more time I spend with him, the more perfect I realize he is for me. I want us to be a couple even though all the odds are stacked so high against us. Odds that I pushed firmly out of my own favor.

Swallowing my dessert, I decide to rip the Band-Aid off. "While I was living with Luke, we started to understand each other better and realized that we had a lot in common." I clear my throat. "And that we were attracted to each other. Not just our looks but the people we are inside. You know?"

Vangie thrusts two fingers toward Yolanda. "I knew it! Didn't I tell you, Yolanda? I told you I thought so much more was happening between Kennedy and ..." She drops her voice to a low whisper. "Luke."

Yolanda closes her eyes as a pained expression masks her face. "Please tell me that the two of you aren't dating." She opens her eyes and looks at me like I'm insane. "That would be crazy, considering you are suing the man for his land!"

"So, we're not dating," I say.

"Oh, thank God," Yolanda says, then looks smug at Vangie.

"We've just been getting to know each other over the past few weeks," I say, avoiding their gaze.

Vangie bounces in her chair as she points her fingers back and forth between me and Yolanda. "Told you! I told you. I told you!" She grabs my chin and jerks my face up to look at her. "Is it wonderful? Tell me he's wonderful."

"He is. I've never been involved with a man like him before. It's different and refreshing, and it's everything I could ever want. I mean, he like truly likes me for me. Everything that drove my boyfriends crazy in the past, doesn't bother him. He actually likes my personality. The good and the bad," I say, then shrug.

Yolanda grabs a macaron and stuffs it into her mouth. Then another and chews frantically as if she's punishing the poor dessert.

"I am so happy for you," Vangie says, then lowers her voice. "You and Luke make a beautiful couple."

"We're not a couple. At least not yet—"

"Because you are suing the man for his land," Yolanda says, punching the table with her finger as she says each word. "Come on, Kennedy. How do you think this is really going to play out? Hmm. Or are you too giddy to see the massive train wreck you're heading toward?"

Vangie rolls her eyes. "Do you have to be a Debbie Downer?"

"I'm being realistic. What will happen when the judge awards the land with your grandmother's orchard to Luke and his family?" Yolanda asks, then softens her voice. "Have you really thought about how that'll make you feel? Will you really be able to get past all that and look at him the same way?"

I poke my bottom lip out and grab another macaron. "Guess I'll know the answer to that soon."

"Why? What happened?" Vangie asks.

"Judge Barnes told Lance that both sides have had ample time to gather evidence, if it exists, to prove their ownership claims," I say, then take a deep breath. "The final court proceeding where she'll rule on ownership is scheduled for Monday."

"Oh," Yolanda says, then leans back in her chair. "And Timmy Quinn has proven to be a useless private investigator. He hasn't found anything to help with your case."

"I know," I say, then bite into the macaron. "Luke told me his lawyer didn't bother hiring a P.I. because the burden of proving that the land is mine is on me. Without compelling evidence, Judge Barnes is highly unlikely to hand over the land to new owners just based on the identical deeds."

"So, in a matter of days, you could lose the land and your man." Vangie shakes her head and pops a whole macaron into her mouth.

"Exactly." I blink back my tears. "Now you see why I sent the SOS."

They nod at me.

"Is there any chance that Judge Barnes would rule that the land should continue to be half-owned by you and Luke?" Yolanda asks.

"Lance was brutally honest. He said I have about a five percent chance of getting the land and a ten percent chance of sharing it." I shrug. "It doesn't matter that I believe with every cell in my body that some kind of way Zebediah Abbott or Frank Diamond scammed the land away from my great grandfather. There isn't enough evidence to prove that's true. It doesn't look good."

Vangie finishes off her last two macarons and then gives me a bright smile. "Well, the path forward is simple."

"It is?" Yolanda gives her a side-eye.

I'm too upset and confused to not hear Vangie's thoughts. I need a plan, and I'm in no condition to develop one.

"We know you, Kennedy," Vangie says. "The minute Judge Barnes rules that the land is still Luke's, you'll be mad. Angry. Livid. You will resent him, and all these beautiful feelings you have for this man will go up in smoke."

I glance over at Yolanda, who is nodding in agreement.

If my closest friends think this thing with Luke is doomed, how can I dispute that?

My track record in love is abysmal, and the lawsuit makes everything impossible for Luke and me. How did I ever believe we could defy the odds stacked against us?

"Which means you only have one option," Vangie continues, picking up the last macaron on the plate and handing it to me.

I take it from her, then ask, "And that would be?"

"Enjoy every second of your last days with Mr. March."

I inhale a deep breath, then push the macaron into my mouth as I realize my cousin is absolutely right.

CHAPTER 31

L UKE

~

"WE NEED TO TALK ABOUT THE ELEPHANT IN THE ROOM," Kennedy declares, blazing through my front door. She looks stunning, wearing a crisp white blouse, perfectly pressed and accentuating her slender neck and shoulders, and tailored black pants that hug her curves in all the right places. The epitome of sophistication and confidence. A bonafide head-turner for sure.

I reach for her, stopping her inertia, and pull her back to me. Cupping her chin in my hand, I lean forward and devour her sweet lips with a fierce hunger. Kennedy's eyes widen in surprise before she melts into the kiss, her arms winding around my neck. I can feel the tension leaving her body as she relaxes into me. A move that stirs my soul as I try to capture every detail of this moment, burning it into my memory forever.

As Kennedy pushes against my chest, I groan in protest. "No, come back here."

"Do not try to distract me with those unbelievable kisses." Her eyes are frantic with worry as she stares at me.

I'd do anything to make her feel better, but I know there's nothing I can do. No words will make the cloud hanging over us move away any faster.

"Fine. Talk."

"The hearing is tomorrow morning."

"I know that."

"We'll have a final answer on the land. No more living in limbo."

"I know that as well."

"But we'll be in a different kind of … limbo. Won't we?"

I shake my head. "Everything will be settled at the hearing, and we can move on."

Kennedy rakes her hands through her hair, then thrusts her hands onto her hips. "Move … on. What does that mean?"

I try to hide my smile, but it's impossible. "It means we can stop hiding. No more dating in secret. No more pretending that we're not … close. We can finally explore what's going on between us."

"It's not going to be that simple," Kennedy retorts. "If you think that, you're delusional."

"Why can't it be that simple?" I snap back at her. "You know how I feel about you—"

"Our feelings right now don't matter. What matters is how will we feel about each other tomorrow?" Kennedy asks. "The ruling from Judge Barnes could change everything."

"For you, I guess that's true." I turn my back on her as anger flashes through me. After everything we've shared, all the time we've spent together, it may not be enough for Kennedy to put us ahead of her disappointment of losing the land. That truth is like a dagger in my gut.

"And you expect me to believe it's not true for you, too?" Kennedy asks.

I turn around to face her. "You're going to believe whatever you want to believe. I can't change that."

"We never should've done this. We should've stayed away from each other until after the hearing."

"Now, who's delusional," I say, closing the distance between us. "You really think we could've stayed away from each other? Seriously?"

She stands her ground stubbornly, but I can see her resistance and defiance wavering.

"You think this connection that took off like a runaway freight train could be stopped by either of us?"

Her eyes soften as she looks at me.

"We couldn't stop this. We couldn't control it. We only had one option: go along for the ride and enjoy every minute of it," I say, then grab a thick strand of her hair. "But there is something that's within our control."

"Don't say it." She shakes her head.

"What happens next is firmly within our control," I force the words out before she can stop me. "Our relationship doesn't have to be impacted by the outcome of the case tomorrow. We don't have to let it be."

"Our ... relationship?"

"Yeah, the one we haven't let ourselves define ... yet," I say, then clasp her hands within mine. "We can do that now."

"I don't think we should," Kennedy says.

"Chicken ..."

"Bawwk bawk," Kennedy responds, flapping her arms like wings. "I'm scared."

"Me too," I admit. "I don't think we should talk about the elephant in the room anymore."

"Too many animals. This is not a zoo," Kennedy says, then exhales a deep breath.

"But it's kind of a circus, right?" I pull her into my arms and kiss her again. The taste of cinnamon lingers on her lips, sending a tingling sensation through my body as we abandon all hesitation and give in to the moment. Seconds turn into minutes, and we're both breathless when we finally break apart. I can't help but smile at her dazed expression.

Having her pressed against me always feels the same way—perfect.

I swear she's the woman I've been waiting for all this time.

I remind myself that a few weeks isn't enough to learn everything about Kennedy. But what I've learned about this compassionate, fiercely intelligent, spirited, and unapologetically authentic woman has done nothing to dampen what I know in my heart.

"You win," Kennedy says, then steps out of my arms. "So, what should we do on our last night of ignorant bliss?"

"I was thinking a romantic dinner by Diamond Lake catered by Thorn and accompanied by a couple of bottles of Harlow Rose's award-winning Cabernet Sauvignon," I say.

Her mouth drops open, which is the reaction I hoped for.

"Did you really plan this in advance?"

"Every part of it," I say, tickling her sides as she squirms. "Starting with the Kennedy who ignores me all day just to show up at my house after work irate about the hearing part."

She playfully swats at my chest and then pulls me into another embrace. I breathe her in and hold her tightly.

"I don't know what to say. This is so … " her voice trails off.

"You don't need to say anything. Just stay for dinner," I say. "Can you do that for me?"

Kennedy nods her head. "I would do anything for you, Luke Diamond."

CHAPTER 32

K ENNEDY

~

THE SHIMMERING WATERS OF THE LAKE SPARKLE AS IF thousands of diamonds were flung across its surface. My mouth falls open as I take in the sight. Soft white lights are strung around the perimeter of the lake on towering wooden poles placed within the trees, creating a dramatic and romantic effect.

Near the edge of the lake, closest to the tree swing, sits a table adorned with white linens. A vase filled with sunflowers rests in between two candelabras.

"How did you do all of this?" Turning, I stare into Luke's gorgeous green eyes, searching for an answer to explain how anything this magnificent could've been done … for me.

"I was inspired," Luke says with a smile, then tugs on a string of my hair. "And I had a little help from a few friends."

"You told them?"

He shakes his head. "Didn't have to. When you've helped as many people as I have, they are eager to return the favor. No questions asked. I'm sure they wondered, but no one asked what it was for."

"And if they had, what would you have said?" Part of me needs to know, while the other part dreads his answer. Especially since we could be hours away from the end of things before they could truly begin.

"The truth. I'm trying to show a special lady how special she is to me."

I swallow past the lump in my throat, emotions catching me off guard. I nod, then turn back to soak it all in. No one has ever done anything this romantic for me.

Until Luke.

I squeeze my eyes shut and say a silent prayer that, against all the odds, things work out tomorrow in a way that helps to preserve this closeness between me and Luke. This land is important to my family's legacy, but Luke is important to me. I don't want to lose him.

Luke slips his arms around my waist. "Stop thinking about tomorrow. I need you present right here, right now, with me." He nibbles on my ear, soothing the stress threatening to ruin the night.

I wrap my arms around his neck, softly caressing his hair as I look at his gorgeous face. "When all this started, I never could've imagined that we'd end up like this."

"This isn't our end, Kennedy. It's just the beginning. That's a promise."

"Don't make promises you may not be able to keep."

"I'm not."

"I wish I had your confidence."

"I have enough for both of us. Just stay with me."

Inhaling a deep breath, I decide to do what he asks. I'll be in this moment and not worry about what tomorrow will bring. Tonight is about Luke and I enjoying each other without holding back and pretending we aren't what we both want us to be—a couple. Neither of us has to say the words to know our current truth.

Luke takes my hand and leads me to the table. Pulling the chair out, I sit down and marvel at the glorious nature surrounding me as the sun dips low in the sky.

"I'm going to grab the wine," Luke says, then jogs back to the house. Minutes later, he returns, juggling wine bottles, glasses, napkins, and silverware. He artfully arranges them on the table like the best waiter at Thorn, then opens and pours wine into our glasses.

"You never told me what's on the menu," I say, sipping from my glass.

"It's hard to beat our cooking."

"That's for sure." I laugh.

"So, I went for the very best Thorn has to offer." Luke winks. "Golden imperial caviar followed by a peekytoe crab salad with heart of palm and a dijon mustard-citrus sauce. Then the main course is poached lobster with truffled gnocchi." A sexy smile plays on his lips. "And dessert is a surprise."

Tingling flutters race through my body, and I resist the urge to fan myself. "Sounds decadent and expensive."

"You're worth it." He leans forward and brushes his lips against mine in the sweetest kiss. "I'll be back with our starters."

"Okay." As soon as he disappears into the house, I pinch myself. The pain tells me this isn't a dream. But if I'm wrong and this is a dream, I have no plans of waking myself up.

A buzz startles me. I glance at the table and see Luke's phone lighting up with a text message. He must have placed it on the table when he opened the wine.

UNKNOWN NUMBER

Hope you're excited about this. I can't wait to see you. It's been too long. I miss you.

My heart pounds in my chest as I quickly reread the text. I shouldn't spy, but I can't help myself. There's a web link in the message. I whip out my phone and quickly type it in before the screen goes black.

I glance over my shoulder. Luke is still in the house getting the first course for our meal. I type quickly, then frown as the website pulls up on my phone.

"What in the world?" I stare into the lovely face of Madeleine Rice on an online ad for a political fundraiser hosted by David Bell at the Bell Botanical Gardens next week. Her dark green eyes dance with excitement as one hand points to a caption of her campaign slogan.

I'm not big into politics, but Luke mentioned in passing that he worked for Madeleine Rice during her mayoral campaign before he moved to Kimbell. He graduated with a degree in political science from SMU and, at one point, had aspirations of being a top-tier political consultant, working on elections for the highest offices.

I sensed his desire to be in politics ended abruptly, which is why he moved to our small town, but he never told me why. Could Madeleine Rice be the reason? Grabbing his phone, I draw the shape of a clover on his screen to unlock it. A move I'd watched him do too many times to count over the past few weeks.

Accessing the text app, I scroll through the texts from the unknown number. There are a few messages a day, going back weeks to before I filed the lawsuit. Each one is more secretive and intimate than the next and signed -M. I slam the phone back onto the table and then look at the photo of Madeleine. She's probably twenty years older than us, maybe less, but still a beautiful woman with piercing green eyes and a glamorous look. Definitely the kind of older woman who could get the attention of a younger man. All signs point to some sort of secret illicit affair, but that can't be right. Can it?

How could Luke be so into me if he's secretly involved in a relationship with a woman trying to be governor of Texas?

Or is that the answer?

Am I an easy distraction to help him avoid the relationship he really wants? The one with Madeleine. It would explain how he did a one-eighty, from hating me for filing the lawsuit and trying to take his land to liking me.

Luke returns, holding two plates, placing one in front of me and the other on the opposite side of the table. He's changed into a crisp light green button-down shirt that complements his eyes and dark, slim-fitting jeans showing off his incredible legs. I'd swoon if I wasn't so confused.

"Should we toast?" Luke asks as he sits.

I'm struggling to reconcile how happy he looks to be with me and all the texts from Madeleine. Maybe I'm overreacting and misreading things. But I know myself. I have to find out for sure. Mom told me not to read too much into Luke's niceness. Maybe I came around at just the right time to help him cover up his affair with a married candidate for governor.

Pushing the wayward thoughts away, I say, "Sure."

"To finding what we've been looking for." Luke extends his glass, and I tap mine against his. The soft clink reverberates, and I realize I've completely fallen for this man. That's the reason why these pesky insecurities are bubbling up. When things are good, I've been trained by my last six relationships to expect the other shoe to drop.

But if that shoe is the lawsuit, then what is Madeleine?

Luke sips his wine, then eats a spoonful of caviar. He grimaces and grabs for his napkin.

"You ordered caviar, and you don't even like it?"

"I ordered caviar because you love it, and I'd never tried it," he clarifies.

Scooping a spoonful of the orange beads into my mouth, I savor the delectable treat. This is top-quality stuff. The kind I remember having in a fancy restaurant in New York with Mom.

"Well, more for me," I say, swiping the caviar from his plate.

Luke laughs, then says, "This doesn't seem like a fair trade. Give me some of your salad."

I hold up my plate and watch as he scrapes the food onto his.

I decide to make my move now. "Because you're my politics expert, have you heard about the candidate for governor coming to town?" I pause to gauge his reaction. His hand pauses over his plate, and I detect a slight tremor. "Madeleine Rice?" He bobbles his fork before clanking it against his plate.

"Umm … yeah, I told you I used to work for her campaign." He clears his throat. "A long, long time ago."

"Getting the Bell Family to host a fundraiser for her is a big deal. You think she'd be good for the state?"

"Without a doubt," the words are out of his mouth faster than I expected. I'm taken aback by the staunch support in three little words.

"She's done an amazing job as a mayor. Cleaned up the city, crime is down, and she brought in new business that's helping to pay off debt," Luke says, his gaze drifting beyond me. "She's principled and truly cares about people."

With each compliment, I seethe.

"She doesn't give you a fish. She teaches you how to fish so you can care for yourself for generations."

Shifting in my seat, my head throbs as he continues to gush about the woman.

"Not the typical politician at all. She'd be a wonderful governor."

I clench my teeth as Luke finally stops extolling Madeleine Rice's virtues. The words are out of my mouth before I realize what I'm doing. "And you'd make the best governor's boy toy."

"What?" Luke frowns and looks back at me for the first time since he went off on a tangent praising Madeleine.

"You heard me." I slap my fork down. "She texted while you were in the house getting the food. She really misses you. Wants to see you when she comes to town."

"You read my texts?" Luke asks, looking down at his phone resting on the table.

"I know I shouldn't have, but I looked through the other texts, too. The two of you know how to cover your tracks. She texts from an unknown number. You don't respond, so there's no communication trail. What do you do? Call her back from a burner phone?" I push back from the chair and stand up.

Luke presses his hands against the table. His voice is a low growl. "You got this all wrong, Kennedy."

I thrust my finger in his face. "So while you were making me fall for you, behind my back, you're hooking up with a woman who's running for governor," I say, then suck in a deep breath as the truth hits me. "That's why you had to stop working for her, isn't it? People were close to finding out about your illicit and sordid love affair. So you quit to throw them off the tracks. But you didn't quit her, did you?"

Luke stands abruptly, knocking his chair over. "It's not what you think."

I pace around the table, forcing the tears away. "I was so stupid for believing that you were into me. I'm such a fool."

Luke stands and steps into the pathway of my pacing. I stop several feet away, unwilling to get any closer to him. "And after we talked about how our moms cheated on our dads, I'm stunned that you would get involved with a married woman!"

"Kennedy …" Luke reaches for me, but I jerk my arm away.

"My goodness, Luke! Madeleine Rice is an attractive woman, but she's old enough to be your mother!"

My mind races as my words crash into Luke.

His head drops, and he stares at the blades of grass between his feet. Slowly, he moves away from me, grabs the chair from the ground, and sits down.

But there's no way I could be prepared for what he says next.

CHAPTER 33

L UKE

~

STARING AT THE STARS SPRINKLED ACROSS THE NIGHT SKY like diamonds, I'm not surprised I'm lying on a blanket with Kennedy next to me. Our plates, filled with remnants of the expensive meal, rest near our feet.

She took the news better than I expected.

"Madeleine … is my mother," I forced the words out. Kennedy's hands flew to her mouth, covering half her face as she stared back at me in shock. Before she could ask me any questions, I came clean with the story of my complicated past with my mother and how I ended up in Kimbell.

Kennedy dangles a piece of lobster meat in one hand and wiggles the lobster tail in the other. I chuckle under my breath, then lean my head over to press against the strands of her hair spread out like an ebony fan against the gray fleece. Her scent, a blend of honey and lavender, soothes me.

"So let me get this straight—the woman who lit a fire in you about community service and politics ... turns out she's your birth mom? And you didn't even know until you were what, twenty-five? When you were already knee-deep working as the manager for her mayoral campaign?" Kennedy shakes her head, trying to wrap her mind around the bombshell I'd just dropped. "Talk about a plot twist."

"The real plot twist is you being jealous that I was what? Cheating on you with an older woman?" I say, snatching the lobster meat from her fingers and popping it into my mouth.

"Hey!" Kennedy says, then laughs as she tries to make the lobster claw pinch me. "That was the last piece."

"Forget the lobster and answer my question." I raise an eyebrow.

Her gaze softens as she looks at me. "Okay, in hindsight, that's not my finest moment. I'm sorry for snooping through your phone and jumping to the biggest wrong conclusion ever!"

"But you were really ... jealous?"

"A little bit ..."

I grab the lobster claw from her hand and use it to pinch her arm.

"Ouch! Fine, yes, I was greener than your eyes with envy. There, satisfied?"

"Good to know that the idea of me with another woman made you crazy with jealousy," I say, turning over to look at her. "Not sure what I'd do if I thought you were interested in another guy. It wouldn't be pretty."

"You're too nice to do anything to tarnish your good guy brand," she teases.

"Normally, that would be true. But you've changed things for me."

"Is that so?"

I nod my head in response.

She bites her bottom lip. I brush a stray curl from Kennedy's face, my hand lingering on her cheek. She leans into my touch, her eyes fluttering closed. I can tell she's not convinced. I don't mind. I'm going to enjoy proving her wrong and getting what I want.

A cool breeze rustles through the air. Kennedy shivers, giving me an excuse to pull her close. The moment feels fragile, precious, and fleeting. I don't want it to end, even though I know it will.

Kennedy shifts in my arms, glancing up at the sky. Her expression turns thoughtful. "Luke," she says softly, "You never said how you found out Madeleine Rice was your mother."

"Eavesdropping."

"Seriously?"

"Not on purpose." I exhale a deep breath, then continue. "Madeleine was missing from the celebration after her big win. I went to look for her and overheard her talking to someone whose voice I recognized—my dad's. I was confused. My dad didn't even know her. He always had difficulty remembering the name of the woman I worked for and was never interested in any details of my job. But here he was at the campaign office, huddled up with her and having an intense, hushed conversation."

"They were talking about you," she surmises.

"And how I could never find out the truth. I stood in the darkened hallway, waiting for them to slip up and say what that truth was. When I heard it, I wasn't ready for it at all."

The memories are fresh in my head as if they happened hours ago.

My dad was angry, accusing Madeleine of playing with fire. He told her how much I looked up to her and thought of her as a mentor. Finding out the truth would crush me.

Heart pounding in my chest, I was on the verge of panic, wondering what was going on. Then Madeleine said, "You think I want my son to hate me? I'm never telling him the truth. I would lose him for good."

"Oh, Luke," Kennedy says, her hand resting against my chest.

"I walked out of both their lives that very night. Didn't look back."

"You must have felt so alone and betrayed. Those relationships were built on lies because they didn't trust you enough to handle the truth. It's horrible. Enough to wreck your whole life," Kennedy says.

I stare into her dark eyes, amazed that she completely understands me. I didn't need to explain why I left or justify my actions. She gets it, and that's a huge comfort to me.

"I was lost," I admit. "I needed to go to the one place where I knew I could hide. My dad and Gramps had been estranged for years. If I could find him, I knew he wouldn't tell anyone where I was." I grip Kennedy's hand in mine, feeling none of the angst or fear about sharing my truth with her. "When I knocked on his door, he instantly recognized me. Not a surprise since we Diamond men all look alike."

"So your dad is hot like you?" Kennedy raises up, eyes wide.

"He's better looking than me," I say grudgingly.

"Good to know I don't have to worry about you turning ugly on me in your old age." She laughs.

My heart skips a beat to hear her true thoughts. Despite her fears, she wants us to be together for the long haul, just like I do.

"Nope. I'll be hot when I'm ninety." And I'll only have eyes for you, Kennedy. But I don't say that. Things are going too good for us right now. "Anyway, he guessed immediately that I'd found out the truth. My dad cut him off because Gramps disagreed with them lying to me. Turns out I never received any scholarships to go to private school. Madeleine had footed the bill from the very first day of pre-school all the way through to SMU."

"Wow, I don't even know what to say." Kennedy shakes her head as she wraps her arms around me. We lay beside each other in comfortable silence as she processes the skeletons in my closet. She's so strong and resilient. I know none of this would scare her away.

"So, did you ever respond to any of Madeleine's texts?"

"No, but I talked to her husband. He wants me to work on her campaign, but there's an ulterior motive."

"Because being Madeleine Rice's secret love child could destroy her political career. It helps them if you're on their team."

"I wish it was that simple. They want me to lie about how I found out I was her son. Tell a story that's more palatable to the voters and not wreck everything she's built," I say.

"What does she expect you to say happened?"

"I met Madeleine for the first time when I was thirteen. She became a formal mentor to me and changed my life. I remember wishing that my real mother, who I thought had abandoned me and my dad, could be as amazing as her." I chuckle under my breath, shaking my head. "Anyway, that's the story they wanted. I'd tell the world all the good parts and pretend Madeleine had come clean to me back then. But I was a kid and worried about all the attention I'd get if people knew the truth, so I thought we should keep things a secret."

"So, you tell everyone it was your idea that your parentage remains a secret. The world will think that she was a good mother, protecting her teenage son from the scrutiny that would've come from being the illegitimate child of a political figure. Her career is salvaged, and you're the scapegoat. What a great mother," Kennedy says.

I can feel the anger wafting from her.

I'm touched, but things aren't that simple. "Madeleine isn't a terrible person. The truth is, she was an exceptional mentor to me. I learned so much from her. A huge chunk of the man I am is because of the wisdom and guidance she gave me growing up. Plus, her resume is stellar. Her contributions to the communities she's touched dwarf others. We need more people like her in politics."

"More liars?"

"Come on, Kennedy. It's not all black and white," I say, trying to get her to understand. "I could never do anything that would stop Madeleine's work. Too many people need the good that she would bring to their lives. I did the right thing. You look up how much things have changed since she became mayor, and you'll see that I'm right. It's better that I stayed quiet and moved away."

"It's still crappy that she doesn't take responsibility for what she did. She's pushing that burden onto you. I don't like it," Kennedy says, then takes a deep breath. "But no one will find out the truth from me. I promise you I won't tell anyone about this. Ever. No matter what."

"I know you won't." Deep in my heart, I know Kennedy would

never tell my story, which is why I felt so comfortable telling her everything. "Nate knows all this, but I've never told anyone else."

"If she wins the primary runoff, reporters will start digging into every aspect of her life, and they'll find out about you. Are you sure you're ready for that?"

"No, but if I have you and Nate in my corner supporting me, I can deal with anything," I say.

Kennedy caresses my face and leans her forehead against mine. "I will always be in your corner," she whispers.

Those are the only words I needed to hear.

Gently leaning in, I press my lips against hers, savoring the softness of her skin and the warmth of her breath. My hands roam down her back as our kiss intensifies. Kennedy moans, her hands tangling in my hair.

I can't help but feel a surge of gratitude for the woman in my arms as I trail feather-light kisses down her neck. She listened to my story with an open heart and mind. Her fierce protectiveness of me didn't stop her from offering unwavering support and that means the world to me.

Our kiss lingers with a tenderness that holds every ounce of our unspoken longing for each other. I can't get enough of her. Deepening the kiss, I hope Kennedy feels how much she means to me. I want to leave no room for doubt that I'm nothing like the men who left her in the past. I'm going to be the man who sticks around for good.

CHAPTER 34

K ENNEDY

~

"H EY, IT'S GOING TO BE OKAY," L ANCE SAYS, REACHING over to squeeze my shoulder. "You look like you're going to pass out."

My body trembles uncontrollably as we sit in a waiting room outside the only courtroom inside the Kimbell Courthouse. Memories of Luke cloud my mind. Holding him in my arms for what felt like hours before we finally decided it was time for me to go home. Walking hand-in-hand, we tried to delay the moment, knowing that today has the potential to change everything between us.

And by change, I mean obliterate, demolish, destroy, and murder beyond recognition the connection forged between us over the past month or so.

Part of me wishes I'd never pursued this lawsuit.

That I'd dropped the whole idea when Luke tried to tell me it was ludicrous that both deeds were real. Still I was stubborn, determined to reclaim the land I felt had been stolen from my family.

Now I'm at a crossroads, knowing I could walk out of the courthouse in a matter of hours having lost … everything.

My grandmother's orchard will be once again owned by the Diamond Family.

Out of my reach.

I won't be able to protect it or share it with the world.

Because it will belong to Luke.

A fresh wave of nausea hits me.

As much as I wish it wasn't so, part of me will hate him for having my family's legacy on his property. A big part of me. So big I'm not sure the feelings I have for him, which are stronger than I've ever had for any man, can survive the anger and disappointment.

"Just nervous," I say, unable to hide the quiver in my voice.

"Preparing for the worst?" Lance asks, easing into the seat next to me. He wraps an arm around my shoulders and tugs me close. "I'm sorry I got your hopes up. I really thought Timmy would find something … anything … that could help bolster your position."

"It's okay. I had to try," I say, blinking back the tears. I'm not sure if they threaten to fall because of losing the land or because I'll be losing Luke.

A knock at the door causes me to jump.

I glance toward the opening and see a friendly face.

"Hey," I say, rising from my chair.

"Checking on you," Dillon says, his lips curved into a slight smile.

Lance brushes past me, giving my hand a squeeze. "I'll give you two a moment alone. I'm going to see if Timmy has arrived."

I don't respond. I'm second and third-guessing Lance's decision to go with the local private investigator. I get that having someone with strong connections in the community should be a benefit, but Timmy is notorious for botching investigations. I can't help thinking about how he missed finding Joe Little after Elm Street Brewery burned down.

Dillon pushes the door closed after Lance leaves. "Must be torture. I know how much you hate waiting."

I nod my head.

"Can I give you a hug?" He asks.

"I'd like that." For some reason, having my first love here to support me is calming. Dillon steps closer and wraps his arms around me. I lean my head on his shoulder. His embrace is so different from Luke's. When Luke holds me, it's like he wants to send a message to the world that in his arms is the only place I belong. With Dillon, the hug feels familiar and sweet. But lacks the intensity and passion.

I pull away after a few seconds. "Are you sticking around for the hearing?"

"Of course. There's no way I wouldn't be here to support you," Dillon says. "Don't freak, but it's like the whole town is here to watch. Most of them will be sitting with Luke. I'm going to balance out your side."

"I need it," I say, not looking forward to the cheers and hollers that will ring out in the courtroom when Judge Barnes rules that the land still belongs to Luke. I just hope my family can whisk me out of there before I completely break down in front of everyone. "Not sure my dad will appreciate you being here as much as I do."

"He has good reason to hate me," Dillon says, raking a hand through his hair. "Most days, I hate myself for how I treated you. You didn't deserve that."

"And the other days?" I ask, curiosity getting the better of me.

"I realize I wasn't ready for where we were headed. Either way, the outcome would've been the same," Dillon explains. "I wish I'd been the man I am today when we were together. I promise you things would've turned out much differently."

I chuckle. "Like what? We'd be an old married couple right now?" More laughter bubbles out of me until I see the sincere seriousness on Dillon's face.

"I can only wish," Dillon says, shaking his head slightly. "I loved you, Kennedy. Don't ever doubt that, no matter how stupid I was back then. I one hundred percent loved you."

"I guess sometimes love isn't enough."

"Strange but true," Dillon says, then walks past me to sit at the table. "I'm really sorry. If I could go back in time and change things, I swear I would."

I follow him and sit in the chair next to him. "I appreciate that."

"And you forgive me?" He asks, eyes filled with hope.

"I forgave you a long time ago. You just didn't stick around to find out."

"Good point. Well, I'm back now." He leans back in his chair. "For good."

"For good? What does your mom think about that?"

"She's skeptical and cautiously happy. Of course, she tries to hide all that behind her curmudgeonly crankiness." Dillon snorts a laugh.

"She wouldn't be your mom if she didn't," I say, then squeeze his hand. "You were always her favorite."

"I know," Dillon says. "That's part of the reason I came back here. She's home for me. After being lost for so long, when I finally found myself again and got a new purpose, this is where I wanted to be. Close to her, you know."

I nod, feeling strangely proud of him. I can see how much he's changed, and a part of me wishes he had been this guy all those years ago. Or that Luke hadn't hijacked my heart so I could see what the future could hold for Dillon and me.

"What are you going to do with yourself?"

"I'm taking over managing Crockett House from the company Mama hired, and I'll still be doing the Firefighter Hunks calendar plus some companion events—"

"Wait! You're behind the Firefighter Hunks calendar? I didn't know that."

"So you bought a copy?"

"Technically, Vangie bought it for me. I waited too late, and they'd sold out in Kimbell. So she picked one up for me when she was in San

Antonio for a tax conference." I flush as Luke's picture flashes in my head. "It's very well done."

"Thank you." Dillon beams, obviously proud of his work. "And I make sure that half the proceeds go to charity. It's a way to entertain and give back to small-town communities like Kimbell. Hope I see you at my first event."

"What's your first event?"

"Date auction," Dillon says, leaning closer to me. "I'll put myself up if you'll bid on me—"

The door swings open.

I look up to see Lance staring at me with an unreadable expression. Timmy Quinn stands behind him, looking like the cat who ate the canary.

"Hey, umm, Dillon. Would you mind?" Lance asks.

"Yeah, of course," Dillon says, then leans over to hug me. "See you after the hearing."

When Dillon is gone, my gaze jerks back and forth between Lance and Timmy. "What's going on? The hearing isn't starting for another twenty minutes."

Lance says, "Timmy has … news …"

CHAPTER 35

L UKE

~

THE GASP FROM THE CROWD PACKED IN THE SMALL
courtroom at the Kimbell Courthouse roars in my ears. My head drops
into my hands as physical pain wracks through my body. A sucker
punch knocked all the air from my lungs and sent me free-falling into
an abyss.

For the first time, I stop stealing glances at Kennedy.

Across the courtroom, she radiates an effortless grace. Her rich
brown skin glows under the harsh fluorescent lights, and her wavy hair
seems to dance with each slight movement of her head. Despite the
circumstances, I can't help but marvel at how she manages to look
both formidable and utterly captivating. Most of the morning, I'd been
lost in the emotions that tethered me to this woman, feelings that had
grown deeper as we spent time together over the past several weeks.

Memories of being happier than I've ever been and not wanting that to end because of the lawsuit.

I thought I knew why she wouldn't meet my gaze.

I was dead wrong.

Timmy Quinn clears his throat. "As I was saying, this sales document clearly shows that Frank Diamond sold five of the fifty acres of land to Alice Butler thirty years ago at a price almost double the market value at the time. That is perplexing given his widely known staunch refusal to part with any of his land. I wondered how she convinced him to sell when no one else had. It caused me to dig deeper into what happened when he first came to Kimbell in light of the identical deed found by Ms. Tarkington. The evidence has been authenticated by Mary Jones, curator of the Kimbell Historical Museum. She's also willing to let a third party review the historical documents if Mr. Diamond chooses …"

The judge murmurs legal statutes about admitting the documents into evidence, then urges Timmy to proceed.

He unveils his story in dramatic fashion. Each detail like razor blades slicing through me.

Confirmed with the Galveston Historical Society that the gambling house where Frank Diamond encountered Zebediah Abbott didn't open until three years after the deed was dated.

Impossible for him to have owned the land on the date identified on the deed.

A hand clamps on my shoulder. Nate gives me a firm squeeze of support. My best friend knows exactly where this is headed. I turn slightly to look back at him as he sits beside Ronan, Wiley, and Darren. All four men give me nods of confidence and encouragement, but can't hide the pity in their eyes.

Clearly, Zebediah swindled Frank, tricking the young man into buying land from an invalid deed. It was the only way Zebediah could pay off his own gambling debts.

Frank Diamond didn't realize the problem with the date until he arrived in Kimbell to claim his land, which Cornelius Butler had lived on for three years.

Olivia squirms next to me, then feverishly writes on her notepad.

She's preparing for a cross-examination that will be pointless. The impossible has happened. All I can do is watch it unfold like a bad car accident before my eyes.

Journals maintained by the renowned judge have notes on Mr. Butler and Mr. Diamond bringing their grievances over the land to the court.

The judge pitied Mr. Diamond—a young man of barely twenty who'd been abandoned and alone, taking care of himself on the streets since he was twelve years old ...

The judge took pity on Frank ... words explicitly contained in the journal ... even though it was clear he was not the rightful owner of the land.

Believed that the Butler Family could bounce back from losing the land. But losing the land would steal hope from Frank Diamond and he might not ever recover. It would destroy his life.

Lance says, "Please read the page submitted from the judge's journal, which has been submitted as exhibit fourteen."

The pen falls from Olivia's hand and she leans back in her chair. I don't have to look at her to see the defeat. There's nothing she can do to counter the bombs Timmy has dropped. The only chance I have is if the historical documents obtained from the Kimbell Historical Museum and Galveston Historical Society are determined to be inauthentic.

I know in my heart that will never happen.

I know Timmy's next words will be the final death knell that causes Judge Barnes to rule against me and give my land to Kennedy.

Timmy clears his throat, then reads from the page in his hand. "The judge wrote, 'May the good Lord forgive me for what I've done. I just couldn't bear to see a young man's future crushed because of a despicable liar and cheater. I ruled in favor of Frank Diamond, taking land away from a good family. Please bless them and make amends for what I've done.'"

Olivia stands and cross-examines Timmy Quinn. She does the best she can, getting Timmy Quinn to acknowledge that his investigation identified a large tax bill and the later construction of the house on the Diamond land in the same year as Gramps sold the land to Alice

Butler. Facts that explain why Gramps pushed for the higher market value sales price. My lawyer makes a strong argument that Butler's willingness to overpay for the land was due to her belief, although unproven, that the land belonged to her family.

Still, I fear it's too little too late. The discrepancy between when Gramps bought the land from Zebediah Abbott with his gambling winnings and the date on the deed three years earlier is unreconcilable. Gramps was tricked, and now, all these years later, the land he loved, the land I love, could be snatched away from us.

After closing arguments by both attorneys, which triggers a new round of chatter and murmuring within the crowd inside the courtroom, the Judge demands silence.

I close my eyes.

I can see Gramps sitting on the porch, his weathered hands cradling a mug of coffee as he gazed out at the land. "This place," he'd said, his voice thick with emotion, "gave me a reason to keep going when I had nothing else."

"Because you'd been on your own for how long? Like eight years?"

Gramps grunted. "Since I was twelve … ten years of fending for myself with no one to help me. I didn't blame Ma. She had eight other kids to feed. She was tired and needed to lighten the load."

"Still sucks that she left you at the train station," I said, pained for what my grandfather endured.

He shrugged. "She knew I could handle it. I was a beautiful boy. If that's one thing Diamond men can count on, it's our good looks. I charmed my way in and out of situations and kept myself fed and a roof over my head most nights."

"That couldn't have been easy." I shook my head, knowing he was downplaying what he'd endured.

"No … and the years wore on me. All I wanted was a place to call home. Somewhere I could settle and stop moving around. I needed some place permanent to call my own." Gramps sniffed, then wiped a hand under his nose. He took a long sip of the coffee. "Got into poker and found I was pretty good at it. One night, this guy came in, and he lost everything. Heavies were about to rough him up. Guy was desperate for help and had some land in Kimbell. A lot of acres. He needed to offload the land, or he wouldn't survive the night."

"Good thing you'd had a lucky night," I said, remembering how Gramps boasted about his winnings. "You were flush with cash to buy the land."

"And I never looked back. I finally had stability and a place that was all mine." Gramps gazed out onto the land. "Every tree, every blade of grass - it's more than just property. It was my second chance. My permanent home. And now that you're here," he reached over to squeeze my neck. "You showing up on my doorstep was the best gift I could've ever gotten. I love you, kid. And I'm glad I have something to leave you so you remember me when I'm long gone."

"Don't talk like that." I punched him lightly in the arm.

Gramps leaned over and kissed me on the head like I was a little boy. "I ain't going nowhere soon, but it brings me so much joy to know I have something worthwhile to leave you. This land will bring you as much happiness as it brought me. I know it."

"I am prepared to make my ruling," Judge Barnes says. Her words slice through the fog of memories in my mind. "Given the compelling evidence presented to the court, I believe it is clear that a horrible injustice was done to the Butler Family. A ruling that never should've been made in the face of clear evidence of the contrary. I am proud to rectify this grievance and award the fifty acres of property between Abbott Road and Lake Lasso to the family of Cornelius Butler."

I cover my face in my hands as my entire world shatters. Gramps' dream of leaving his land to me has vanished into thin air, and it's all my fault. I should've done more to fight harder for it.

Instead, I wasted time consumed with Kennedy.

I forgot what was really at stake.

Gramps's land.

My land.

Now it's gone, and there's nothing I can do to change that.

A roar rumbles inside me. I clench my jaws, refusing to let it out.

Cheers erupt from Kennedy's side of the courtroom while I can hear a pin drop behind me.

Judge Barnes looks at me, her voice soft, "Luke, I will give you sixty days to vacate the premises."

I push up from the chair, knocking it over with a loud clatter.

"Don't bother. I'll be leaving tonight." Ignoring the protests of my friends and well-meaning townsfolk, I walk out of the courtroom without looking back.

CHAPTER 36

ENNEDY

My cheeks ache from smiling.

The jubilant mask of happiness on my face mirrors the emotions my family and closest friends expect me to feel. I look around the ornate wooden table covered with the finest linens inside the private dining room of Thorn, one of the Hill Country's best restaurants, and try to force myself to feel a fraction of what I should.

I'm flanked by Daddy on my right and Mom on my left, gorging themselves on slices of the forty-five-ounce Tomahawk steak on a platter in the center of the table. This is by far the most decadent meal I've ever had. Vangie and Yolanda sit across from me with Lance seated next to Yolanda and Timmy Quinn, our guest of honor, on the opposite side of Vangie.

For the past couple of hours, we've indulged in a six-course meal paid for by David Bell because of the injustice my family endured after having our land taken from us.

"Uh oh, Sugabean. Looks like your glass is getting low," Daddy says, reaching for a bottle of Harlow Rose Merlot, which we all agreed we liked better than her award-winning Cabernet Sauvignon.

"Well, how did I let that happen?" A fake laugh escapes my lips. I give him an even bigger smile, if that's possible, as he pours my glass full of red wine. Taking a sip, I ask, "How do you like the lobster macaroni and cheese?"

"Definitely feel like I can give them a run for their money, but it's really good," Daddy says, staring at the noodles on his fork before taking another bite. I can imagine he's trying to dissect every ingredient in the dish so he can prove to himself that he can make it better than the world-renowned chef at Thorn.

"Would you expect your father to say anything less?" Mom asks, shaking her head. "How are you feeling, Ken? Do I need to pinch you?" She teases as she reaches her long nails toward my arm.

I jerk away, remembering the move that used to punish me when I'd misbehaved as a young child. "Get those fingers away from me!" I take another long sip of the wine, then turn toward her. "I think I'm still in shock about everything that happened."

Luke's face, devastated and destroyed, flashes in my mind. I stole a glance at him at the exact moment Judge Barnes gave her ruling. There was no hiding his disappointment. Everyone in the courthouse could literally see his whole world imploding.

And that's all my fault.

Mom nods her head. "I mean, we all believed that the land was ours. There's no way you would have forced the issue if you thought you would be disrupting a man's life for nothing." She takes a sip of wine. "Still to have the truth corroborated by authenticated solid evidence. Not the circumstantial stuff, but real proof. It's beyond what any of us thought was possible."

Daddy leans over, his voice just above a whisper. "I'm just glad Timmy Quinn isn't as incompetent as the whole town thinks he is."

I swat a hand at his arm. "Dad!" I glance at Timmy, who is beaming as he regales Vangie, Yolanda, and Lance with another extraordinary tale from his private investigating adventures. He is the picture of a man vindicated from a string of past failures.

Not unlike myself.

Six failed relationships, blindsided by each one, had almost come to an end with lucky number seven—Luke Diamond. But Luke and I will never be in a relationship. I'm the last person he wants to see now and maybe ever.

Lance clears his throat. "Well, just got a text that Olivia Garnet has appealed the judge's decision, as I expected."

Yolanda leans forward. "What exactly does that mean?"

Everyone leans in, eager to hear Lance's response.

"Basically buys them time to validate the evidence Timmy found and see if they can find anything to dispute it," Lance says.

"Which they won't. Trust me. I had the best historians in the state authenticate the information I presented in court today. There's not a single hole in the information I found. That property is Butler land," Timmy says with confidence.

Vangie gives Timmy a side-eye, then turns to Lance. "Does this mean Kennedy doesn't own the land anymore?"

Lance shakes his head. "She owns the property and can do whatever she wants with it. This appeal is a move of desperation. Olivia is a brilliant attorney. Once her team of investigators corroborates Timmy's findings, she'll drop the appeal."

Dad pumps his fist in the air. "Glad to hear it because I happened to have another conversation with Simona at the courthouse after the ruling—"

"Oh, you just happened to run into her, did you?" Mom says, a tinge of anger in her tone.

"What?" Dad shrugs. "Anyway, she gave me a little more insight into how much Zaire was willing to pay for the land when they were working on a proposal to present to Luke. It was a hundred thousand dollars per acre! Can you believe that?"

I groan and cross my arms over my chest. "Granny's orchards make up the bulk of the land. I plan to meet with the board of Bell Botanical Gardens to see how I can have it preserved as part of the Alice Butler Center for Horticulture."

"I completely understand that Sugabean," Daddy says, squeezing my hand. "But the orchards are roughly thirty-five of the fifty acres. That leaves fifteen acres that could be sold. Think about it. That's one and a half million dollars!"

"I can't sell that land." The words are out before I can stop them. In my periphery, I see Vangie and Yolanda exchange a look. They know the real reason for my outburst. Part of the fifteen acres contains Luke's home, Diamond Lake, the hill overlooking the orchards, and the barn that Luke and his grandfather spent a year building. Those are the most important parts of the land to Luke, where most of his memories with his grandfather are tied into every tree, blade of grass, and ripple of water on the lake.

How could I ever hurt him by selling that land to Zaire?

Lance speaks up, "It's not a bad idea, Kennedy. I can reach out to Zaire and gauge interest if you'd like. That's not the kind of money you want to dismiss so easily."

Timmy whistles. "I know I'd sell in a heartbeat, especially since Luke is long gone—"

"What do you mean?" I ask, heart thundering in my chest. "Where did Luke go?"

Timmy's eyes grow wide, and he chews on his bottom lip. "Okay, don't spread this because I was kind of eavesdropping after the hearing this afternoon—"

Vangie shoves Timmy in the arm. "Just say it. Where is Luke?"

"We all saw how devastated he was after the ruling. How he raced out of the courthouse like the devil himself was after him," Timmy says, then swipes at a bead of sweat on his brow. "As I was leaving, I overheard Nate asking Ace Lallo to gather some men to pack up Luke's house. Then he told Ronan not to be surprised if Luke didn't show up to work in the morning. He was pretty sure Luke was leaving town for good … tonight."

I clutch my chest, then drop my head in my hands as tears sting my eyes. Mom's arm slides around my shoulder as she hugs me tightly.

"Ken, this is not your fault. You do not have to feel guilty about doing what was right for your family," Mom whispers as she caresses my arm.

"I just feel so bad … he's lost so much," I say, and I'm not talking about the land.

The connection I felt with Luke overshadowed every relationship I'd had in the past. For the first time in a long time, I was optimistic that I might get my happily ever after with a man who appreciated me unconditionally.

Rationally, we knew the risks of getting close with the lawsuit over our heads, and we were both naive enough to believe the connection between us was strong enough to survive it all.

But we were wrong.

And Luke is gone.

CHAPTER 37

LUKE

~

The grand salon suite inside Crockett Manor is
pitch black. The minute I arrived, I closed the blackout curtains and
placed a towel at the crack in the door to block the light filtering in
from the hallway. The bedroom has old-world charm and luxury.
None of it matters to me as I push up on the bed to peer at the
door.

I had finally stopped my mind from racing over the day's events and
was about to drift off to sleep when a loud, persistent knock
interrupted me.

The door opens slightly, and a head pokes inside. Alma, the long-
time cook, and housekeeper at the bed and breakfast, backs into the
room, flipping one of the soft overhead lights on with her elbow, then
turns to face me, carrying a wooden tray with several covered plates
on top.

Alma asks, "When was the last time you ate? Before the hearing? You must be starving."

My mouth feels like cotton, and the jackhammer is having its way with my head, so food is the last thing on my mind. Still, it was sweet of Alma to think of me and make the trip to the third floor to hand deliver dinner.

"Thanks," I say, reaching over to turn on the lamp on the night table. "Not sure I'm going to eat much. I'm actually not hungry."

"You will be once you see what I brought you," Alma says matter-of-factly. "It's good you didn't come down to dinner. Too many people around who could spread the word that you haven't left town like your best friend wants everyone to believe."

I shake my head and inhale a deep breath. "Nate probably went overboard with that. I just asked him to help me get some space to process what happened today. Everything is so raw. I can't deal with … people … right now."

Balancing the tray in one hand, Alma moves deftly across the room and places it on the night table. She removes the stainless steel cloches from the plates of food. The smell hits me like a freight train. My stomach growls.

I continue, "I'm sure that sounds crazy coming from me. I'm the guy who's always swooping in when disaster strikes to offer a helping hand."

Alma levels me with a compassionate stare. "That's because you're a good man. The best kind."

Sitting up straighter, I glance at the food on each plate. It looks like she's brought enough for the entire fire station and not just me.

"I never realized how annoying that could be," I say, unburdening myself on the unsuspecting hospitality manager of Crockett Manor. "Never even thought that people might just need time to deal with things on their own before I tried to save the day, you know?"

"No, I don't know," Alma counters, pointing a finger at me. "I don't know a single person in town who was ever upset that you wanted to help them in their time of need. Not one."

I look away.

"But that doesn't mean that you need the same things they did in times of trouble. You have a right to space if that's what you want. Between Nate and me, we'll make sure you get all the space you need." Alma busies herself with arranging the plates in an order only she understands, then says, "Tonight's dinner is meatloaf with garlic mashed potatoes and sauteed green beans. For dessert, I made apple pie. But I've heard you make a pretty decent tres leches, so I whipped up my special recipe to show you how it's done."

I laugh, appreciating her thoughtfulness. "Nate should keep his mouth shut." Swiping a finger across the moist cake and icing, I lick it from my finger and swoon with delight. "Maybe I'll start with dessert first." I grab the plate and a fork and take another bite.

"I won't tell anyone," Alma says brightly. "It's better than yours, isn't it?"

I shrug in defeat. "Yeah, I'm taking another loss today."

Alma looks mortified. "Oh, Luke, I didn't mean it like that."

"It's okay, really. I'm good, and I know when my dessert has been bested by a master." I laugh and see the distress leave her face.

She wipes her hands on her apron, then sits on the edge of the bed next to me. "Is there anything the lawyer can do to help you hold onto some of the land?"

The cake soaked in three milks quickly disappears from the plate as I shovel more into my mouth. After several minutes, I respond, "My attorney, Olivia Garnet ... she's from Austin. Anyway, she filed an appeal before the courts closed today. But no one at the firm is optimistic that their private investigators will find evidence to dispute what Timmy Quinn uncovered."

"What a time for him to do a decent job," Alma mutters.

"I'm glad he did. The truth needed to come out, and the wrong needed to be rectified. I know that in my head ..."

"But your heart is still breaking."

"Shattered," I admit. I place the empty plate onto the table, then lean back on the bed in no mood to eat dinner. "Olivia also brought up countersuing for all the taxes that Gramps and I paid on the property. We weren't the rightful owners and technically did not owe the taxes. She said there is precedent already on the books from other cases."

Alma's mouth drops open. "So, Kennedy would be on the hook to repay you for decades worth of taxes. That seems so harsh, but I guess that's why you pay the fancy lawyers from the big city."

"I'm not going to do it," I say with a firm finality. "I already told Olivia to drop that idea. I don't want to do anything that would cause Kennedy and I to interact with each other again. I don't want to see her … at all. Ever."

"That's understandable," Alma says, squeezing my hand.

"You know, she and I lived in this town for over five years and never crossed paths," I say, still amazed. Kimbell is a small town but not so small that everyone interacts with everyone else. There are still so many people who've lived here for years or their whole lives who I've never met. "Our worlds literally never intersected. Then, one random day, she finds a document in an old trunk, and our worlds crash into each other and burn."

But the burning only came earlier this morning.

Before the final hearing and the ruling from the judge, our worlds didn't crash.

They merged.

Seamlessly. Effortlessly. Perfectly.

Kennedy was everything I knew I wanted in a woman and all the things I never knew I needed. She was passionately infuriating me one minute and harmoniously in sync with me the next.

She made me happier than I ever remember being in my life.

All in a matter of weeks.

But now, as I cycle through all the memories of the times we spent together, secretly seeing each other without the townsfolk finding out, I put all my efforts of concentration into conjuring how she made me feel.

But they are gone.

The memories are there, but the emotions have disappeared.

All I feel is numb.

Underneath the numbness is a simmering and irrational anger that she is the one who cratered my life. Changed everything in a blink, snatching away my home and leaving me with nothing.

I hate her for doing this to me.

But I won't unleash this chaos onto her.

It wouldn't be fair.

She doesn't deserve my wrath.

What happened between our ancestors long before we were born isn't her fault or mine. But we do have to live with the consequences of those actions.

And the only way I can live with them is by returning things to how they were before.

When I didn't know her and she didn't know me.

When there wasn't a billboard of her beautiful face calling to me like a siren on my way to work every three days.

I need to erase every memory of Kennedy from my head.

And the faster I do that, the better.

"Good thing you know how to handle things that are burning. Putting out fires is your specialty," Alma says, then chuckles. "I have no doubt that you'll find a new normal. It may not look like what you shared in the past with Frank, but it will ease this pain and help you focus on the family you still have here."

Nate, Ronan, Wiley and Darren come to mind—all like brothers. I wouldn't have survived today if it wasn't for them. They arranged my escape and cared enough to give me space, even from them.

"Eat some dinner. It will make you feel better," Alma says, standing. "Should I bring breakfast to your room in the morning? Or will you be going to work?"

"Ronan gave me the day off, so I'll hide here. Breakfast would be wonderful," I say.

"Don't hide for too long. It's not healthy."

"I'll emerge in time for the date auction on Friday," I say, but the fundraising dinner for Madeleine isn't far from my head. With everything going on, the last thing I need is to deal with her, too.

"Dillon got you to do that silly thing?" Alma looks surprised, then smiles. "The ladies will fight all over you, especially after what happened today. You'll bring in a lot of money for the community center."

"That's the plan," I say.

"Good night, Luke," Alma says, heading to the door.

"Night, Alma." Alone in the room, I suddenly remember I never told Kennedy about the date auction. Clearing my events with her is pointless. Everything I thought we would be is dead now.

CHAPTER 38

K ENNEDY

Knocking lightly on the frosted glass door, I step inside the modern office of Zaire Kincaid of Kincaid Real Estate. The space is massive, with modern sophistication and luxurious high-end touches that perfectly match the powerhouse business woman. Floor-to-ceiling glass makes up two of the walls, giving her an unobstructed view of the prettiest part of Lake Lasso. This place makes my office look like something a hobbit would waddle out of, even if it is in a building that her company designed.

Zaire twirls around in her chair like some real estate fairy godmother and gives me a welcoming smile. "Kennedy, please come on in."

I cross the room and perch on the edge of one of the chairs in front of her desk. "Thanks for meeting with me on such short notice."

"Of course, I'd do anything for Yolanda. She said you needed help with some real estate questions," Zaire says, then places her elbows on the desk and leans her chin on her hands. "Congratulations, by the way. I'm so happy that everything worked out for you. It's hard to believe a judge would circumvent the law and give your family's land to someone else. The whole town is shocked and grateful that the land is back in the right hands."

"Thank you," I say, not sure that the entire town is in my corner. I'm sure there are still more than a few folks who would've preferred that I lost my lawsuit. "It's exactly what I wanted, but it's surreal at the same time. I'll admit that I'm struggling to wrap my mind around this new normal and all the things I have to do."

"Ah yes, the bureaucracy of rectifying the situation with officially changing paperwork and getting correct versions on file. That's step one and probably the easiest. The hardest part is figuring out how to do what you want with the land now that you have it."

I nod slowly, not surprised that she knows what I'm dealing with. "The tax aspect alone is a nightmare. Vangie and I have been pouring over all the details, working through options and alternatives to not pay my annual salary to the government to cover them." I let out a heavy sigh. "It's a lot to take on, even for a finance and accounting professional like me. My head is literally swimming."

"Good thing is that you don't have to have all the answers at once. Slow down. Take your time," Zaire says, then smiles. "What can I help you with on the real estate side?" She holds up both her hands. "And don't worry. Yolanda already gave me a stern warning not to try to buy the land from you. She made it clear you're not selling. I'm not going to push. I'm offering my expertise as a consultant."

I grimace. "Yolanda's not exactly on the same page as me about selling the land."

"Really?" Zaire raises an eyebrow.

"I'll be honest. If my grandmother's first orchard design wasn't on the property, I don't know if I would've been so tenacious about pursuing the lawsuit ... even with the deed. I was so concerned that her work could be damaged or destroyed and not available to be shared with the world as part of her legacy. That part of the land was the most important to me," I explain.

"And the rest of the land?"

"Doesn't feel like it could ever be mine. I knew the lawsuit would result in a winner and a loser. I didn't realize how horrible it would feel to know that getting my family's land back would mean that Luke loses his home and the property he and his grandfather bonded over."

Zaire leans back in her chair. "That's tough. Anyone with half a heart would feel the same way. So, you're looking to divide the land? Keep the parts that are meaningful to you and sell the rest."

"That's right, and that's where you come in ..."

"You want me to buy the rest of the land?" Zaire looks hopeful.

"No." My words are more blunt than I intend. "Well, you're not my first choice of buyer. But if that person declines, I would be open to selling the land to you." I reach into my purse and pull out my stack of research. "I've been digging into the valuation of my property. The numbers are astronomical. Everything I find factors in the increased property values since your developments have taken off." I pause, then give her a slight smile. "Everything you're doing for our community is wonderful, but it doesn't come without some consequences that aren't good for everyone."

"Townsfolk love the increased property values if they're trying to sell. But those who aren't are hit with higher taxes because of the increase," Zaire looks contemplative. "Trust me, we get calls almost weekly complaining about that. Progress does come with challenges."

"As an accountant, I understand the valuation of a property has a lot to do with what the buyer will do with the land. So, for example, you might pay a lot more for land around the lake because of what you can earn from it than someone who just wants to keep things as is and not develop it."

"Why are you here? You obviously don't need my help."

"But I'm not a valuation expert," I say, then spread out the numbers I've been researching almost nonstop since the celebration at Thorn. "I don't know how to get to a fair market value of the land for someone that's not ... well, you. There's no information out there to help me do that."

Zaire perks up. "I see. So you want a non-commercial property valuation for a residential sale with no improvements?"

"Yes, I think so. Is that something you'd be willing to help me with?

"And this would be how much you want the mysterious potential buyer number one to pay for the land," Zaire says, a mischievous glint in her eyes.

"Right ..."

"You're going to offer to sell the land to Luke, aren't you?"

"I have to! He is homeless, and it's all my fault. I never wanted to take the home that means so much to him. Or Diamond Lake, where he and his grandfather would race in swimming during the summers. Or the barn he and his grandfather spent a year building. Or the hammock where he falls asleep on lazy afternoons. Those parts of the land mean way more to him than they ever would to me or my family." I run my hands through my hair. "I'm going to at least make the offer."

"Sounds like you know Luke extremely well. He's not the type to accept the land as a gift or for an amount below it's worth."

"But he also can't afford to pay what you would," I say. "He lost his home, and that's why he left town. Maybe if I could find a fair way for him to get it back, he'd come home to Kimbell for good."

Zaire flips her hand at me. "Luke didn't leave town. He's at Crockett Manor."

"What?" My heart flutters. "He's still ... here?"

"Like you said, Kimbell is Luke's home. That man isn't going anywhere. Wiley says he just needed some space to process what happened."

A fog of confusion floats in my mind. "But everyone said he left the same night of the hearing."

"That's vintage Nate. He forced Luke into hiding so people in town wouldn't bother him. Wiley says it was actually a good move. Luke seems to be coming to terms with everything slowly but surely."

"Luke is here …"

"Come on," Zaire prods. "You can't really be surprised."

"Why do you say that?"

"After how close the two of you got, I'm sure you're the biggest reason he would never leave Kimbell."

"Wait? Why do you think … I don't understand … who told you?"

Zaire bursts into laughter. "Wiley, of course. My man can't keep a secret. At least not from me." She leans back and twirls her chair from side to side. "He said after the lawsuit, Luke was suddenly M.I.A. from the guys' usual hang outs because he was spending time with his new neighbor. Nate threatened them if they teased Luke about it, so they kept quiet. But it was obvious to them how much he was falling for you."

"You've got to be kidding? They all noticed?"

"Mmm hmm," Zaire says, unable to hide her glee. "Yolanda let a few things slip. Stuff that other people wouldn't have noticed, but since I had all the tea from Wiley, I could put it all together. Not even a lawsuit could stop true love."

"I don't know about that," I say, almost choking on the idea that Luke and I found true love. If we had, the judge's ruling wouldn't have torn us apart. "Whatever Luke and I were building was instantly destroyed when the judge awarded me the land. I'm the last person he wants to see. He hates me now for good reason."

"Maybe …"

"The only thing I want to do is give him an opportunity to buy part of the land," I say with wavering conviction.

"He would become your neighbor again."

"With forty acres of land separating us." I thrust my arms out wide to prove my point. "Trust me, we would only run into each other if we wanted to. Luke clearly doesn't want that." The man is hiding at the local bed and breakfast so he won't have to see me again. "I just need a fair value to put on the sales documents."

"You do know that I would pay you a hundred thousand dollars per acre for as much of that land that you want to sell," Zaire says, her eyes narrowing.

"And if Luke turns me down, I will sell it to you. But right now, I really need—"

"Okay, okay," Zaire says, giving me a look that I can read easily but refuse to acknowledge. She reaches for the phone and gives pointed directions in the nicest way, then turns her attention back to me. "I'll have a number for you in thirty minutes. While you wait, can I give you some unsolicited advice?"

"How can I say no?" I laugh.

"Don't let Lance present the offer to Luke. You need to do it. It's the only way he'll accept it. Trust me."

"He doesn't want to see me ..."

"You don't know that for sure. But let's say you're right. Then, he'll turn you down to your face and you'll never have to wonder if Lance pitched the offer like you would have. You can be at peace knowing that you did everything possible to make things better for Luke."

"That makes a lot of sense."

"And maybe if the two of you talk, Luke will come to his senses. He's hurting from losing the land, but not as much as he's hurting about losing you. I have that on good authority. If you make the first move, he might just make the last one and fight for the relationship you both deserve."

I shake my head. "I can't let myself hope for that."

CHAPTER 39

L UKE

~

A SOFT DRIZZLE COATS MY FACE AS I WAVE GOODBYE TO THE
guys who'll be part of the date auction on Saturday night. Turning, I
head toward Bell Park instead of Crockett Manor. After being cooped
up in the suite for the past four days, it felt good to be out with people
again. The organized chaos of the date auction rehearsal injected a
sense of normalcy. No one brought up the court ruling or my
disappearance. But they made it clear I was missed and welcomed me
back into the fold as if nothing had changed.

But the truth is … everything has changed.

Tonight proved that Kimbell doesn't feel like home anymore.

I'm a shadow of the man who found solace in this community. My
place here was changed forever by one ruling from the judge. One
selfish move made by the grandfather, who helped me heal and gave
me a new home when I needed it the most. Anger and

disappointment strangles my heart. I can't seem to shake these feelings.

Stuffing my hands in my pocket, I trudge slowly toward the faint glowing lights of the gazebo nestled near the back of the picturesque Bell Park. The pristine white fence surrounding the town's haven of activity beckons me to enter. I zip my windbreaker and pull the hood over my head as I walk across the damp grass. The night is peaceful and quiet. The only sound is the soft patter of rain gently falling to the ground. Jogging up the three steps into the octagonal gazebo, I sit on the wooden bench that lines the interior and gaze into the dark copse of towering oak and pine trees, contemplating what could be next for me.

The truth is, Judge Barnes's ruling didn't blindside me. It was the logical conclusion to the evidence Timmy Quinn found. Evidence that proved my grandfather was so desperate for a new life that doing the right thing never crossed his mind. He knew the land didn't belong to him. He'd been swindled by Zebediah Abbott, and he didn't care.

He prioritized his own wants and needs over the truth.

The crankiness and aversions to folks in town were probably triggered by guilt or, worse, a refusal to let people close for fear they would discover he didn't belong on the land.

And when I showed up on his doorstep, he had no choice but to double down on the lie he'd lived for decades. Of course, he wanted it to be mine after he was gone. But it wasn't his to give—

"Hey ..."

My muscles tense at the sound of her voice.

I turn toward the entrance to the gazebo and rest my eyes on Kennedy. She stands like an angelic vision on the steps, holding an umbrella over her head. Her dark skinny jeans and tank top amplify her gorgeous curves. There's no doubt she's as beautiful as ever, but the rush I used to feel being around her has diminished.

I look at her but can't find any words to say.

I'm not ready for this conversation, but it's happening whether I like it or not.

"I'm sorry to bother you," Kennedy says, fumbling with her words. "I was at the bridal boutique with Yolanda and saw you head to the park … not that I was looking for you. I was looking for you … eventually, but not tonight specifically. I was just gazing out the window … and … " She pauses and takes a deep breath.

"It's fine." My words are monotone. I push the hood of my windbreaker off my head and lean back onto the bench. She steps onto the gazebo, resting her umbrella on the white wooden planked floor.

"I know I'm the last person you want to see right now," she says, then reaches into her purse. She lifts out a stapled stack of papers.

My chuckle has no mirth. "More papers from your purse? I don't have the energy for another one of your surprises."

"I'm hoping this time will be different," she says.

"Whatever it is, I don't want to know."

"Please, hear me out."

I recognize that defiant, determined look in her eyes. She's strong and fierce, qualities that make her a phenomenal woman … for someone other than me. Not in the mood to battle with her and knowing she'd win anyway, I acquiesce.

"Go ahead," I say, becoming unsettled by the compassion in her eyes. The tenderness I see reflected back at me that I can't return.

"We were dealt a crappy hand with this land situation. Now that it's behind us—"

"Behind … us?" I scoff. "Nothing is behind me, Kennedy. All that's ahead of me is the daunting task of packing up my whole life and figuring out where to land next. Glad to hear you're moving on. I'm not there yet."

"That's not what I meant. You don't have to twist this around to make me the bad guy. All I wanted was to get to the truth, no matter what."

"Yeah, no matter what was sacrificed to do that," I say, a dull ache building in my heart for what could've been between us. Kennedy was perfect for me until she did the one thing that hurt the most—took away my life here in Kimbell.

A flash of regret and disappointment crosses her face as she avoids looking at me. "I didn't come here to upset you." She looks down at the papers in her hand. "I know you're probably thinking about finding another place to live in town, but I have an alternative for you to consider. I'd like to sell part of the land to you," she says. "The house, the hammock, the tree swing, Diamond Lake, and the barn sit on five acres of the property. Your grandfather sold my grandmother five acres. I'd like to extend the same offer to you …"

I squeeze my eyes shut as her kindness pierces the cloak of disappointment around me. She, more than anyone, knows the parts of that land I hold most dear. Of course, she would be generous and try to make this easier for me. Did I really expect anything less? Maybe this specific offer didn't come to mind, but I can't say I'm surprised that Kennedy was still thinking of me as she celebrated her win.

When I open my eyes, the sales agreement is resting on my lap. "That's a sweet gesture. I truly appreciate it," I say, my words careful and measured. "But I'm not interested in buying any of the land."

Her eyes grow wide. "It's a fair price. I promise. It might feel weird buying land you thought was yours." She tucks her hair behind her ears and takes a step closer. "I could give it to you if that's easier."

"Nothing about this is easy," I say. How could she possibly understand the torture I'd go through living so close to her. The tug-of-war I'd fight daily with my conflicting emotions, wanting her one minute and needing to be far away from her the next. It's too much for me. The only way to solve the problem is to start over someplace new. "I've had time to think over the past few days since the hearing. I'm leaving. Moving away from Kimbell. At least for a while."

"No. This is your home," Kennedy says. In an instant, she's sitting next to me, her hand resting on my thigh. "You can't leave. Not because of this."

I don't know if this is the judge's ruling or the end of what could've been between me and Kennedy, but both warrant a need to move on.

"I don't have a home in Kimbell anymore. It's too hard to keep living here. I said I'd be off your property days ago, but I need the sixty days to settle everything and move out."

Kennedy is silent, her mahogany eyes imploring and pleading for a different answer. One I can't give.

"Where are you going?" She asks.

"Some place where I can start over," I say. The only answer I can give to a question that has no answer.

"I'm so sorry," she says.

"Don't be. I'll be fine," I say, then add, "thanks again for the offer. It means a lot even if I can't take you up on it."

"Okay ..." she looks stunned. Standing, she crosses the gazebo and picks up her umbrella. "But if you change your mind ..."

"I won't."

She nods slowly, then walks out of the gazebo toward Main Street. I watch her grow smaller and smaller in the distance until I can't see her anymore. The tension eases from my muscles. I drop my head in my hands and say a silent prayer for an escape from this situation. One where I can find happiness again—

"Lucas Lorenzo Diamond, you can't avoid me forever ..."

CHAPTER 40

L UKE

~

Lifting my head, my gaze falls on the piercing green eyes of Madeleine Rice. Eyes exactly like mine, the only physical attribute I inherited from her. Too bad the rest of me is one hundred percent her—from her innovative problem-solving skills to her never-met-a-stranger personality to her boundless compassion for the underserved. We're exactly the same that way.

She stands where Kennedy had been, wearing an expensive trench coat over dark slacks and sensible heels. Long waves of brown hair cascade over her shoulder. A hint of a smile curves her lips.

What's with this night?

Forcing me to be with the two women I'd rather avoid.

Stuffing the sales agreement into an inner pocket of my jacket, I say, "Madeleine. Surprised to see you in town so early. The fundraiser isn't until Saturday."

"When David Bell mentioned a legal case that involves my son, I figured I could spare a couple of days to come down and check on you." She walks into the gazebo and sits on the wooden bench directly across from me. Ten feet separate us for the first time in years.

"I'm fine."

"Tell me what happened," Madeleine says.

Her request is familiar and comforting, reminding me of old times we shared before I found out the truth. My anger wavers. My staunch wall of defense crumbles. After seeing Kennedy, I don't have the energy to fight. Instead, I take Madeleine through every detail of the land dispute, from stopping Kennedy from falling on the slick grass in Bell Park to racing out of the courtroom after Judge Barnes had given her ruling.

"Interesting ..." Madeleine says, then cocks her head to the side. "Is there more?"

"Well, Kennedy offered to sell me part of the land. Not a big chunk, just all the parts that mean the most to me." I rake my hand through my hair. "I turned her down."

"Because the price was too steep?"

"I can't live next to the woman who ..." my voice trails off, knowing I'm getting into territory I don't want to share with Madeleine.

"Made you fall in love with her."

"Where are you getting that from?"

"From you, Luke. If you could've heard yourself telling the story of the last month or so. Kennedy this and Kennedy that. You didn't talk about her like she was an enemy trying to wrestle the land from you. You admire and adore her. And because in love, you're much more like your father than me, I just put the pieces together."

"None of that matters because we were destined to fail. I wish I hadn't even gotten close to her." A pang of regret slices through me, intense and jarring. Keeping Kennedy at arm's length had never been my plan, even though I knew our situation was impossible. I was too attracted, too intrigued, too drawn to her. I didn't think things through rationally and objectively like I should have.

And this is the result.

A hollow ache in my chest from missing her filled with a burning anger at her for taking my land away.

"Do you really?"

I pause as her question rattles around in my brain. Knowing how things turned out, would I give up all the memories of the times I shared with Kennedy? It bothers me that an answer isn't clear, but I force my thoughts away.

"Well, you see I'm fine, and it's getting late." I stand, in no mood to let the conversation continue.

"Why don't you walk me back to Crockett Manor? David offered to host me at his home, but it's far from town and the people. I want to be in the community and meet the townsfolk, so I booked a room at the bed and breakfast instead." She rises and walks toward me, unwilling to take no for an answer.

I can't really turn her down since I'm rooming there myself. I shrug, then fall into step with her as we exit the gazebo. The rain has stopped, and a brisk, warm wind blows. An uncomfortable silence settles on us.

After several more minutes, Madeleine clears her throat and asks, "Were you ever going to respond to my texts?"

I don't look at her as I respond. "Probably not."

"Well, that's honest. I would have left you alone but then I found out my husband went behind my back to ask you to join my campaign team," she explains. "At first, I was furious, considering what happened the last time we worked together."

"You mean when I overheard you and my father conspiring to keep me in the dark about you being my mother?"

"Not my finest moment."

"And asking me to lie about how and when I found out about you being my mother. How does that rank on your list of finest moments?" Anger laces my words.

"Tops the list of most regrettable," Madeleine says. "I had everything at that moment—a landslide political win with my son at the helm of my campaign driving me to victory. I'd mentored you since you were a teenager. We'd grown close over the years. I didn't want to lose that. I panicked, trying to find a way to keep it all. But, of course, that backfired, and you walked away. As you should have."

"That close relationship was built on a lie—I had no clue that the woman who was my hero was also my mother. It could've changed things if you'd had the courage to tell me back then."

"I know, and I'm so sorry."

I stop and look at her. The sincerity in her gaze rattles me. I'm blindsided, reeling, and unable to respond.

"Your father thought it was a mistake for me to swoop in and try to be a mother. He warned me that things wouldn't turn out like I dreamed, but I wanted to be more than the person writing the checks for your private school tuition. When I heard about this visionary kid who'd already been a force for change at the high school, winning class president elections and working with the administration to uplift and make student life better, I knew it was you. I had to meet you."

"And I'd always wanted to meet you," I admit. "I remember seeing you on the news, working in the community, helping, and never asking for anything in return. I wanted to do the same thing for people."

"It's crazy that I didn't raise you, but you're so much like me. Except you would never have lied like I did. I let you down. I know that. I live with that every day. But I won't let you down again. I will own up to everything I did in the past and accept the consequences."

"The consequences could ruin your chances of winning the primary," I say. "You made some crappy decisions when it comes to me, but that has nothing to do with all the good you've done in the community. You've been the best mayor that city has ever seen, backing up every one of your campaign promises with real action that made a difference. You can do the same thing with the state as governor if this ... scandal doesn't get in the way."

A bright smile spreads across her face. "You've been keeping tabs on me?"

"I worked hard on that campaign. I needed to make sure you didn't botch it once I was gone. I was glad to see that you didn't. You continued to be the same Madeleine Rice who inspired me as a teenager and young adult."

"Just not so inspiring as a mother." Her smile fades. "Anyway, like I was saying. I was upset at first when Herbert reached out to you, but then I realized my campaign could use your political savvy and strategic thinking."

A spark of excitement flares beneath my devastation. The prospect of diving back into the political world. One that had been a driving force in my life years ago. A career I left behind not for professional reasons but because of personal disappointments. Leaving Kimbell has already moved to the top of my to-do list, even though I have no idea where I'll go. This could be the answer I'm looking for.

She continues, "You've always had an inherent knack for this and the right balance to ensure every move you make is for good. You're never tempted to cut corners or play nasty political games."

"And it wouldn't hurt the campaign as much if I was working for you if the truth came out about me being your son," I say.

"You'd work behind the scenes as a consultant. I meant what I said. I will own my mistakes and the truth if it comes out." She sighs. "But we both know my chances of winning the primary run-off aren't good."

"We also both know this can't possibly be your end game."

"Told you. That brilliant political mind of yours."

"This is the right step to increase your notoriety across the state. I'm guessing you'll give it a hard push for lieutenant governor in four years, which you'll have no problem winning. Then after that, you'll target ... what?"

"U.S. Senate."

I nod, impressed.

"You could come along for the ride. Especially since you might need a break from this town," Madeleine says. "Then you could return here refreshed and step into your real destiny."

"What does that mean?"

"You should set your sights on being mayor of the town. I was only here for a few hours, but everywhere I went, people gushed about you without being prompted. The current mayor isn't as popular as you are."

"I don't know ..." I look away. It's not a bad suggestion. Just horrendous timing. I don't want anything that could tether me tighter to this town. I've lost everything that truly mattered—my normalcy, land, and sense of belonging. It all slipped away with one ruling from a judge.

"I could give you the money to buy that land from Kennedy, or you could take a break from this town to work on the campaign with me. That will give you time to figure out your next move."

The idea of working with Madeleine again should be repugnant. But instead, I'm intrigued and ... interested. "Why are you doing this?"

"Because I've never seen you look this lost. Whether you like it or not, I'm your mother. I want to be your mother. And this is what mothers do."

"A change of scenery might be good," I say, but don't tell her I had already planned to move on. "It's too hard to be in Kimbell right now."

"Too hard to be in Kimbell or too hard to be near Kennedy?"

"Both, maybe?"

"So, let's get you some distance."

"But if I do this, we can't sit around and wait for the truth to be discovered. We should go on the offensive and release the story ourselves. That way, it elevates your media profile and quickly fades as a non-event."

"I don't want to put you through that."

"As your political consultant, I'd insist that it be done. And I know the perfect journalist to break the story," I say, thinking of Ciara Thompson.

"Well, this particular political consultant has never steered me wrong." Madeleine smiles. "I'd love to have you on my team, but you must be convinced it's what you truly want."

CHAPTER 41

ENNEDY

~

"AND THAT'S HOW DAD ENDED UP WEARING MOM'S favorite dress to the grocery store grand opening," I say, doubling over with laughter as pain pierces my side. The guffaws from Yolanda and Vangie are louder than mine. "Needless to say, Mom wasn't too happy about that public display of affection."

"Your poor dad." Yolanda chuckles, dabbing at a tear in the corner of her eye. "Do you think he'll ever move on? Try to find love with someone new?"

Vangie scoffs. "Never! That man is incredibly stubborn."

"And not easy to get along with. Combine that with the ridiculous hours he works at the grocery store, and it would take a special woman to put up with him," I say as my chuckles subside. "But we could be wrong."

"Well, I can definitely say I'm glad I was wrong about you," Vangie says, jumping up from the couch to grab a handful of fried catfish nuggets.

"Wrong about me? What does that mean?" I ask.

It's Saturday night, and I didn't want to be alone. So I invited my two favorite people in the world over for a late-night movie marathon with enough food to make us all gain five pounds. I probably went overboard with the fried delicacies. Along with the fish, I made fried green tomatoes, fried pickles, onion rings, and fried apple turnovers for dessert.

Nothing says indulgence better than a Texas-fried meal.

"When you texted us, I thought we'd find you in a pool of tears. I have a value pack of tissues in my trunk and slices of cucumber in a Ziplock bag in my purse to treat your puffy eyes from crying all day. No lie. But you don't need either one. You seem to be handling everything as best as can be expected," Vangie says. "I'm proud of you."

"Is she really getting sappy over there?" I turn to Yolanda. "Wait! Are you getting mushy, too?"

Yolanda says, "Kennedy, the last time we talked to you was after Luke turned down your offer to sell him part of the land back. My heart broke for you because we all know you did that out of love. To have it dismissed so quickly by him had to be devastating."

Vangie adds, "But you know what's not devastating? You can sell that land to Zaire now and put millions in your bank account. That'll get you over heartbreak or at least distract you from it."

"How are you so together about all this?" Yolanda asks.

I inhale a deep breath and ponder the question. They aren't wrong. I'm at peace about how things have turned out or not turned out between Luke and me. I could tell he was touched by my offer but couldn't hide that it wasn't enough to change things for him. Deep down, I knew I had to respect that and move on.

Finally, I say, "I think it's because of something your good friend Zaire told me."

"Oh goodness, what did she say?" Yolanda asks.

"She told me that I should make the offer to Luke myself. Not through Lance. And that if he turned it down, I'd know I did everything I could to mend things between us." I reach for a fried pickle spear and take a bite. "There's no doubt it was a long shot for Luke to get past me owning the land he thought was his. What man could ignore that and still be interested, you know? But I gave it my best try, and I failed."

"No, ma'am! You did not fail. Luke is the only failure here because he's too caught up in his feelings to realize that he could have the best of both worlds," Vangie says, flopping back down on the couch.

"Vangie, what are you talking about? He doesn't own anything anymore. No land. No house. How can you spin that into something positive?" Yolanda asks.

"If he followed his heart, that would lead him to Kennedy," Vangie responds. "And Kennedy is the new owner of a lot of land that's important to him, which she would freely share. So, he wouldn't have lost anything in the end. In fact, he would've added an incredible, beautiful, intelligent woman to his life. That's real winning."

I frown as I finish off the pickle spear. "You have a good point," I admit.

Yolanda concedes with a shrug. "He's smart but not smart enough to figure that out."

"Honestly, I think this rattled him so much because he never thought, not once, that he would come out on the losing end," I say. "I mean, how many times did we sit together talking about every possible outcome—good or bad. I was prepared no matter what happened."

Vangie shakes her head. "Nothing could prepare you for Luke leaving town for good because of this. That never came up in any of our scenarios."

"Please do not tell anyone!" I give my cousins a stern look. "I don't think it's public knowledge yet."

"When I met up with Zaire today, she didn't mention anything about Luke leaving town. But she did say that Luke may take on an additional job as a political consultant for that woman who's running for governor. Can't remember her name," Yolanda says.

"Madeleine Rice!" Vangie screams. "I need you to care more about the candidates and who could potentially control our state."

"I'll care when it's time to vote in November," Yolanda insists.

"Are you sure Luke is going back into politics?" I ask, mind racing. What could have happened in one week that would have caused Luke to reconcile with his mother? They've been estranged for five years. Still, when he talked about her, there was always an air of awe, reverence, and fondness for Madeleine. Despite her lies, some part of Luke still looks up to her.

"The information came from Wiley, so who knows," Yolanda says.

"Well, here's what I think," Vangie says. "Luke would've jumped at your offer if this was just about the land. All the places he loved most on the property were on those five acres, except the orchards, of course."

"I agree. This is about you, Kennedy. He's torn up because the woman he was starting to fall for is the same one who took the land away. That's what he can't get over," Yolanda says.

"I don't disagree," I say, in no mood to debate a point that won't change anything.

"But you don't seem upset about it either," Vangie says. "Why aren't you doing more to fight for Luke?"

"Because he's not doing more to fight for me. This isn't like the relationships I had in the past. He didn't wake up and realize there was some flaw in my personality or behavior he couldn't stand. He knew this lawsuit was hanging over our heads. So, the fact that he's unwilling to get past this says a lot," I say. "I truly care about him, and that's not going away any time soon. But this isn't another tally under the Kennedy the Dumpee column. I'm okay."

"So, you wouldn't be interested in trying to talk things out with him one more time?" Yolanda asks.

"There's no point—"

"Yes, there is!" Vangie says. "Your last conversation with him was all about property and contracts and deeds and monetary transactions. It wasn't about what matters the most—the connection the two of you have. I don't think it's gone."

Yolanda nods her head. "Neither do I."

"I cannot believe you two. I'm finally okay with the end of a relationship that never actually became one, and y'all aren't satisfied. Do you want him to break my heart? Because I promise you, if I do what you ask, that's exactly what'll happen." I push off the couch and stalk toward the bookshelf lined with figurines.

Vangie races to my side. "Don't you think this is why Zaire pushed you to make the offer yourself? It wasn't just to literally make the sales offer. It was to put the two of you in the same place so you could talk about what really mattered. The beautiful future you could share if you two fools would get out of your own way!"

Yolanda approaches me from the opposite side. "Vangie's right. You didn't quite follow Zaire's advice. But you might have another shot to do that before Luke leaves."

"Really? How?" I ask.

Vangie whispers, "The date auction."

Yolanda giggles. "It's starting in an hour. We have plenty of time to get glammed up and make it."

"Wait … you want me to bid on a date with Luke, so he'll be forced to spend time with me?"

"Exactly!" Vangie and Yolanda say in unison.

"And because half the proceeds are going to charity, if you win the date fair and square, he would follow through," Yolanda says.

"It's the perfect solution," Vangie insists.

"I don't know about this …" I say.

"Well, let's just say there are some other guys in the auction that Yolanda or I might want to bid on. You can come along and decide later if you're going to bid on Luke," Vangie says.

I ask, "Who are y'all going to bid on?"

"Mr. June and Mr. November will be up for auction. I'm focused on them," Yolanda says.

"And I have my eyes on the Baker Brothers. Dillon added them to the auction with the firefighter hunks. Any of them would suit me just fine," Vangie says, winking. "What do you say?"

"Fine, I'll go. But no promises about bidding on Luke."

CHAPTER 42

L UKE

~

I SIT ON THE COUNTER THAT LINES ONE SIDE OF THE hallway, which connects the kitchen of Baker Bros BBQ to the restaurant dining room. Normally, this space would be bustling with waitresses and busboys carrying plates of hot food. Tonight, the area is packed with a different kind of hotness. The kind that's driving a packed dining room of hundreds of screaming women from all across Texas wild.

I listen as the bachelors who've already been auctioned give advice to others still waiting for their time in the spotlight. Most of the suggestions are hilarious but some are worthy enough that I take note.

"What's the latest tally?" Asa Baker asks, wiping his hands on his apron.

I look up at the oldest of the triplets who own Baker Bros BBQ, the one known for running the back of the house and keeping the team of cooks on task with optimal effectiveness to crank out dish after dish for the demanding crowds.

"Getting close to twenty-five thousand by my rough count." Tracking the winning bids of each bachelor in the date auction was a welcomed distraction, at least in the beginning. My concentration has waned as it gets closer to my turn on the auction block.

Asa looks pleased with my response.

The kitchen door swings open, and Rusty Baker, the middle Baker triplet, walks through like a man headed for the guillotine. He stops next to Asa. "I'm nervous. I shouldn't be nervous, but I am. Like, I wish I'd gotten it over with early like you did, Asa. Then this would be behind me, and I could go back to doing what I do best ... smoking brisket." Rusty's award-winning brisket has put the restaurant on the map. Rumor has it that only the triplets know Rusty's complex seasoning recipe and smoking technique to keep the crowds coming back for more.

Before I can respond, the youngest triplet, Chaz Baker, joins us from the restaurant. As the marketing guru and official face of the restaurant, he's been stirring up excitement for the date auction and the restaurant all week. Hopping on the counter next to me, Chaz says, "If the lady who won the date with Asa is any indication, I don't think there's anything to be nervous about. She's quite the looker."

Asa says, "She drove all the way from Lubbock for this. Can't say I'm mad about that at all. It'll be a fun date."

Chaz grips the back of his brother's neck. "Relax, Rusty. There's not a troll in the place."

Laughter erupts from my mouth. "Chaz, you're horrible."

"Did I offend your sensitive ears, Mr. Diamond?" Chaz quips, giving me a side-eye. Turning back to Rusty, he says, "Now, just work the angles a bit." Chaz jumps down from the counter to thrust and roll his hips. "Make sure you bring in at least five hundred bucks. This is partially for charity, after all. Don't forget that."

"Charity, right. Five hundred bucks," Rusty says, stiffly mimicking Chaz's moves as he grows pale. As the introvert of the triplets, I'm not surprised he's got stage fright. The exact opposite of Chaz, who never seems to be able to get enough attention.

Chaz unbuttons Rusty's shirt, tosses a small bottle of baby oil at his brother, and then mimes how to rub it over his chest.

"You'll be fine, Rusty," I say, encouraging him as he's the next bachelor up for auction.

The door that leads to the restaurant opens, but it's not the return of the last bachelor from the stage. Nate pushes through the crowd of guys, yanking at the tie around his neck. He makes a beeline toward me. If looks could kill, I'd be six feet under.

"Seriously? You drop a bomb like this over a text message? What is wrong with you?" Nate asks.

Chaz, Asa, and Rusty look back and forth between me and Nate, confused.

"Why don't we discuss this outside?" I jump down from the counter and lead Nate to the back alley. Smoke billows toward the sky from the massive smokehouse twice the size of the restaurant.

"You're leaving," Nate says, throwing his arms up.

I turn slowly and look at my best friend. "You're disappointed that I'm going to work with Madeleine again after everything that happened five years ago."

"Am I disappointed that you're finally going to spend time with your mother and try to rebuild the trust that was broken between the two of you? Absolutely not," Nate says, glaring at me as if I had two heads. "Luke, this is the woman you watched on television as a kid, wishing for a mother like her. I know how much Madeleine means to you despite her lies. Having a complicated relationship with my own mother, I'm not one to judge."

"So why are you so upset?"

"Besides the fact that my best friend is abandoning me?" Nate leans against the wall, pounding it with his fist.

"You know a few hundred miles won't change anything between us. Nothing will stop us from being as close as brothers. Plus, like I said in my text, I'm not sure I'll be gone for good. After the primaries in May, I might come back to Kimbell."

"But that's not what you're going to tell Ronan tomorrow," Nate says. "You're not asking for a leave of absence. You're quitting the fire department."

"Would it be easier if I asked for a leave of absence instead?"

"What would make it easier is if you stopped running every time a woman in your life disappoints you," Nate says.

I bristle. "What are you talking about?"

"This sudden shift back to politics and moving away from town has nothing to do with losing the court case and everything to do with Kennedy Tarkington."

"She's the reason I lost the land."

"Don't be obtuse. The court case is why you feel you have no choice but to walk away from Kennedy even though every part of you wants to be with that woman," Nate says. "You love her, idiot."

I don't deny it. "Sometimes love isn't enough."

"It's the same thing you did with Madeleine. Instead of staying put and doing the hard work to forge a new relationship with your mother, you ran away. Now, five years later, you're doing what you should've done back then. I just hope it doesn't take you five years to come to your senses about Kennedy. She's been unlucky in love, but with Dillon back, she might be married to the guy before you realize your mistake."

A surge of jealousy roars through me. "She would never marry Dillon."

"Who knows what she's open to now that you're being a jerk to her? Can you imagine how hard it was for her to offer to sell part of the land to you? Wiley told us Zaire came up with a fair price for the property she knew you could afford at Kennedy's request. And what do you do? Throw it back in her face like it meant nothing."

"I didn't throw it back at her literally. I thanked her for doing it, but …"

"But nothing," Nate says. "I need to get back to your mother's fundraiser. Try not to make any more boneheaded moves while I'm gone."

I lean against the cool brick wall, letting out a long breath. Nate's accusation echoes in my mind, forcing me to confront the pattern I've been blind to. I've always prided myself on facing challenges head-on, but maybe I've been fooling myself all along. Maybe he's right—maybe I'm running ... again.

The door bangs open. Dillon pokes his head out. "Hey Luke, you ready? You're almost up, and the ladies are about to go crazy."

"Yeah, I'm ready." And that's a complete lie.

CHAPTER 43

K ENNEDY

"SHOULD I JUST GIVE UP?" YOLANDA RANTS, SLAMMING HER
bidding paddle on the table.

Vangie glares at the raucous crowd of women seated at tables behind us. "We're outnumbered. These city girls have descended on this place like vultures. They have big purses and even bigger pocketbooks, and they're trying to take our men!"

"Calm down, ladies," I chuckle, sipping Elm beer. Despite my initial hesitation, I'm glad my cousins dragged me out of the house to attend the bachelor date auction. The all-you-can-eat barbecue has been stellar, and the auction wildly entertaining. "At least we got the hometown perks of one of the best tables in the restaurant."

It's true. At the table to my right, Mya, a client and new friend whose personal fitness business is taking off, sits next to Kimbell librarian, Odalis, and ER nurse Avril. To my left, the best cooks of

227

Kimbell are crowded around a table: Raven and Brianna representing Elevation Cupcakes, Ivy representing Gwen's Country Café, and Fiora from Resviglio Italian Restaurant.

Kimbell women are at all the front tables with the best vantage of the stage and the delicious parade of men.

"That's the fifth guy I've lost out on. Mr. November from the calendar. I really wanted that guy," Yolanda complains as she yanks a piece of rib meat from the bone and stuffs it in her mouth.

"Yeah," I say, wrapping my arm around her shoulder. "You just didn't want him enough to drop thirteen hundred dollars on a date with him."

"Absolutely not." she shakes her head. "I don't care if half the money is going to charity. That's just too much."

Vangie says, "I completely agree. I wanted to bid on Asa Baker, but the bids got out of hand before I could jump in. There's no way I was spending six hundred bucks for a date with him."

I pick at a brisket burnt end, wondering how I'll feel when Luke gets on the stage. "I still haven't decided if I'm going to bid on Luke," I admit. "He might not want me to ..."

"Don't overthink it," Vangie advises. "Just go with your gut instincts when the time comes. Now, let's see how much the last Baker brother will command from the crowd."

"Talk about swoon-worthy," Yolanda says, fanning herself. "Adding the triplets to the auction block was one of Dillon's better ideas."

Vangie reaches for a napkin and pretends to faint. "They are drop-dead gorgeous. I predict the blonde from Grapevine will pull out all the stops to win since she lost out on the other two."

"I bet you're right," I say, glancing back at the woman who looks ready to charge the stage.

Dillon says, "Alright ladies, the second to last man up for auction is the youngest of the Baker triplets by nine minutes. Guess he really didn't want to be out of the womb—"

Chaz grabs the mic and says, "I just wanted to make a grand entrance. Saving the best for last."

Cat calls, and hollers ring out from the ladies.

Dillon laughs, then adds, "He is co-owner of this fine dining establishment, which has graciously agreed to host our festivities this evening. Chaz likes extreme couponing, training squirrels to do tricks, and perfecting his impressions of every Disney prince. Rules are the same. You get six months to plan and complete your date with Chaz. All dates must cost our bachelors less than two hundred dollars and take place in Kimbell. Got it?"

The crowd cheers in answer.

"Alright, let's start the bid at one hundred dollars," Dillon says.

The music starts and Chaz jumps from the stage to work the crowd. Maneuvering through the room, he pauses as women pull him into hugs and take selfies with him, all the while driving the bids higher.

"He's good ..." Yolanda says. "I think every woman in the room has put a bid on him."

Dillon continues to call out bids, increasing in ten-dollar increments until the bidding hits six hundred forty dollars, and Chaz Baker is covered in lipstick kisses on his face and arms.

"Can I get six hundred fifty?" Dillon asks. Murmurs ripple through the crowd. The Beaumont blonde looks eager to claim her prize as the last highest bidder.

Chaz walks back up to the edge of the stage and turns toward the crowd. His gaze lands on our table, but he's not looking at all of us.

Just my cousin, Vangie.

He walks over and kneels down in front of her. "Did you bid on me?"

Vangie flushes, eyes wide in shock as she shakes her head.

Chaz gives her a sexy smile. "I think you should ..."

The crowd goes wild, chanting Vangie's name.

For the first time, my brash and boisterous cousin is speechless.

Dillon eggs her on. "How about it, Vangie? Will you bid six hundred fifty for the incomparable Chaz Baker?"

The chemistry between Chaz and Vangie sizzles through the air. Yolanda and I exchange excited looks.

Vangie reaches for her auction paddle, fumbling it before raising it. "Six fifty," she says.

Chaz winks at her, then jumps onto the stage. Grabbing the mic from Dillon, he says, "Sold to the beautiful woman in orange." Blowing a kiss at Vangie, he drops the mic and disappears into the dark hallway.

"OMG …" Vangie sputters. "What just happened?"

Yolanda and I jump up and hug her.

"Looks like you got your Baker brother after all," I say.

Vangie gets high-fives from the women around our table, then we settle back into our seats.

"Now for the moment you've been waiting for," Dillon announces to the crowd. "Mr. March himself … Luke Diamond!"

The sound is deafening as Luke emerges from the dark hallway and steps onto the stage. Cheers, chants, and delighted screams erupt from the women in the restaurant as if Luke is some kind of star, which I suppose he is. A small town, viral social media sensation since the calendar was released. His photos on the Firefighter Hunks garnered the most likes and shares, but I don't think we were prepared for this.

Definitely not me or my heart, which seems to be beating a mile a minute, threatening to burst from my chest. I'm thankful nurse Avril is nearby in case I pass out.

My gaze lingers on Luke, dressed in dark cargo pants and a neon yellow firefighter windbreaker, as he waves and smiles at the crowd. A tasteful view of his bare chest peeks through his open jacket. He's the most beautiful man I've ever laid eyes on.

A man who captured my heart and made me feel hopeful about falling in love again.

A man who could've been mine.

Before the judge's ruling on the land stole my hope away.

But maybe Yolanda and Vangie are right. Maybe I should try one more time to see if the feelings Luke and I developed for each other can be salvaged.

Feelings?

Who am I kidding?

I fell in love with Luke. More importantly, I have no doubt that he fell in love with me first.

That's got to be worth fighting for.

As Dillon starts the bidding at five hundred dollars, my arm shoots into the air. Vangie and Yolanda hoot next to me, clapping their hands in delight.

I look up at the stage and see Luke staring back at me.

The emotion in his eyes says it all as a wide grin spreads across his lips. We lock eyes. It's as if we are the only two people in the room. A mischievous twinkle in those emerald orbs urges me on. He wants me to win the auction.

Emboldened, I glance at my cousins for support, then hunker down to win the date with Luke no matter what. The minutes pass in a blur as Luke quickly surpasses the highest paid for any other man in the auction. Ivy, Odalis and a woman from Beaumont are my biggest competition. I'm not deterred. Every time I rise to the challenge and bid higher, I get a jolt from the excited look in Luke's eyes. He struts across the stage, urging the crowd for higher bids, but there's no denying that his gaze lingers on me far too often and far too long to mean anything else. We want the same thing right now.

More minutes pass, and Ivy drops out of the bidding.

"Sixty-five hundred!" The not-so-frumpy librarian says, waving her paddle in the air. Odalis is proving to be a bigger threat than I realized. Who knew she was this interested in Luke?

"Seven thousand five hundred!" Beaumont woman calls out, increasing the bid by a thousand.

"Why won't these chicks give up?" Vangie whispers angrily. "Everyone here can see Luke wants you to win the bid."

It's true. The Kimbell women have been cheering me on in hopes that winning the bid will heal the rift the lawsuit caused in town. They have no clue how much more this will mean.

Luke glances at me. He knows the price is getting steep. A tilt of his head tells me he'd understand if I bowed out.

Instead, I say calmly, "Eight thousand."

The claps and cheers go wild in the restaurant. Odalis shakes her head in surrender, then pretends to bow down to me. Beaumont woman slams her auction paddle onto the table and claps with the rest of the women. My bid for Luke is twice the previous highest bid. But he's most definitely worth it.

"That's eight thousand," Dillon says, scanning the crowd as he paces the room. "Going once. Going twice."

A jangle of the chimes on the entrance door to the restaurant pierces the air.

"Twenty thousand dollars."

All eyes jerk toward the door. You can hear a pin drop as we see Ciara Thompson, Channel 4 News for You Houston reporter, and Kimbell's darling, standing at the door. "And don't even think about challenging me, ladies. There's no way I'm leaving here without a date with this man."

The crowd goes wild as Luke beams.

Ciara jumps onto the stage and wraps Luke in her arms. He returns the embrace. They stand there looking like a celebrity couple. Women all over the restaurant whip out their cell phones and take pictures.

Dillon jumps excitedly. "Sold to Ciara Thompson!"

Lowering my auction paddle, the smile fades from my face.

I'm not the only former love interest hoping for a reunion with Luke.

I'm just the losing one.

CHAPTER 44

L UKE

~

Tugging the baseball cap lower, I slip sunglasses over my eyes and head in the opposite direction of the town center. Taking the long route from Crockett Manor to the Fire Station is my only hope of avoiding the throngs of women who stayed overnight in Kimbell after the date auction. It was a massive success, bringing in over fifty thousand dollars. Half of the money will be donated to the charities of the bachelors' choice. The Kimbell Community Center will get a ten thousand dollar donation thanks to Ciara Thompson.

But the best part of the night for me was Kennedy sitting at a table near center stage. Her long, thick tresses were pulled into a genie ponytail on her head, showcasing her breathtaking face. I couldn't take my eyes off her. Nate's warnings went off like sirens in my head. The only question I kept asking myself was ... what are you doing?

Do I really want to leave Kennedy behind to be a political

consultant for Madeleine? Will that make me happy? Or am I avoiding what I really want because I don't see a way for Kennedy and me to be together after she won the legal battle?

As Kennedy's auction paddle raised in the air when Dillon asked for the opening bid, I felt a surge of conflicting emotions. The fact that she openly bid on me, not caring what the townsfolk would think about her actions, touched my soul. At that moment, as we locked eyes, I questioned everything I'd told Nate.

Love not being enough?

I'm not so sure about that.

Every time Kennedy increased the bid to win the date with me, I felt a pull to be close to her again. I imagined our date and all the things in my heart I'd finally get to tell her …

Until Ciara showed up.

"The route to work is good, but that disguise needs a lot of work."

I smile and turn to face Ciara. "You're a stellar reporter. It's time they stop giving you fluff pieces and let you handle tougher assignments."

Ciara grins. "Already in motion. I was going to fill you in last night, but the autograph session with the ladies lasted too long. I figured the best shot I had of talking to you would be this morning before you got to work."

"That was an extremely generous bid. I get the feeling your motives weren't entirely altruistic … or romantic," I say.

"Correct on both accounts. I think every woman in the place knows that something deeper is going on between you and Kennedy Tarkington despite what happened with the legal case. I won't be cashing in on my date, so she can have it if you like," Ciara says. "Care to fill me in?"

"I'd rather not," I admit, then head along the sidewalk toward town.

Ciara falls into step next to me. "No problem. Small-town love isn't exactly newsworthy."

"But Madeleine Rice's push to win a surprise primary run-off is," I say, guessing Ciara's real reason for returning to her hometown. "Can't believe the station assigned you to cover a fundraiser."

"They didn't. I paid out of pocket for a ticket to be there."

"And between that exorbitant cost and the twenty thousand you dropped on a date that you have no plans of doing with me, was it worth it?"

"Depends on how you answer my next question." Ciara gives me a sly look.

"You found out, didn't you?" My heart thuds in my chest as I wait to hear her response.

She nods. "You have a connection to Madeleine that could benefit my career. As her former campaign manager, you could introduce me to her. Maybe even an interview. All I got last night was an obligatory thanks for contributing and platitudes. I need this. If I can get even a short interview with Madeleine, it could change everything for me at the news station. Will you help me? Please?"

I relax as I realize Ciara doesn't know the truth about Madeleine and me. Breaking the news that I'm the candidate's son would most definitely put Ciara on the map as a top investigative journalist in the state. But Madeleine still isn't on board about revealing the truth.

And I'm not sure I want to be a political consultant for her run at the primary run-off after Kennedy bid on me at the date auction.

That doesn't mean I can't help Ciara.

"I haven't worked for Madeleine in over five years," I hedge, wondering if this is a good idea or if I'm about to stir up a hornet's nest.

"I heard you were the driving force in getting her elected as mayor. She must have fond memories of the two of you working together. Who wouldn't? You're such an amazingly gifted and kind man," Ciara says. "Maybe it's been a while since the two of you talked, but I'm sure she'd take a call from you. All I need is an introduction. I'll do the rest. You can't make her agree to an interview with me—"

"Actually, I can."

"Seriously?"

"I can get you an interview with Madeleine. Just give me a couple days to set everything up."

"Luke!" Ciara leaps into my arms, wrapping me in a bear hug. "I could kiss you, but I'd like it too much, and knowing that you probably would wish it was Kennedy kissing you instead just doesn't work for me."

I laugh as I lower her back to the ground. "Makes sense."

"You love her?"

"Yeah."

"Does she know?"

"I think so," I say, but that's a lie. I knew when Kennedy fought to win the date with me that she knew how I felt about her. I fell in love with her, and she fell in love with me. What other reason explains her generous offer to sell part of the land back to me? An offer I refused to accept.

Ciara slaps at my arm. "That's not good enough, Luke. The land is just … land. Look, I get it. You and your grandfather shared some good times there. It was your home. But what made it a home wasn't the land. It was the person you shared it with. People mean so much more than material things. Make sure Kennedy knows for sure how you feel about her."

"Love advice from the woman who has no time for love? That's rich."

"Do as I say, not as I do," Ciara retorts. "Do you really think you can get me an interview with Madeleine? You're not just …"

"It's as good as done," I say as we reach the entrance to the fire station. A few of the holdovers from the date auction are standing behind a barricade. They scream my name and wave, frantic for me to come over. "Sorry ladies, I have to be a real firefighter now. No time for autographs or pictures."

They groan in disappointment, then reluctantly walk away.

"Thank you, Luke. I'll pay you back. I promise."

"I think the twenty thousand bid and all the kids the money will help feed over the summer holidays is payment enough."

Ciara hugs me goodbye, then heads toward Gwen's Country Cafe.

I open the side door of the fire station and walk inside.

The alarm blares, and red lights flash on and off.

Racing toward the garage, I arrive just as Ronan, Wiley, Darren, and Nate burst into the space. We change into our gear at warp speed.

"What happened?" I ask.

Ronan's face is grave. "Fire at Oakbrook Senior Living Facility. Five alarms. Not sure all the residents got out. It's going to be a tough one. Let's get going."

I take my place in the fire truck and glance back at the locker.

The resignation letter I typed up to give to Ronan will have to wait.

CHAPTER 45

K ENNEDY

"HAVE YOU DECIDED WHAT YOU WANT TO DO NEXT? YOU know, now that Dillon is moving back to Kimbell," I say as I pour more tea into Mrs. Crockett's cup. The petite sandwiches, scones, and fruit tarts are almost entirely devoured. For a diminutive woman, she has a healthy appetite.

"I'm not leaving Oakbrook if that's what you mean," Mrs. Crockett says, raising an eyebrow. "My son may be turning his life around, but living with him would be foolish. He's a young man trying to re-establish his life. I'm an old woman. I don't want to be a burden, especially since his hopes of getting back together with you aren't going to happen."

I take a few gulps of my tea, knowing where Mrs. Crockett is going next. We've been catching up for the past hour in an attic nook she had designed specifically as a condition for signing a long-term resident agreement at the senior living facility. The place is a serene hideaway with walls painted in soothing pastel hues, adorned with framed pressed flowers, and accented by gilt-framed mirrors reflecting light from crystal sconces. The furniture is a collection of antiques from Crockett Manor, each holding memories of Mrs. Crockett's past.

Our Sundays together revitalize both of us, but I'm not sure I'm ready for a dose of Mrs. Crockett's tough love.

Last night at the date auction, I did what Vangie and Yolanda wanted me to do … followed my heart. I was close to winning the date with Luke until Ciara Thompson showed up with her record-breaking bid. No matter what Luke told me about their relationship, I couldn't shake the feeling that it was similar to how we described ours. There could be so much more between Ciara and Luke than what he told me, considering their intimate embrace after she won the date.

I was too upset to stick around, bolting before the after-auction autograph and picture session with the Firefighter Hunks.

I thought I'd feel better in the morning, but I don't.

The ache in my heart over Luke is growing, and now I wonder if going to the auction was the right thing to do.

"Kennedy, don't go quiet on me," Mrs. Crockett says. "I know all about you bidding on Luke Diamond at the date auction."

"How in the world did you find out?"

"Gossip travels fast in a small town. Most people are proud of you and see it as a gesture to mend things with Luke after the court ruling. But we both know that you bidding on that man is about so much more," Mrs. Crockett says. "I'm guessing you still haven't told him you're in love with him. You wanted to win the date and do it then, but Ciara stopped that. I knew she was up to no good when she left Madeleine Rice's fundraiser dinner early."

"That's why she was in town?"

"You don't think she really came here for some long-lost love of Luke, do you? That woman is too ambitious to be a sucker for love. She was here for one reason—to get an interview with the candidate.

When all her angling and manipulation didn't work, she decided to try a different approach."

"Luke … " I say. But there's no way Ciara knows the truth. She wouldn't need an interview if she knew Madeleine was Luke's mother. That bombshell would be a big enough story to launch her career. "I guess she thought since Luke worked for Madeleine in the past, he could help her get the interview."

"Exactly. So don't let your mind go crazy thinking it's more than that. Luke told you they never got off the ground as a couple, unlike the two of you."

"Technically, we never got off the ground either."

"Just because you kept your relationship a secret from the town doesn't mean the two of you weren't in a relationship. No matter what ridiculous term y'all used to describe it," Mrs. Crockett says.

"Luke didn't look upset when I started bidding on him," I admit, then grab the last scone. "I thought he might be. Our last conversation was so impersonal. I wasn't sure. But instead, he looked … pleased. Happy almost."

"That's good. So what are you going to do about it?"

"Nothing," I say as a decision solidifies in my mind. "I put myself out there last night in front of everybody. I waited, thinking that Luke would call me to talk, but he didn't."

"And you're done making all the moves," Mrs. Crockett nods, understanding. "I don't blame you, Kennedy. Luke really should make the next move. But the truth is, sometimes men are too stupid to realize what they should do."

"He told me he was leaving Kimbell. Maybe if he decides to stay, that could mean … something. I don't know." I shake my head.

"Luke would be a fool to leave town now. But my boneheaded son made that same mistake with you years ago and lived to regret it. Luke could find himself in the same boat—"

"Mrs. Crockett … do you smell that?" I ask, turning toward the door.

She pauses, growing quiet. "Smells like smoke, doesn't it?"

"Wait here. I'll go check it out," I say, rising from my chair. I walk over to the door and reach for the knob. It's warmer than I expected. My heart pounds in my chest as I slowly open the door. Smoke fills the room. I push the door back closed and turn to Mrs. Crockett. She's gone pale as a ghost.

"There's a fire, isn't there?" She asks, her voice trembling.

"I think so," I say. My mind races, trying to figure out what our best move is. We are far away from the rest of the residents, trapped in the attic. Depending on where the blaze is, we may not be able to get out.

Grabbing my phone, my hands shake as I dial 9-1-1. I take a deep breath to steady my voice, then explain our situation to the operator. Seconds later, my worst fears are confirmed as the emergency respondent informs me that a fire has already been called in, and firefighters and EMTs are en route.

The operator says, "Check the hallway. If you don't see the fire, try to exit the building using the pre-determined emergency escape plan."

Following her directions, I open the door and look toward the end of the hallway. Orange flames lap against the wall in the distance. I swallow past the lump in my throat. "I saw a flicker of flames near the stairs leading up to the attic. That's our only way out. It's a long hallway, though. The stairs aren't close to the room we're in. Maybe a hundred feet or so away." The distance does little to comfort me. It's no match for an intense fire.

"Are there windows in the room?" asks the operator.

"No, there are no windows in the room." I turn in a slow circle as if one would magically appear, but I know it won't.

"Do you have access to water?"

"No ..." I say, panic rising within me. "We don't have any water."

Mrs. Crockett waves at me, pointing to the extra pitchers of water we brought up to the nook with us for our tea.

"Wait, yes, we have a limited amount of water," I say.

"Any towels or linens?"

"A tablecloth."

"Good, use the water to wet the tablecloth and stuff it under the door to keep the smoke out," the operator says. "I'll inform the first responders that the two of you are in the attic."

Placing my phone on speaker, I take the additional precautions doled out by the operator. Removing the tablecloth, I drench it in water and put it along the gap under the door. With nothing left to do but wait, I huddle with Mrs. Crockett on the settee as we stare at the door.

"Don't worry, Kennedy. We're going to get you and Mrs. Crockett out of there."

CHAPTER 46

L UKE

~

AN EXPLOSION RIPS THROUGH THE MORNING AIR, HURLING me face-first into the scorched earth. My helmet clatters away as the blast wave rolls over me, thickening the sweltering heat. Even through the layers of my turnout gear, I feel the burning intensity on my skin. Shattered glass rains down in a deadly cascade, bouncing off the sunlit ground and biting into my jacket. I shield my face, squinting against the blinding brightness, and wait until the shower of debris finally stops.

I haul myself up, vision blurred by the smoke already thickening around us. Nate is a few feet away from me, fumbling for the specialized pocket on his turnout gear. His helmet and breathing mask are strewn across the ground near mine, knocked from our heads from the blast.

"You alright?" I ask, as he pulls the rescue inhaler from the pocket.

He scowls, takes a quick puff, then scrambles to his feet. "I'm fine. You?"

I nod my head, knowing how irritated my best friend would be if I asked about his asthma. He's dealt with it his whole life and doesn't need me nagging him.

"Yeah, I'm good," I say. Nate grabs our gear from where it landed, tossing my helmet and mask to me. I yank them back onto my head, securing the chin strap with practiced efficiency. The sound of roaring flames, hissing water streams, and distant sirens blend into a chaotic symphony of destruction.

We were the first crew to arrive at the scene, but several other units are here, doing everything they can to fight back the blaze. The senior living facility—a sprawling Mediterranean-style complex—burns like a tinderbox. The stucco walls have buckled in places, blackened and crumbling under the relentless assault of the fire. The iconic red-tile roof, though partially intact, hides the real danger—the wooden framing, dry as kindling, is feeding the fire inside.

Across the street, a mass of displaced residents and staff gather in shock, their eyes fixed on the devastation. I spot a few EMTs attending to the more vulnerable residents, but there's no time to process the scene further.

Nate's already scanning the building, eyes sharp. "That last explosion took out the east wing entry."

I follow his gaze. Windows have blown out, and the doors are a molten wreck. Smoke pours out in thick, roiling clouds. We've lost our primary access point.

"Plan B?" Nate glances at me.

I look toward Ronan, our captain, who's already reading my mind. "We can try the roof," he says, voice clipped. "But listen—the fire's working through the attic spaces. If the framing's gone, those red tiles could give way at any second."

"The tiles themselves will hold heat longer than the wood," I say, thinking it through. "But if we're wrong, we could break through into active fire..."

Ronan gives a tight nod. "It's a risk. The ventilation is tricky, too. We breach that roof, we'll pull oxygen into the attic. It could flash over."

I take a steadying breath, focusing on the here and now. "We've got no choice. We'll cut through and drop down directly where they're trapped."

"Do we have an ID on who's trapped in the attic nook with Mrs. Crockett?" Nate asks, wiping the sweat and soot from his brow.

I read Nate's mind. We need to gauge the physical abilities of both trapped victims to formulate the best plan to get them out. Dillon must be going crazy with worry over his mother. They've just reunited after years of being estranged. Having reconnected with my mother over the past few days, I know how much that means. I'm not going to let him lose his mother just when they are finding their way back to each other.

I ask, "Is it another elderly resident or a worker?"

Ronan's eyes flicker—just a fraction of a second, but it's enough.

His hesitation settles like a lead weight in my gut.

But it's his refusal to look me in the eyes that pushes me over the edge.

I grab at his shoulder, jerking him to face me. "Ronan! Who is trapped in the attic with Mrs. Crockett?"

I know it's wrong, but I silently pray that it's not—

"Kennedy," he says quietly.

The world narrows, sound fading into a muted hum. Kennedy. In the attic.

I turn back to the building, my chest tight. The fire's spreading too fast—we're running out of time. If we don't move now ...

"Deploy the ladder. I'm getting her out," I say, voice firm despite my rising panic. "I won't lose her."

Ronan grips my shoulder briefly. "Just don't lose yourself, too. Let's keep our heads here."

I give him a nod, already turning to Nate. "We have to go through the roof. It's the only way. You with me?"

"Always," Nate responds.

We haul the ladder up, setting it against the unscorched side of the building, aware that the roof's integrity is likely compromised. We don't have time to guess. Every second counts. I grab the chainsaw and start the climb. Each rung groans under the weight of my gear. My breathing mask seals to my face, the filtered air a thin barrier between me and the thick smoke rising to meet us.

The tiles are hot beneath my boots as I reach the top. Nate's right behind me, eyes scanning the surface. We both know the risks—tile roofs like these can trap heat, creating a literal oven beneath. But if the wooden beams holding them are weak, the whole section could drop us straight into the fire. It's a gamble, but we've got no choice.

I pull the chainsaw's starter cord, and it roars to life. The blade screeches as it tears into the tiles, sending ceramic shards flying. Each strike makes me hyper-aware of the flames lurking beneath. We can hear the fire crackling below us now, a monster we can't see but feel in every tremor of the roof.

A hole opens beneath my saw. The second the tile gives, a burst of heat and smoke escapes, but no flames—yet. I glance down, seeing the wooden framing. "Wood's still intact here. Dropping down," I shout over the noise.

I lower myself through the opening, landing in a crouch on the wooden beams of the attic. My flashlight cuts through the smoke, revealing the dark, cramped space. No flames, but the air's heavy with heat, smoke swirling around me like a living thing.

"Clear," I call up.

Nate secures the roof hooks, drops the ladder through the hole, and descends into the attic.

We need to move fast. The temperature is rising—thermal imaging tells me we're just shy of a flashover point. One wrong move and the entire attic will ignite.

I glance at Nate. His breathing seems more labored than usual, but I chalk it up to the intense heat and pressure of the situation. Getting Kennedy out of this burning building is my only priority.

"We're not where we need to be," I say, consulting the building layout on my radio. I relay our location to Ronan. "Ronan, call Kennedy. Tell her to bang on something—loud. We're close, but we need to pinpoint her."

A moment later, we hear it—a dull, rhythmic thud. Metal against wood, faint but distinct. She's alive.

"This way!" I motion to Nate, and we swing our axes into the drywall between us and the sound. Plaster and wood splinters fly as we chop through. Each hit is deliberate—we can't risk breaching a wall that's shielding us from the fire on the other side.

Finally, a hole opens, and I hear her voice.

"Luke!" Kennedy's voice, weak but clear, cuts through the smoke.

My heart skips. I reach through the opening, tearing the last pieces of the wall away. Kennedy stumbles forward, wide-eyed and trembling. I quickly assess her for injuries, relieved that there are no signs of physical trauma.

"I thought we weren't going to get out ..." Her voice cracks, but I pull her tight, just for a second. A momentary indulgence that is against every protocol, but I need to feel her in my arms to know for sure she's okay. To let her know I will never let anything hurt her.

"I got you," I whisper. "I'm getting you out of here."

The look of complete trust in Kennedy's eyes melts away any hint of doubt lingering in my mind.

There's no way I could ever leave this woman.

I love her more than any land deed and too much to be apart from her.

"And I'm never letting you go."

"Never?" Kennedy asks, a slight curve to her lips.

"I was so stupid, Kennedy. Now is not the time to get into all this, but you need to know one thing."

"What's that?"

"I love you," I say, then push past her to enter the attic nook.

Nate's already with Mrs. Crockett, sitting upright and looking shaken but physically okay. "No injuries," Nate says, through labored breaths as he helps her up. "She's fine, but we need to move."

"Are you alright?" I ask, noticing my best friend's strained breathing as he assists Mrs. Crockett. The woman is petite and couldn't weigh enough to be a difficult move for him.

"Don't worry about me." He wheezes slightly. "Just the gear acting up. I'm good." His hand briefly moves to his face, but he stops himself, clearly resisiting the urge to remove the mask. An asthma attack is imminent but removing the mask to use his inhaler would be too time-consuming and dangerous with the level of smoke in the attic. The only thing I can do is get him out of here first.

I glance at the hole we made in the roof, calculating the best way to get us all out safely. Nate's breathing is becoming increasingly ragged. "Nate, you go up first, then Kennedy. I'll follow with Mrs. Crockett."

Nate starts to argue but then relents, giving a quick nod. "Fine." He moves up the ladder slower than usual, each movement a struggle. Once he's back on the roof, I turn to Kennedy.

"You next," I say.

"Luke ..." She hesitates.

"Go Kennedy. I need you out of here and safe on the outside," I insist.

Kennedy squeezes my hand before moving to the ladder. She navigates the rungs up toward the hole easily. Nate's waiting at the top to pull her the rest of the way. He leans in, grabs her arms, and helps her over the ledge. His breathing is audibly strained even through the mask. Relief floods me as she disappears into the bright sunlight.

"Your turn," I say to Mrs. Crockett. I take a steadying breath, then hoist Mrs. Crockett up, guiding her as she reaches for the ladder rungs. I stay close, keeping a firm grip on her waist as she pulls herself up toward the opening at a glacial pace.

The heat intensifies. My muscles scream in protest as I hoist her higher, helping to navigate her up the ladder. A crackling roar erupts in the air. I look to the left. Part of the attic crumbles under bright orange flames. Mrs. Crockett is almost at the top but unable to reach Nate's outstretched arms. I follow close behind her, almost shoving her to the top.

Nate grabs hold of her and lifts her out through the hole.

One glance back, I see the flames licking at the wooden floor.

I rush up the ladder, grateful to see Kennedy, Mrs. Crockett, and Nate halfway to the ground, assisted by other firefighters. Nate's finally removed his mask, using his inhaler as they descend but I'm not sure it's working.

I race across the tiled roof toward the ladder—

An explosion rocks behind me, and everything goes … black.

CHAPTER 47

K ENNEDY

~

The small chapel is draped in somber hues, with dark wooden walls and pews. The haunting melody of organ music drifts in the air, wrapping around me like a shroud. Flickering candles cast long shadows, their soft light illuminating arrangements of white lilies and roses. The air is heavy with the scent of incense and grief. As I stand in the corner, my heart feels cold and lifeless, like the marble floor beneath my feet. My eyes burn, refusing to shed tears I'm not ready to release.

A fresh wave of memories slams into my head.

Luke's body falling like a rag doll from the roof of the senior living facility. When he landed on the inflatable rescue cushion, I expected him to jump up and dust himself off.

But he didn't move.

He lay there still and quiet, face down, as EMTs and firefighters rushed to him.

My legs turned to lead. I couldn't move.

I didn't want to see him like that.

Couldn't bear to see the sweet, kind, funny, and infuriating man, so full of life that I'd fallen in love with, a shadow of who he was.

"Luke is a fighter," Vangie whispers in my ear. She stands on my right, holding my hand. Yolanda is on my left, holding the other one. My two rocks keep me upright as I struggle with the lack of information on Luke's condition. The hospital staff won't even let me into the ICU waiting room with the firefighters because, to them … I'm nobody to Luke. Worse than that, I'm more an enemy than a friend. The person who sued him for his land and the reason he's leaving Kimbell.

They don't know our truth.

They didn't hear the words he said to me before he rescued me from the fire.

Yolanda adds, "He's going to be fine. He will come back to you."

I nod my head robotically and try to smile. But I can't prove I'm okay. Not when every ounce of me is focused on Luke.

"Why don't y'all go back to the waiting room? Maybe someone has heard news about Luke and may let it slip," I say, suddenly wanting to be alone in the hospital chapel. "I just need … a moment."

"Of course," Yolanda says, giving me a hug.

I hug Vangie next, then watch them leave the serene space. My gaze lingers on the flames of the flickering small white candles. Flames no different from the ones that burned Oakbrook to the ground.

Memories of our times together flash through my mind—laughter, arguments, culinary explorations, tender moments sitting out on his back porch in comfortable silence. Luke's selflessness in putting everyone's needs above his own shined through today. He protected his best friend from the onslaught of an asthma attack and saved my life and Mrs. Crockett's. But he's so much more than his good deeds.

And I vow to cherish every second with Luke if he pulls through this. No, when he pulls through this.

Satisfied that my prayers will be answered, I turn to head out of the chapel and nearly collide with a woman barreling inside.

"Oh!" She says, steadying herself by holding onto me. "Just the person I'm looking for."

It only takes a second for me to recognize Madeleine Rice, Luke's mother. "You were looking for me?"

"Yes, Kennedy," Madeleine says. "Nate has Luke's medical power of attorney. As soon as the doctors got his asthma attack under control, he informed the head of the ER that both you and I should have access to visit Luke and receive updates on his condition."

"That's wonderful," I say, wrapping my arms around her. "When can we get an update."

Madeleine chuckles. "He really does love you if he told you about me."

I look into her emerald eyes that are so much like Luke's. "I need you to know that I love your son very much. We may have been forced to deal with each other under unusual and challenging circumstances, but it didn't take us long to realize we're a perfect fit. Maybe perfectly imperfect because he and I can argue over anything and everything."

"He needs someone strong like you who can let him have down days or be mean occasionally."

I laugh. "This town has no clue how mean Luke can be. But I'm grateful he opened up and showed me every part of him—the difficult and compassionate, caring and loving side."

Madeleine gives me a warm smile. "Come on, let's go see the doctor."

Minutes later, Madeleine and I sit across from Dr. Jasmine Jones in her private office. I don't know the formidable and terse head of ER well, but I do know she's the best doctor St. Elizabeth's has. Luke is in great hands with her directing his treatment.

Dr. Jones's eyes narrow as she looks back and forth between Madeleine and me. The head of ER can barely hide her confusion over why she's sharing an update on Luke's condition with a gubernatorial candidate and the woman who sued Luke and took his land away. Still, she remains the consummate professional as she gives us a thorough and complete assessment of Luke's condition.

"Bottom line is he's very lucky," Dr. Jones says. "He has a concussion and was a bit disoriented. He displayed a few unusual behaviors and personality changes, so we took him away for a battery of tests to be sure nothing more serious was happening. I'm happy to report those came back clear."

"So, he's awake?" Madeleine asks.

"Yes, he woke up shortly after the EMTs brought him in. That was the first good sign. The rest of the tests confirmed no other concerns from the fall. I will keep him overnight for observation, but I'm comfortable enough to allow him to have visitors now."

Madeleine turns to me, and we break into warm smiles as we hug each other.

"You should go first," I say to her.

Madeleine looks conflicted, possibly torn between wanting to see her son and respecting my closer connection with him.

"Actually, Luke has been causing quite a raucous about seeing you ... Kennedy, very unlike his usual personality. But he did fall off a building," Dr. Jones deadpans.

Madeleine says, "You have to go first. Luke is expecting you. Just let him know I'm here, and I'd love to see him if he feels up to it."

"I'm sure he'll be up to it. He may not realize you're still in town," I say, careful not to give away any details about their relationship to Dr. Jones.

"Good point," Madeleine says.

Dr. Jones rises from her chair and walks us to the door, giving us Luke's room number as we head out. Madeleine and I hold hands as we walk through the ER toward Luke's room. Stopping at the door, I take a deep breath.

"Go on .... go," Madeleine urges me.

I push the wide door in and stop, my mouth dropping open.

"Luke Diamond! What are you doing?"

Luke stands in the middle of the hospital room, wearing dark jeans as he pulls a Kimbell Firefighter t-shirt over his ripped chest.

"Getting out of here." Luke gives me a sexy grin.

"Take those clothes off right now!" I say, pressing my hands on my hips.

The look Luke gives me sends fire blazing through my body.

"Wow, Kennedy, I've never seen this side of you," Luke teases. "Kinda like it. I could get used to you bossing me around." He winks at me as a mischievous sparkle dances in his green eyes.

"Luke! You know what I mean. You know what I'm really talking about. Dr. Jones has not released you. Get back in the hospital bed."

"There's no way I'm spending the first day that you know how much I love you in the hospital away from you."

"Dr. Jones says you have to stay here overnight for observation. I'm not letting you leave this place," I say, then point a finger in his face. "And don't think you're going to get away with dropping an 'I love you' bomb on me in the middle of a raging fire. Who does that?"

"Someone who was scared out of his mind that I might not get the chance to tell you at all," Luke says, sobering me.

We walk toward each other, stopping with only inches separating us.

"I was so angry at everything and everyone after the judge's ruling. I was mad at you. Mad at Gramps. Nothing turned out how I thought it would. I lost the land, and in my head, that meant I couldn't have you either," Luke says, his fingers playing with strands of my hair. "But then I realized nothing turned out how I thought it would."

I tilt my head but stay quiet, waiting for his new revelation.

Luke says, "You suing me was the second best thing that could've happened to me."

"Do I even want to know the best thing?" I ask, frowning.

"The best thing is that I owe all this to the one person who showed me the most love. Gramps. Every move he made decades ago set up this situation between you and me. If it wasn't for him, I never would've come face to face with the undisputed love of my life. So, instead of focusing on what I lost. I'm choosing to focus on the gift I gained from this whole crazy situation. Loving you, Kennedy, no matter how you feel about me, was worth all the pain and stress of that lawsuit."

"No matter how I feel about you? Luke, are you crazy? Can't you tell I'm so in love with you, too?" I ask, slapping at his chest.

He grabs my hands and pulls me even closer. "But is love enough for you to believe in us?"

"I've had more than my fair share of relationship disappointments," I say, trembling slightly. "There always seems to be something that makes men fall out of love with me. I know that could happen with us—"

"No—"

"Let me finish!" I demand. "I'm not afraid to keep trying. You are definitely worth risking my heart again. So, yes, love is enough for me to believe this relationship can last. That you could be my one."

"Could be?" Luke scoffs. "I am your one, and you are mine. I know that as surely as I'm breathing. And I look forward to proving that to you every day."

"Well, I like the sound of that." A smile bursts onto my face. "Now kiss me."

"Gladly," Luke says.

Luke's lips capture mine in a passionate kiss that makes my knees weak. His arms tighten around me as if he never wants to let go. I melt into his embrace, savoring every sensation. The kiss feels like coming home, affirming our love and the beginning of our new life … together.

CHAPTER 48

K ENNEDY

"I NEVER KNEW THIS WAS ON THE OTHER SIDE OF THE electric fence ..." Luke says, staring at the octagonal basin centerpiece of Granny's backyard garden. The water ripples gently in the breeze, bobbing the water lilies dotted along the surface—the view reminiscent of a Monet painting.

I can't help but smile as I watch the familiar look of awe and amazement as he takes in one of Granny's most impressive works. His gaze slowly drifts across the landscape, taking in the spouting fountains of the basin, the manicured trees stationed like sentries watching over the stone sculptures nestled between. In the distance, Lake Lasso emerges, stretching as far as the eye can see.

Granny saved her best work for her enjoyment. No matter how often I see someone discover the beauty of her gardens, the impact and impression it makes on them never gets old. I love seeing her designs through the reactions of others. This is why preserving her first orchard was so important to me. Despite everything, I will never regret securing her orchards for future generations to enjoy.

Luke completes his canvassing of the backyard garden and rests his eyes on mine.

"Beautiful, isn't it?" I say, beaming with pride.

"The most beautiful thing I've ever seen ..." His words are low, barely above a whisper, and I know he doesn't mean the garden. Heat flushes my face as tingling butterflies skitter across my skin. I want to pinch myself, but I'm sure Luke would think I was crazy. It's surreal that we are sitting at a stone table with the broad branches of a live oak tree shading us from the afternoon sun.

Luke rests his open palm on the table, and I place my hand on his.

"Does the garden look familiar to you?" I ask, wondering if he picked up on Tulieries Gardens as the romantic inspiration. He responds with a subtle shake of his head. "Paris?" I prod.

"I've never been," Luke says, a wistfulness in his face.

My mouth drops open. "Seriously? You've never been to the city of love?"

"Well, I didn't grow up knowing I had a wealthy mother. There were no family trips and vacations with my dad," he explains without a hint of resentment or disappointment. "I didn't go outside of Texas until I was in college. That was just to party places like Miami and Cancun."

"I'm sure you have some wild stories from those days," I say, not wanting to think about what kind of trouble Luke and his friends got into back then. "But with Nate as your best friend, I figured you might have gone—"

"To the city of love? With him?" The sexiest frown creases his forehead. "No way. It's not exactly a city for a guys' trip."

I concede his point. "Well, we'll have to change that. Paris is beautiful." Reaching for my glass of lemonade, I take a sip and imagine Luke and I on a stroll along the Seine with the backdrop of the Louvre and Notre Dame behind us. I have no doubts that a trip like this and many others will happen in our future.

For the first time, I genuinely believe that my string of abrupt and unexpected breakups is over—

"Maybe we could go on our honeymoon ..."

The glass of lemonade slips from my hand. The liquid sloshes onto the table as the glass falls onto the grass near my feet. I stare at the juice dripping down the linens, unable to process Luke's unexpected statement.

Is this really happening?

Luke erupts in laughter. "Do not panic. I'm not proposing ... yet." He grabs our cloth napkins and cleans up my mess since I seem frozen in shock.

His face turns serious. "But the question is coming."

I swear I forget to breathe.

He adds, "Sooner rather than later."

"You want to get married?" I choke the words out. "I mean not specifically to me but just in general. Is it something you want? That you see in your future?"

"There's nothing more that I want than to settle down with a beautiful woman I love with all my heart," he pauses, then points his finger directly at me. "We'd get married, then have a few kids and enjoy life the way it was intended to be enjoyed—sharing moments with the people you love most."

"I want that same thing." The words rush from my mouth.

"I think you're supposed to point at me," Luke says with a sly smile. "Just to eliminate any doubt about who you want it with."

I raise both my arms and point at him over and over.

Luke rises, leans over the table, and kisses me. His lips are soft, and his touch is gentle and tender. He takes his time showing me exactly how much he loves me.

But he breaks the kiss too soon for my liking. Dazed, I stare into his forest-green gaze.

"There's something we need to take care of first," Luke reminds me.

"The elephant in the room."

"It's not that bad anymore. I'd say it's more like the butterfly in the garden," he says, placing a document face down on the table between us.

"Glad the papers didn't get wet," I say, suddenly nervous. I wasn't sure what to expect when Luke called to tell me he was being released from the hospital and needed to talk to me about his future in Kimbell. I'd spent enough time with his mother to know she fully expects him to leave Kimbell and join her as a consultant on her gubernatorial campaign.

Luke is a man of his word.

If he makes a commitment, he won't renege later, especially now that he's opening his heart to build a relationship with the mother he's always admired.

As much as I don't want him to go, I'd never do anything to stand in his way. "Can I say something first?" I ask, feeling the need to make sure he knows that.

"Of course," he says, a curiousness crossing his face.

"Winning the land in the lawsuit had consequences that I never wanted. Knowing that I was the reason that you'd lost your home and the parts of the land you adored most was extremely hard for me. I know, not as hard as it was for you, but I never wanted that."

"I know you didn't. You just wanted to preserve your grandmother's orchards. I don't blame you for that."

"But it doesn't change that you're leaving Kimbell because you lost your home. Who knows what will happen once you go to work on your mother's campaign," I say, then take a deep breath. "Even though it's not ideal for me, I love you too much to not give everything I have to make a long-distance relationship work."

"But will you give everything you have to make me stay?" Luke asks.

"I don't understand."

He turns the papers over and I realize for the first time what they are—the sales agreement I had drawn up for him to buy the five acres of land from me.

I grab the papers from him. "You don't need these. I'm happy to sign over these five acres to you." I turn the papers to the side, ready to rip up the old document.

Luke snatches it from my hand. "Don't do that."

"Why not?"

"Because I need to buy them from you. I was going to ask you to agree to sell it again since I turned you down abruptly when you first offered it to me at the gazebo."

"You don't need to buy them from me, Luke."

"Yes, I do, Kennedy." He reaches into his pocket, pulls out a rectangular paper, and then places it in front of me. It's a check for the amount I offered to sell him the five acres of land.

"I don't want your money." I push the check back toward him. "This feels wrong."

"It has to be this way. I need to buy the land from you. I don't want a gift. I want to own it fair and square."

"But if you propose to me, then this will be pointless. We'll both own the land."

"Not if we get a prenup, which you should," Luke says, pressing his hands on the table. "Why are you fighting me on this? Take the money so we can move on and start our lives together."

I squeeze my eyes shut as the old fears dart through my mind. As much as I try to convince myself I'm being irrational, I can't get them to stop. "Is this a backup plan? Your security in case you discover something that makes you want to walk away from this ..." I blink back the tears. "At least you'll be able to walk away from me and still have the land." I bolt up from the table, putting distance between us.

"I'm never walking away from you," Luke says. His words hit me with a finality that makes me feel foolish.

"I'm sorry," I mutter.

"Don't be sorry." He joins me near the basin, reducing all the space

I'd erected. "You can always share your feelings with me. Raw, unfiltered, crazy, or sane. That's what we do for each other. That's why we work."

"So help me understand why this is so important to you," I say, willing myself to trust in Luke's confidence in us despite my past.

"I'm trying to preserve a legacy, too. Gramps's greatest joy was passing down this land to me. It meant the world to him, and it meant the world to me, too," Luke says. "No matter what this town thinks about my grandfather, he truly believed he'd made a valid purchase of the land. If he was still alive, it would devastate him to know the truth. And you know what I'd do?"

"You'd repurchase the land for him. Even if it was just a part of it," I say, getting everything Luke is saying.

"I'd have to buy it. A gift wouldn't satisfy him."

"And it's not going to satisfy you either."

"So, will you take the check and sign the agreement?" Luke asks.

"Yeah, I get it. This has nothing to do with us and everything to do with your family."

He hands me the check, then grabs the papers from the table. "That's not entirely true."

I watch as he signs the document and then hands it to me.

"Not true?" I add my signature to the document and hand it back to him.

"I asked if you'd be willing to do everything in your power to get me to stay," Luke reminds me. "And you just did the only thing I needed."

"So, you're not going to leave Kimbell?" Happiness bubbles within me.

"I was a fool to think I could walk away from you. I'm staying here, and because of this, I still have a home to move back into," Luke says.

I squeal and leap into his arms, peppering his face with kisses. "Welcome back, neighbor!"

"Thanks, neighbor," Luke says, grinning from ear to ear.

"And while we are neighbors, I've been meaning to talk to you about that pesky electric fence your grandfather put up …"

Luke laughs. "That's technically your property, not mine."

"But as you and your family were the property's caretakers, I believe you have a duty to help rectify the problem." His laughter tickles my ears as I continue. "You see, I have grand plans for a jacuzzi oasis where we can float and relax, enjoying this beautiful view. But it can't be built because of the electric fence. So, I thought you might be kind enough to turn the electric part of the fence off?" I ask, wrapping my arms around Luke's neck.

"Since you asked so nicely, how about I tear the whole thing down?" Luke asks. "I don't want any barriers between me and you."

"Neither do I," I beam.

"Consider it done," Luke says. "I love you, Kennedy."

"And I love you, Luke."

Want more of Luke and Kennedy?
Get their swoon worthy bonus story delivered straight to your email inbox!
https://BookHip.com/TXVLMSK

Next up to find love in Kimbell, Texas is Luke's friend Nate Bell.

Nate's goal: prove he's worthy of running the family business at any cost. Love? Not on his agenda. But when an elevator traps him with a beautiful stranger full of optimism and a smile from the heavens, he starts questioning everything. Can this sunshine-in-human-form break through Nate's grumpy armor? Or will ambition keep his heart locked up tight?

Check out the next book in the Kimbell Texas Sweet Romances …
BREAKING FREE!

https://amzn.to/3XYUBh5

ABOUT THE AUTHOR

Angel S. Vane never imagined she'd stumble into becoming an author. An avid fan of books her whole life combined with an active imagination were the right ingredients to embark on a single goal of completing one book.

Now she's written several books and has tapped into her love of Jane Austen novels by writing her own brand of satisfyingly sweet romances. Learn more at Angel's website.

ABOUT THE PUBLISHER

BONZAIMOON BOOKS

BonzaiMoon Books is a family-run, artisanal publishing company created in the summer of 2014. We publish works of fiction in various genres. Our passion and focus is working with authors who write the books you want to read, and giving those authors the opportunity to have more direct input in the publishing of their work.

For more information:
www.bonzaimoonbooks.com
info@bonzaimoonbooks.com

facebook.com/BonzaiMoonBooks